Pra all

"A major talent of the genre."   —*Publishers Weekly*

"[Ball] knows how to keep a tale moving."   —*Kirkus Reviews*

"Donna Ball has created a delightful world in her Ladybug Farm novels. Her characters are lively and endearing, and readers will feel a longing to join the girls on the front porch in the evenings as they reminisce about the day's activities."
          —*Fresh Fiction*

"A must-read."   —Examiner.com

Berkley Books by Donna Ball

A YEAR ON LADYBUG FARM

AT HOME ON LADYBUG FARM

LOVE LETTERS FROM LADYBUG FARM

KEYS TO THE CASTLE

Keys to the Castle

DONNA BALL

BERKLEY BOOKS, NEW YORK

A BERKLEY BOOK
Published by the Penguin Group
Penguin Group (USA) Inc.
375 Hudson Street, New York, New York 10014, USA
Penguin Group (Canada), 90 Eglinton Avenue East, Suite 700, Toronto, Ontario M4P 2Y3, Canada
(a division of Pearson Penguin Canada Inc.)
Penguin Books Ltd., 80 Strand, London WC2R 0RL, England
Penguin Group Ireland, 25 St. Stephen's Green, Dublin 2, Ireland (a division of Penguin Books Ltd.)
Penguin Group (Australia), 250 Camberwell Road, Camberwell, Victoria 3124, Australia
(a division of Pearson Australia Group Pty. Ltd.)
Penguin Books India Pvt. Ltd., 11 Community Centre, Panchsheel Park, New Delhi—110 017, India
Penguin Group (NZ), 67 Apollo Drive, Rosedale, North Shore 0632, New Zealand
(a division of Pearson New Zealand Ltd.)
Penguin Books (South Africa) (Pty.) Ltd., 24 Sturdee Avenue, Rosebank, Johannesburg 2196,
South Africa
Penguin Books Ltd., Registered Offices: 80 Strand, London WC2R 0RL, England

This book is an original publication of the Berkley Publishing Group.

Copyright © 2011 by Donna Ball
Cover art: château by Peter Richardson/Getty; key by Gunnar Pippel/Shutterstock; frame by Sanjar/Shutterstock
Cover design by Annette Fiore DeFex
Text design by Laura K. Corless

First edition: January 2011

Library of Congress Cataloging-in-Publication Data

Ball, Donna.
  Keys to the castle / Donna Ball— 1st ed.
    p.   cm.
  ISBN 978-0-425-23930-8 (trade pbk.) 1. Single women—Fiction. 2. Americans—France—Fiction.
3. Life change events—Fiction. I. Title.
  PS3552.A4545K49   2011
  813'.54—dc22   2010030818

PRINTED IN THE UNITED STATES OF AMERICA

10   9   8   7   6   5   4   3   2   1

Long Ago and Far Away

· ONE ·

When she closed her eyes, her dreams were of summer seas and the call of gulls, and the sound of someone's laughter . . . laughter, which, each time she dreamed of it, seemed to grow farther away and more indistinct until sometimes she couldn't be sure whether it wasn't, in fact, nothing more than the cry of the gulls. Sometimes she would close her eyes and try desperately to bring those dreams to mind: the sound of laughter, the taste of salt and sunshine, days so blue they could make your eyes ache. The feeling of being utterly, wantonly, outrageously loved.

When she opened her eyes, the ocean was gray and the wind was biting and all she saw was the worry in her sister Dixie's eyes. It was an expression Sara had seen far too much of over the past year, and she hated herself for having put it there.

"Sara?" prompted Dixie, her short legs struggling to keep up with Sara's long stride across the damp sand. "Are you listening?"

The two sisters could not have been more dissimilar. Sara, with her long legs and windblown mahogany hair, had a figure that was made for skinny jeans and haute couture. She had turned forty-six last year, and even though the winter had left her heart-shaped face pale and pinched and had leached too much of the joy from her blue gray eyes, the resulting fragility seemed almost to have subtracted years, not added them.

Dixie was short and round and three years younger than her sister. A lifetime of ocean air and beach sun had bleached her bouncy yellow curls and added color to her face that even the gray winters of the Outer Banks couldn't strip away. She was mother to twin four-year-old boys, wife to a good and solid man, and owner of a thriving downtown business. Most people, seeing the two women together, would have guessed that Dixie was the older sister.

"Sara?" she repeated now, taking a single running step to close the ground between them.

"Right." Sara shoved her hands deep into the pockets of her oversized gray sweater—Daniel's sweater—and wished she had worn a scarf. "Three p.m. flight out of Charlotte, connections in Atlanta. Next stop Paris."

"You don't have to sound so excited about it. And could you slow down? You're not *walking* there, you know!"

Sara dredged up a grimace of a smile, and she slowed her pace. "Sorry. I just don't see why this all couldn't be done via e-mail. Good God, I've handled multimillion-dollar contracts by e-mail. Why the French government can't manage to settle one man's pathetic little estate without dragging me across an ocean . . ."

"I thought you said it had something to do with the house, and the property taxes, and it's not as though a trip to the French countryside in the spring is a punishment, you know."

The wind whipped Sara's hair across her face, and she combed it back with her fingers distractedly. "I don't know. The trip sounded like a good idea when I booked it, but now . . ." She gave a brief, bracing shake of her head, and her hair flew into her eyes again. "Sorry. I guess this gray weather has got me down. It's depressing, isn't it?"

The ocean rumbled behind them, and the wind sent rivulets of dark sand scurrying across the deserted beach. The sky overhead was the color of lead, with darker clouds banking to the north. It had been a long ugly winter, and this day, this sky, seemed to epitomize all of it.

Dixie's smile was as bright and bouncy as the curls that peeked from beneath her stocking cap, and a good deal more genuine than Sara's. She replied, "In the Outer Banks of North Carolina, maybe. But in the French countryside, I hear the weather is gorgeous! It's going to be a wonderful trip. You're going to drink fabulous wines and eat French food and take tons of pictures of churches and châteaux and sunflowers. Sara, you deserve this. Please try to enjoy it."

Sara stopped walking suddenly and turned on her sister. The buffeting sea winds tore at her dark hair again and she caught it wildly between both hands. "It's not a vacation, okay?" She could not believe the voice that came out of her mouth, raised and shrill over the crash and mutter of the waves, was her own. "I'm flying across an ocean to settle the estate of a husband I barely knew, and I *don't* deserve it, okay? I didn't deserve to meet Daniel, I didn't deserve for him to die, and I for damn sure don't deserve that *stupid* house in a country where I don't even speak the language. Stop trying to make this fun for me, Dixie, could you just do that? It's not going to be fun!"

Her sister endured the onslaught patiently, as she always did. Her eyes were filled with compassion, her wind-chapped face softened with understanding. She was the caretaker, the comforter, the patient, sympathetic friend. It was a role she had had to play all too often since Sara had come back to Little John Island almost a year ago, and life had changed for all of them.

She said gently, "You know you need to do this, Sara. You know you need to say good-bye."

Sara drew in a breath for another sharp reply, a dozen angry retorts bubbling to her lips. How could she say good-bye to a place she had never been, a man who did not belong there? What was there to say good-bye *to*? Daniel wasn't there. Daniel was here, on this island, in her memories, in her heart. Lawyers weren't going to change that. Signed papers weren't going to change that. And flying to Europe for damn sure wasn't going to change it.

And neither was screaming at her sister on a beach in North Carolina three thousand miles away. Sara released her breath, closed her lips, and started walking again.

Dixie slipped her arm through her sister's in easy, companionable comfort. "Jeff said he'll be glad to drive you to the airport," she said. "There's no need for you to leave your car in long-term parking."

"That's okay." Sara's reply was wooden. "I don't want him to miss a day of work." Although she imagined her brother-in-law would be more than glad to miss the work and make the trip if it meant having his house—and his wife—to himself again for a few weeks. She released a breath, pushing back the tangle of her hair again. "I'm sorry I yelled at you."

Dixie patted Sara's arm. "I know you are."

"It's just . . ." She hesitated, not certain she wanted to put her thoughts into words, and, even if she did, how they would sound once spoken. She tightened her fists inside her pockets. "God, this doesn't even feel like my life!" The words burst from her lips in a single breath, and once she had spoken them she didn't seem to be able to stop. "Here I was, plain old Sara Graves, middle-aged workaholic, my entire life devoted to making the world a better place for useless household gadgets that break the minute the warranty runs out, and I had this one outrageous, incredible chance for adventure and I took it and that was crazy—it was crazy I would even do such a thing!—and suddenly I'm the widow of a man I've only known three months—a Frenchman, for God's sake, with a whole heritage and culture and past I know nothing about . . . and it turns out there's no one, no one in this entire world, left to deal with what he left behind but me. Me! They sure don't prepare you for that in the romance novels, do they?" She wasn't even aware of the tears that were streaming down her cheeks until a cold gust of wind stung her face, and she swiped the moisture away impatiently. "It's like some great big sick cosmic joke. God, I am so tired of crying!"

Sara pressed the heels of her hands against her eyes to stop the flow of tears, and drew in a breath through parted lips. "It isn't fair."

She whirled away from her sister then, facing the ocean, and she screamed into the oncoming tide, *"It! Isn't! Fair!"*

The thunder of the water swallowed her words, and when the surf sucked outward again it seemed to take her fury with it, leaving her only tired, and drained. Her shoulders slumped.

Dixie passed her a crumpled tissue from her pocket, and Sara blew her nose. After a moment, they started walking again.

"It's just that . . . I feel like I've used up all my chances, you know?" Sara's voice was quieter now, resigned. "I'll be fifty in a couple of years. Can you believe that? And there's nothing left for me to do, no one for me to be. No more surprises. No more possibilities. I had my shot. And this trip to France . . . it just seems like someone forgot to tell me it's over."

Dixie was shaking her head, curls bouncing in the wind, before Sara finished speaking. "That's why you've got to go, Sara. You know that. Because until you deal with it—with every last single detail that Daniel left you to deal with—it won't be over. And you'll spend the rest of your life wondering why it ever was at all."

They walked in silence for a while, the heavy sand sucking at their sneakers, the whoosh and grumble of the surf their only companion. And then Sara said, "Do you have any idea how jealous I am of you?"

Dixie stopped in her tracks, staring at her. Her astonishment was genuine. "*Me?*"

Sara nodded. "Jeff, the twins, the way your phone is always ringing and it's always someone you want to talk to, the way your house always smells like cinnamon rolls—"

"And wet laundry and burned popcorn," Dixie finished, with a small shake of her head. She looked up at her sister, doubt and puzzlement in her eyes. "I always thought you were disappointed in me," she admitted, shifting her gaze briefly, as though embarrassed. "You worked so hard to get us both out of here . . . it was so important to you that I go to college . . . and what do I do after two years but drop out and marry Jeff and spend the rest of my life trying to have babies?"

Sara and Dixie had grown up in a single-wide trailer home on the outskirts of a fishing town on the mainland. The whole town smelled like diesel fuel and fish guts. Though less than thirty nautical miles from where they stood, it was a lifetime away from the peaceful resort island of Little John.

Sara said, "You live in a place where people ride their bicycles to town. You work in a bookstore. You can walk to the beach. You have macaroni and cheese for dinner." Sara stopped, and took a breath, not wanting to sound maudlin. "You're right. When we were kids, all I wanted for both of us was to get away from this godforsaken coast. I just never intended to go quite so far. That's why I came back here. I know I've stayed too long. But . . . what's here, what you have, is everything I've always wanted. And for a while I almost believed I could have it, too."

Dixie slipped her arm around Sara's waist, hugging her

briefly. "Remember how, after school, we used to ride our bikes over to Sandy Point and build sandcastles on the beach?"

Sara smiled, remembering. "Some of them were really out of control. Huge."

"And you used to tell me stories about the princesses that lived there, and make believe we were them."

"I remember," Sara said softly.

"You," Dixie told her, looking into her eyes, "are the reason I have everything I've always wanted. And you can stay with me as long as you like."

Sara was silent as they climbed the sandy wooden steps that led up to the street, away from the surf and the wind, and made their way back home.

* * *

Sara had met Daniel at one of those ultra-exclusive Manhattan parties for which you had to have not only an invitation, but three references and a bodyguard to get in. Sting was there, and someone said Oprah was supposed to show, but she never did. Sara was there as a guest of a prospective client who wanted to impress her with his connections—or, more likely, didn't want to miss the party and, since Sara was only in town for one night, saw no choice but to bring her along.

There must have been two hundred people in attendance. The party spilled out of the penthouse apartment and onto the rooftop terrace, which was decorated with thousands of tiny white lights and exotic orchids that would never survive the cool, windy spring night. Sara preferred to remain indoors where the party was slightly less raucous, and she was glancing at her watch for perhaps the fifth time in the past half hour and wondering whether she had been here long enough to politely take her leave, or whether anyone would notice at all if she simply slipped out the door, when a voice spoke behind her. It was male, faintly but exotically accented, and gently chiding. "No, no—it's far too early for you to leave. If you do, you'll never be invited to an A-list party again."

She forced a polite professional-party smile to her lips before she turned to greet the intruder. "I can't tell you how unhappy that would make me."

She remembered thinking that he wasn't particularly handsome. His nose was too sharp, his forehead too high, his lips a trifle too full. He wore his dark hair unfashionably long and loose about his shoulders. He was tall and thin, and wore a white silk shirt, light enough to see through, untucked over faded jeans. She thought the embroidery at the cuff was pretentious. But there was warmth in his cocoa eyes, and something that she could only describe as an intense and brilliant interest, as though everything about the world fascinated him; as though he couldn't get enough of learning about it.

She, on the other hand, was carefully cool and precise and disinterested. She wore Vera Wang. Her dark hair was upswept to display her long neck—which she knew was her best feature—and teardrop diamond earrings. Her makeup was impeccable. She was elegant, in control, and unapproachable, a look that she had mastered, along with so many other lies, over the years. Yet somehow the look had not worked with him.

And although she generally would have, at that point,

politely excused herself and moved away, she was intrigued enough to add, "How do you know how long I've been here, anyway?"

"Because I've watched you since you entered," he replied, "forty-two minutes ago. I've watched you check the time on five different occasions and I've watched you finish that silly orange drink a little too fast. So I've brought you another. What is it, anyway?"

She lifted an eyebrow, hesitating a moment before setting aside her empty glass and accepting the full one he offered. "It's a mango martini," she said.

"Sounds dreadful."

"It is."

He laughed. "Then you shall simply stand here and hold it and pretend to enjoy the hospitality and inventiveness of our hosts, *eh bien?*"

"You're French," she observed, placing the accent.

"I used to be," he admitted. "I've lived in North America now for so many years that I have to practice my accent for ten minutes in the morning before I can go about in public."

That made her laugh a little, and the small lines at the corners of his eyes deepened a little as he observed, gently, "There, now. That's so much better. You have the saddest smile I've ever seen."

And before she could even react to that, he thrust out his hand and announced, "I am Daniel Orsay. I am a poet, and currently the darling of the avant-garde literary set, or so I've been told. Please don't apologize that you've never heard of me. I'm a very bad poet."

She accepted his hand, and he held her fingers, in the way of Europeans, as she tilted her head at him in skeptical amusement. "But charming."

"Which is precisely how one gets invited to parties such as this without being either rich or famous."

He held her hand a little too long, which threatened to make her flustered. She withdrew her fingers and dropped her eyes, taking a sip of the too-sweet martini. "I'm Sara," she said, looking up at him again. "Sara Graves. And I'm not rich or famous either, I'm afraid."

"*Impossible*." He seemed to use French pronunciation solely to amuse her, his accent exaggerated. "Do you think we might have stumbled into the wrong party by mistake? Surely, it is so!" Then, smoothly lapsing back into easy cocktail chatter, "What do you do, Sara?"

"I sell things." The stupid martini was giving her a headache, possibly because she was sipping it too fast again.

"What kinds of things?"

"Things that people don't need and don't want."

"You must be very good, then."

Her lips tightened in acknowledgment. "I am."

"But not very happy, I think."

She was annoyed, and wanted to argue, but she didn't know what to say. So she took another gulp of her drink and drew a breath to take her leave but he forestalled her in the very instant she was about to speak. Head inclined toward her curiously, eyes filled with that deep and genuine interest, he inquired, "Where is it that you sell these unwanted things to people who don't need them?"

"Chicago," she told him, finishing off her drink. "I work for Martin and Indlebright Marketing in Chicago." She flipped a business card from her tiny vintage evening purse and gave it to him. "Call us sometime. We'll make people believe you're a *good* poet."

"Chicago?" He seemed genuinely surprised. "How can you be happy there? You have the sea in your eyes."

That took her aback, but she recovered quickly, plastering another determinedly distant smile on her face. "It was nice to meet you, Daniel. Good luck with your poetry."

He fingered her business card thoughtfully as she turned to move through the crowd. "Good-bye, Sara Graves of the sad smile and the sea-watching eyes," he said softly. "I will call you."

But it wasn't that casual promise, which she did not expect to be kept, that caused Daniel Orsay, poet, to linger in her memory long after she left the party, after she left Manhattan, after she returned to Chicago and tried, with grim determination, to step back into the routine. It was that he knew. Even before she did, he knew that the life she had always believed she was meant for was over. And by the time he tried to call her, it was too late.

* * *

Behind her, Sara heard the sliding glass door open, and close. She was surprised, because she knew Dixie was upstairs, wrestling the boys into the tub. And then she heard the click of a lighter, and smelled the first whiff of tobacco on the chill night air. Dixie liked to pretend she didn't know Jeff came outside to sneak a smoke after dinner every night. Jeff liked to pretend he kept a secret. And Sara just kept quiet.

She was in the lawn chair on the patio, bundled up in gloves, a wool scarf, and a stadium blanket, watching the wind toss the stars around overhead. The sound of the surf was like a distant sigh, in and out, in and out. And, from inside the house, there were muffled giggles, Dixie's stern mother-voice, and a television somewhere in the background. Jeff stood silently in the shadows cast by the kitchen light on the patio, and smoked.

In a moment he said, "It's no trouble, you know. To drive you to the airport."

"It's a lot of trouble," Sara said, "and I appreciate the offer. But I'd rather have my own car. Thanks."

After a moment, he came over to her. He was a big man, a high school football star now twenty pounds overweight thanks to Dixie's good cooking. He owned his own construction company, which was no small thing on an island whose off-season sustenance depended entirely on construction and development.

He sat down at one of the little café chairs drawn up at the bistro table near her, dwarfing it with his bulk. The tip of his cigarette glowed orange in the dark, and the fragrance drifted through the night. He said, "You know, it's been good for Dixie, having you here."

Sara tried to smile, even though she knew he couldn't see it. "You mean it's been a royal pain in the ass, for both of you."

"I mean what I say." His voice was mild, Southern-accented, quiet. "You're her sister. She loves you. It's been good for her, and the kids, too." And he added unexpectedly, "I'm right fond of you, too, Sara."

Sara sat up a little straighter, surprised. She almost didn't know how to respond. "Thank you, Jeff."

"What I'm trying to say is . . ." Again the flare of his cigarette tip, faint blue smoke diffusing in the air around them. "I know it's got to be hard on you, flying over to France, doing what you've got to do . . ." Another brief orange flare in the dark. "And I know you haven't exactly made up your mind, you know, about what you're doing next. But if you were figuring on staying here on the island . . . well, it might be good if you felt like you had someplace to come home to."

A pause, too long, and Sara could hear her heart beat in the silence. Her eyes, finally adjusted to the dark, could see Jeff's silhouette, arms resting on his knees, shoulders hunched, head down and gazing at the tip of his cigarette, a faint ember in a vast bowl of windy shadows and sighing surf.

"Joe Peterson's thinking about selling that little yellow house of yours," Jeff went on, abruptly. "The place you were renting before . . . well, before. I think he'd give you a good price on it, and it wouldn't take a whole lot to fix it up."

"Ah," Sara said. And that was all she could manage, because that was all the breath she had.

Sara had moved into the little house with its scrubby yard and faded yellow clapboards less than a month after she'd arrived in Little John. It had brown linoleum floors and a kitchen the size of a linen closet, and it smelled of the sea. Daniel had moved in three months later, and permeated every corner with his presence. They had sat in the porch swing and counted the stars and listened to the surf. They had made love in every room. They sat before the fireplace, wrapped in a single quilt, and whispered their dreams to each other. And then one dark, cold night Daniel was not home when she got in from the bookstore, and he didn't answer his cell phone, and it started to sleet, and then Stu Richman, the island's only police officer, stood on her porch with his hat in his hand, dripping a freezing rain, and said, "Sara, I'm so sorry . . ."

She had not been back in the house since. Dixie had packed up her things. There weren't many; so much of what she owned was still in storage in Chicago. There had been only two sad little boxes labeled "Daniel." Daniel had never owned much at all.

And now Jeff was saying, "Listen, I'm not saying you should make up your mind now. But it might be something to think about, while you're over there, you know. And if you want me to, I'll go in and check it out for you, put together an idea of what it might cost to fix it up nice."

She was quiet for a time. "Daniel . . . never had time to tell me much about his childhood, or the place he grew up. All he ever said about his parents' house in France was that it was old, and falling apart, and had rats the size of house cats." She almost managed a smile at the memory. "He loved our little yellow house." She took a breath—a big breath, a deep breath, a breath whose effort hurt—and corrected deliberately, "My house."

Sara leaned forward, and placed her hand lightly on her brother-in-law's knee. "Thanks for letting me live in your basement, Jeff, and monopolize your wife and steal your kids. Thanks for not saying anything when I didn't show my face at meals for days at a time and worried Dixie sick." And even as she spoke she began to understand how hard these past months had been on her family, even though she had never intended to bring them her sadness, and how much they had given her, even though she had never asked them for anything. She understood, and even though she knew she could never repay them, she vowed in that moment she would not steal any more of their happiness.

She found Jeff's fingers in the dark and squeezed them briefly. "Thanks," she said. "Just thanks."

He looked uncomfortable. "Listen, Sara, it's not that you're not welcome here. You know that. But a person . . . well, a person needs a home. A place of her own."

A *life of her own*, Sara amended silently. She sat back in her chair, and tucked the scarf up around her ears against a gust of salty wind. "What's Peterson asking for the house? Do you know?"

"I'll find out. But whatever it is, you take ten thousand off the top if he doesn't replace the roof." He ground the cigarette out under his heel and sat forward with his elbows on his knees, in his element now. "I was thinking you could bump out the back wall, right where that little patio is now, and double the size of the kitchen. Of course you'll have to redo the plumbing, but you'll get ten times your money out of it when you go to sell. And as long as you're in there, you might as well add another bath. If you decide you want to go ahead with this, I could probably get a crew in there before summer . . ."

Sara smiled and nodded and made appropriate affirmative sounds in the right places, and didn't hear a word he said. Her thoughts were far away, in a country to which she had never been, with a man she had never known. And a future she couldn't even imagine.

· TWO ·

Ash Lindeman's flight from Hong Kong arrived in London a little after three a.m., and by the time he reached his flat and collapsed in bed, it was almost dawn. He had gone through the past thirty-two hours of difficult negotiations on fewer than three hours' sleep and almost nothing at all to eat, living on the exhilaration of risk and success, which was what he loved most about his life. But when it was over, he was exhausted to the bone. And, as often happened on such occasions, he had the dream.

It was a silly dream, about nothing, really, that he had had since he was a boy. A bright green meadow, and sunlight glinting off a river. In the background, a flapping sound, like wings. Two small boys in blue jackets tossed a red ball, and a little girl in pink ran around them trying to steal it. There was a woman in a big hat, someone he knew, seemed to have known all his life, and he was happy standing beside her. As they stood in the sunshine and watched the children play, a breeze caught the wide brim of her hat like a sail and spun it into the air. They both reached for it and missed, and she started laughing, and so did he, and he always woke then, yearning for that moment, and that place, and understanding, for just the briefest of instants, that he would never be that happy again.

As an adult Ash had come to realize that the dream was, in fact, a memory, but the devil of it was that he could not place that meadow, that hat, those children with the red ball, anywhere in his past. And that bothered him. Because if he could recall with such perfect clarity that moment of pure, unadulterated happiness—even if he could not recall exactly when or where it had occurred—didn't it follow that the rest of his life had been, well, virtually downhill from there?

But the worst thing about having the dream was that, having awakened from it, he found himself for days afterward wishing he could dream more.

He awoke now with the memory of leaping to catch the hat, a bright white sail against a cobalt sky, and the fast-fading sense of bliss that he ached to hold on to, and could not. He fully expected the day to be nothing but disappointment from there on.

Moreover, as he showered and shaved and dressed for the day, he was bothered by a discomfiting sense of unpreparedness, as though there was something he was supposed to have done, or remembered, but he couldn't for the life of him think what it was. He had been out of the country for nine weeks. He hated to begin his first day home this way.

Jet lag was, in a word, a bitch.

Nonetheless, he greeted the sloppy gray London day with a pragmatic equanimity and his secretary with his customary élan. "Good morning, gorgeous," he declared, checking his mobile for e-mail as he strode into the office. "Did you miss me? Lovely to be home, thank you for asking." He tossed his trench coat, still damp from the London rain, on a chair, deposited his briefcase atop it, tapped out a text message, and sent it. "I e-mailed you the contracts from the plane, did you get them? Excellent. Hard copies are in my briefcase. Work your magic on the computer, won't you, darling, and fax them out for signature before nine U.S.? Anything urgent overnight?"

The middle-aged Mrs. Harrison—he had never called her anything else—maintained a perfectly sanguine expression as she brushed away the raindrops that had splattered from his coat onto her dove silk jacket. She had two suits, which she wore on alternate days with identical white blouses, dark stockings, and sturdy, block-heeled shoes. Mondays, Wednesdays, and Fridays she wore black. Tuesdays and Thursdays she wore gray. It had been so for the thirty-five years she had worked at Lindeman and Lindeman. And for the twenty years since Ash had inherited her from his father, he had found himself looking forward to Tuesdays, and the gray suit that broke up all the black.

She crossed the room, hung his coat on the coatrack by

the door, and said, "Welcome home, sir. I trust you had a pleasant flight."

"Wouldn't know. Slept like a baby the whole way." He pocketed his phone and scooped up a collection of envelopes from her desk, sorting through them absently.

"Which might explain why you've failed to realize it's afternoon, not morning, and already well past nine, U.S. It has been for several hours now."

He glanced at his watch, which had faces for seven different time zones. "So it is," he observed, surprised. "How do you keep up with all of that in your head?"

Patiently, she retrieved the envelopes from him, and rearranged them into their original stack on her desk. "Perhaps five o'clock U.S. would do as well? I've taken the liberty of clearing that with the New York office."

He smiled at her. "Of course you have, you precious thing."

She did not respond with as much as a flicker of an eyelash. "On the subject of the U.S., sir, I was asked specifically to remind you that the young lady is flying out for Rondelais today. I believe you wanted to send flowers?"

He stared at her blankly. "What young lady?" And then, in a sudden flash of chagrined recognition, "Oh bloody hell! Is that today?"

He knew then what he had forgotten. And it sank in his heart like a stone.

"Mr. Winkle reminds you that if you wish him to represent your interests in this matter, you should please pop down to the sixth floor and sign the power of attorney before end of business today, or kindly instruct him otherwise of your wishes. Otherwise he will expect you at Rondelais Friday at noon to take care of the matter personally."

The frown that had started to gather between Ash's brows as she began speaking had settled into a scowl by the time she finished. He had been back in the office less than five minutes and his day was, indeed, on a steady downhill slide. "I was supposed to go to the cricket match with the Swiss ambassador Friday. I don't suppose we could reschedule?"

"The cricket match, possibly. The appointment at Rondelais, no. After all, it did take almost six months to arrange. Shall I send down to Mr. Winkle's office for the documents, then?"

"No." The word came out a bit too sharply and he modified it with a quick, "What I mean to say is, hold off a bit on that. I'll let you know." He thrust his hand through his rain-damp hair in a brief and uncharacteristic gesture of frustration and said, "Damn it all to hell. What a bloody nuisance. The last thing I have time for this week is a trip across the Channel. I haven't even unpacked my cases from Hong Kong."

"Then that should save you some time, sir. And on that subject . . ."

He turned on her with an uplifted eyebrow. "Mrs. Harrison, has anyone ever told you that you are the master of the elegant segue?"

She did not blink. "Your mother called to invite you for the weekend. She is having a few people out. Since you do not intend to go to Rondelais, shall I accept?"

Ash regarded her without expression. "You surely can't be serious."

And she returned, equally sanguine, "She is your mother, sir."

"And I adore her. But her house parties are ghastly—not to mention dangerous. She almost sent the prime minister to hospital with food poisoning that time."

"A regrettable incident," agreed Mrs. Harrison.

"And how she can manage to gather every homely, awkward, tediously unsuitable female in the British Isles all in one place at the same time . . . there must be some sort of directory to which she has exclusive access."

"Shall I ring her up for you, then, sir? You have been away for some time."

He looked carefully for some sign of accusation in her demeanor, and found none. "I sent her a kimono from Japan."

"You are a devoted son." She made a note on her pad. "You've a rather light week, all in all, as you weren't expected back so soon. Regarding the trip to the country . . ."

"Shall I tell you what would make you even more perfect than you are at the moment? You may take this by way of a performance review."

"And what is that, sir?"

"If you could manage, now and then, to at least pretend to be marginally taken by my charm."

"I shall certainly keep that in mind. Now, there are one or two other matters . . ."

"I suppose," he said, resigned, "I have to meet with her."

"If you are referring to your mother, it would be the civilized thing to do," agreed Mrs. Harrison.

He scowled. "I'm referring to Daniel's wife. What *is* her name, anyway?"

Mrs. Harrison gave a slight lift of her brow and informed him, "Madame Orsay."

Ash said, annoyed, "Well, I can hardly call her that, can I? That's Daniel's mother. Besides, I seem to recall she didn't take his name when they married."

He stopped then, shaking his head briefly against the shadow of pain that crossed his eyes. "Damn," he muttered. "I should know her name. I should know the name of the woman who married my oldest friend."

Mrs. Harrison took up another notepad, turned two pages, and informed him, "It's Sara, sir. Sara Graves."

"Sara," he repeated, bringing himself back with an effort from the melancholy place his thoughts had taken him. "Yes, that's right. I remember now. Excellent. Get the number where she's staying, will you? Perhaps I can persuade her to move the meeting to next week."

"Shall I tell your mother to expect you, then, sir?"

He gave her a quelling look. "You may set up a video conference in half an hour with Carlos Antigua in Brazil and Alexandra DesChamps in Switzerland. And then . . ." He sighed. "Ring my mother."

He started toward his office and Mrs. Harrison said, "Also, the former Mrs. Lindeman popped by."

Ash paused with his hand on the handle of his office door, waiting, as it were, for the other shoe to drop. And so it did.

"She's waiting in your office now. Shall I bring tea?"

He gave her a long and steady look. "You," he informed her, "are an evil, evil woman." He started to open the door, hesitated, and turned back to her. "Do not," he said distinctly, "under any circumstances, bring tea."

* * *

Michele Orsay St. Cloud Dupuis—the former Mrs. Lindeman—was Ash's constant reminder that youthful indiscretions did not necessarily fade with youth. He had married her when he was twenty-three, against the advice of his father, his mother, and his best friend, Daniel, who also happened to be Michele's cousin. He regretted the impulse almost immediately, but it had taken him more than two years to divorce her. He had been paying for the mistake, in one way or another, ever since.

"Michele." He closed the door behind him and opened his arms wide in greeting, though the gesture, and his tone, were noticeably without warmth. "What an absolute delight to see you."

The walls of Ash's office were painted a deep gray; the furnishings a postmodernistic mixture of white leather and lime green, with black metal sculptural accents in the lamps and tables. A nine-foot-square glass desk floated in the center of the room, and an enormous Rothko, brilliant in oranges and greens, dominated the opposite wall. It was a perfect backdrop for the exotic beauty of the creature who made herself so perfectly at home behind the glass desk—bold, brilliant, and uncommonly expensive. Ash's tastes were, if nothing else, consistent.

His ex-wife uncurled her long, bare legs from his leather desk chair, tossed a length of straight, fire-red hair over her shoulder, and sauntered into his arms. She smelled as thoroughly, immaculately gorgeous as she looked. "*Mon cher*," she murmured, air-kissing his cheek so as not to smear her perfect lipstick. "You are a heartless liar."

"So I am." He held her shoulders briefly to navigate his way around her, feeling a little claustrophobic in the embrace of her perfume. "What brings you to London, then?"

She tried her seductive smile, cat green eyes slanting up at him as he moved behind his desk. "Why, I came to see you, of course. Do I need another reason?"

"For your sake, I certainly hope so." He sat down behind his desk in the chair she had just vacated, folded his hands across his chest, and regarded her evenly. "Now, if it isn't too much trouble, could we get on with it? I've just returned from abroad and I've a mountain of work to get to, so if you could just tell me what you want, I can say No, you can have your tantrum, and we can both move along with our days."

She switched to a pout, trailing her pink-painted fingernail along the curve of his desk. "You are a cruel man, *mon cher*."

"I believe we've established that." He glanced pointedly at his watch.

"I rang your mobile dozens of times while you were away."

He inclined his head. "Clever of you."

"And always I get a recorded voice, never your own."

"Which is one of the many benefits of modern technology."

"And never do you bother to ring me back."

He glanced again at his watch. "I may have mentioned, my love, busy day."

She dropped the seductive air and cast him an impatient look before flinging herself into the stylish lime green chair that was arranged at an angle to his desk. *"Et bien sur,"* she said, spreading her hands. "You force me to be direct. I have for you a proposition."

He raised one eyebrow. "Of a purely business nature, dare I hope?"

Her slitted eyes glittered, evidence of the effort she made to control her temper. That alone intrigued him.

"Sadly," she murmured, "that is all that remains for us, yes?"

He said nothing. He could see the muscles in her lovely, oft-retouched jawline tighten as she waited for his reaction, and received none.

"Chéri," she said at last, and there was a distinct edge in her voice now, "enough foolishness, eh? If it is business between us, then business it shall be. I am interested, as you know, in Rondelais."

"Then you're in the wrong office. Winkle is handling that matter." He reached for the single-page agenda Mrs. Harrison always printed out and placed on the corner of his desk each morning. It was a redundancy left over from the time of his father, since his agenda was instantly e-mailed to his home computer and his mobile phone before he even got out of bed in the morning, and he had memorized it before he left the flat, but it was a tradition he liked. It also came in very handy at moments like this, when he lost interest in a conversation and simply wanted something to do.

"I understand the matter will be settled very soon, *n'est-ce pas?*"

"Very likely."

"I would like to help you bring the situation to a happy conclusion."

He tossed the agenda aside and sank back in his chair, letting his impatience begin to show on his face. "Could you kindly get on with it? This isn't even original, Michele, and I really am out of time."

She lost all pretense of being pleasant. When she abandoned sultriness, all that was left was a face with too many harsh angles, and eyes as hard as granite. She said, "Daniel's little American has no claim to Rondelais. All you need do is persuade her to abandon her interest in my favor, and all of our problems will be solved."

"Your problems will be solved," he replied. "Mine will be only beginning. What is your fascination with that old place, anyway? Believe me, it's far more trouble than it will ever be worth."

"It is my home!"

"It was Daniel's home," Ash pointed out patiently. "It never has been and never will be yours. But all other considerations aside, what in the name of all that is holy would ever make you think I'd want to go into partnership with you?"

She gave an impatient flick of her wrist. "Do not be difficult, Ashton! You know the property has been a—what is that word? A bird around your neck . . ."

"Albatross?" he suggested, trying not to smile. Sometimes

she could still be quite enchanting, even when she wasn't trying. Mostly when she wasn't trying.

"*Exactement!* An albatross about your neck for years, and nothing would make you happier than to be done with it. While Daniel lived nothing could be done, but if the two of us go into partnership, we can attract investors, we can leverage our shares, we can use the property as collateral . . ."

"We could sell at a profit," he suggested. His tone was thoughtful, his expression carefully neutral as he watched her.

"There, you see, we think alike, you and I!" She beamed at him, pleased.

"So much for your great attachment to your ancestral home," he observed.

"It is more mine than yours!" she snapped back. "Or hers!"

He shook his head a little, laughing softly. "Michele, Michele. After all these years, you still haven't learned how to manage me. Never overplay your hand, my dear. It's boring."

"Very well." She carefully rearranged her features into a cool semblance of pleasantness. "I will try not to be boring."

Tucking one foot beneath her, she leaned forward in the chair, affording him another waft of her perfume, and an unabashed view of a long and slender thigh. "You are clever; I am clever. We think alike, and we have the courage to do what needs to be done. We would be good in business together, *cher*." She gave him a small and secret smile. "As we were good together at so many other things."

He took up a Montblanc from the chrome stand on his desk and began to twirl it absently between his fingers, his expression implacable. "I wonder what Daniel would think of your proposal. Or his parents, for that matter."

"What do I care what anyone in that family ever thought? Daniel was a careless fool who never deserved his good fortune. And his little American whore . . ."

"Have a care, madame," Ash warned, his eyes growing cool. "You're talking about the woman Daniel married."

"Daniel, Daniel!" She threw him an angry pout. "I think sometimes you loved him more than me."

He pretended to consider that. "You don't want me to think too long about that one."

"She is a rich American!" Michele continued, giving a contemptuous toss of her head. "What use has she with property in France? She will let it out to Japanese tourists and have rock concerts on the lawn and build a car park in the garden!"

"Perhaps," agreed Ash. "Or perhaps she will find the same uses for it you have. On the other hand, she may take one look at the place and adore it. You know how absurdly romantic Americans can be about old houses."

"Then you will persuade her differently," said Michele, leaning in close again with those green, greedy eyes. "This is what you do so beautifully, is it not? You make people think what you wish them to think, and want what you wish them to want."

He returned a wry half smile. "In a word," he acknowledged. "But even if I were the slightest bit interested in your scheme, there remains one problem: I work for the other side.

It would be completely unethical of me to try to persuade a client of a course of action I know to be against her best interests."

"Posh!" She gave another one of those uniquely French and highly expressive turns of her wrists. "Ashton Lindeman works for Ashton Lindeman, and I know this to be true. You have big talk about doing what is the right thing but in the end everyone does what is right for *you*. That is what makes you brilliant."

"Flatterer." But he could not resist a small smile.

"No more games, then, darling. You know Daniel would have sold the place a dozen times over if the legacy had allowed it, and now that he is gone his widow will do what she likes." She gave an elaborate French shrug. "She will want to be rid of it, of course. I will make her a very . . . reasonable"— the smile that accompanied the word was smug, as though it were already fait accompli—"offer, and you will point out that it would be far more costly for her to attempt to maintain the property than to sell it at a loss. This is true. This is in the *best interests* of your client."

He tapped the pen lightly alongside his nose, his expression contemplative. "What makes you think I won't try to buy her out myself, if she's inclined to sell?"

She laughed throatily. "Darling, that would make me very happy! Rondelais remains very close to the family, and I remain . . ." Her eyes narrowed in such a way that might have been interpreted as a threat, or a promise. "Very close to you."

He regarded her thoughtfully for another long moment.

"You," he observed softly, and the note of admiration in his voice was not entirely feigned, "are a piece of work."

"Thank you," she murmured, with another upward, cat-like glint from those green eyes.

"No. Thank *you*. For a thoroughly entertaining"—he glanced at his watch—"twelve and a half minutes. However . . ." His tone became brisk as he stood up. "I'm sorry to say it has been a waste of time on your part. I'm not interested in your proposition, Michele, so, as I predicted from the outset, I'm afraid the answer is no. Do feel free to call again, though, when next you're in town." He crossed the room toward the door. "Good day."

The expressions that warred across her face were too swift, and too volatile, to be deciphered in their entirety, but Ash knew her well enough to read each one. A lesser man would have been brought to his knees.

In an instant, with a strength of will that was classically Michele, she smoothed her expression into easy nonchalance, and uncurled herself from the chair with a long, lazy shrug. "*Eh bien.*" She smiled. "It was, as you say, worth the try. We shall live to fight another day, *alors?*"

Ash opened the door. "I look forward to it."

She slung her bag—a bright yellow, crushable Prada—over her shoulder and sauntered past him. Just before exiting the door she paused, and turned a curious look on him. "This Mrs. Daniel, the American," she said. "Do you intend to tell her about the brat?"

Ash's expression remained as pleasant as ever, but he could not disguise the wariness that crept into his eyes. "I can't imagine the subject would come up."

She smiled, insincerely. "You are no doubt right." Coming close to him, enveloping him in her scent, she placed a sharp-nailed hand alongside his face. She leaned in close, emerald eyes fixed on his, and brushed a quick, light kiss across his lips. "Au revoir, *mon cher*. Think of me."

Ash waited until she had gone, then he removed a hand-kerchief from his pocket and blotted his lips. He walked into the outer office and stood thoughtfully beside Mrs. Harrison's desk for a moment. "Do you know what my father taught me?" he said, at length.

She did not look up from her monitor. "Everything you know, sir."

"Quite. More to the point, he had a saying he was fond of repeating: An ember that's allowed to smolder overnight will oft be a blazing inferno by morning. You'd best cancel my date with the Swiss ambassador, and give my regrets to my mother. And clear my schedule for the week, will you? I'll be leaving for Rondelais on the evening train."

"Very good, sir." One hand continued to type as, with the other, she offered him a slip of paper. "The young lady is staying at the Rosalie in the village. Here's the telephone. She's expected to arrive by five."

He took the paper, tapping it absently against his hand as he gazed out the window at the rain. "Sara," he murmured. "Her name is Sara."

"Yes, sir."

He turned from the window to Mrs. Harrison with brisk resolve. "Let's see what we can do about upgrading our Sara's accommodations, shall we? Call in a staff, and get that chef—

what's his name? The one who catered that affair for the museum we had there last spring."

Mrs. Harrison raised an eyebrow but did not glance up as she jotted notes on her pad.

"Have them put her up in the Queen's Chamber," he went on. "Yes, that will do nicely. And flowers, mountains of them. Make the place look like a bloody church. Candy, champagne, the full VIP treatment. And get Winkle up here. Tell him to bring the file on Rondelais. I think I'd best handle the matter personally after all."

· THREE ·

There was not one single thing that Sara could look back on and say, *Yes, that was it; that was what happened*; no precipitating event or specific moment. After the party in New York, she flew back to Chicago, approved the final revisions on the Super Bowl launch campaign for New Blue Microbrew, and three days later woke up in her plush lake-view apartment to the horrifying, paralyzing awareness that she couldn't do it another day.

She couldn't make herself get out of bed. She couldn't make herself get dressed. The telephone rang, and she didn't care. Her cell phone rang, and she didn't care. Her BlackBerry buzzed. She didn't answer the banging on the door. For forty-eight hours she lay in bed and stared at the ceiling and barely noticed the changing patterns of light and dark. She just didn't care.

Exhaustion, they called it. Stress and overwork. Take a vacation. She would be fine.

Sara nodded and smiled her wooden smile and pretended to listen to all the careful concern and well-meant advice. But even as she boarded the plane for the coast of North Carolina, Sara knew that the only way she would ever be fine was if she never came back.

And she didn't.

She moved into Dixie's basement guest room. She took long walks on the beach. She played endless games of Chutes and Ladders with the twins. She started to laugh again.

She accepted a generous settlement package from her employer, and transferred her two suitcases and a garment bag to a one-bedroom 1940s rental on Ocean Avenue with hideous linoleum and yellow clapboard siding. She helped Dixie with the bookstore in the height of tourist season.

And then one day she noticed a publisher's flier in the mail: Daniel Orsay presents *Ribbons of Light*, Sonnets for a Modern Age. "Well, I'll be damned," she had muttered out loud. "He *is* a poet after all."

On a whim, she had contacted the publisher to schedule a signing. And six weeks later, Daniel Orsay himself had stood backlit in the open door of Dixie's Books and Nooks, looking for all the world like a knight in shining armor in his white jeans and open-throated shirt with his dark hair flowing over his shoulders, and he had said, softly, "Now, *that* is a beautiful smile."

It had been the most successful event Books and Nooks had ever hosted. The women attendees swooned over his

French accent and his dark Gaelic good looks, and the store sold every copy. Sara, as hard as she tried to maintain a professional distance, was as caught up in his charm as any middle-aged tourist. And when he invited her—no, he insisted on taking her—to dinner to celebrate the evening's success, she didn't have a hope of resisting.

Looking back, she saw she hadn't had a chance since the moment he appeared in her doorway framed by the sun like some hero of yore, ready to sweep her away. She was forty-six years old, and falling for a fairy tale.

He told her about his travels—to Nairobi, Bali, India, Hong Kong. He made her laugh until she was giddy with his tales of his multiple attempts to climb Everest, each one funnier—and more outrageous—than the last. His dark eyes softened and his fingertips touched her cheek as he told her that if he could paint her laughter, it would be musical notes bursting against a crystal sky. He took her breath away.

They walked on the beach, they went sailing, they held hands at outdoor concerts. Neither Dixie nor her customers saw much of Sara that enchanted summer, and when Sara looked back on it now she realized that was exactly what it was—an enchantment. Daniel was a force of nature, a small sun that pulled everything into its gravitational path, and she had absolutely no desire to resist his magnetic power. She tumbled willingly, gladly, into the madness that was loving Daniel.

She had lived half a lifetime without trust, without commitment, without love, and there was a part of her that knew this mad, wild adventure was completely reactionary, was totally insane . . . and that sanctioned it anyway. The little girl who had cowered in a closet, holding her sister tight in her arms, while her mother's latest boyfriend shouted and broke things in the next room, disappeared when Daniel was with her. She did not have to prove anything. She did not have to be anything. She believed in fairy-tale endings.

There was another part of her that knew, of course, that he was the type of man who would break her heart, and so he did. But first he married her.

Because the real wonder of their entire, magical courtship was that this incredible man had, for some reason, fallen as much in love with her as she had with him.

She didn't know much more about him on the day she married him than on the day she had first read his publisher's brochure. He told her that his parents had died, suddenly and tragically, in the 2002 bombings in Bali, where they had been on their first out-of-the Continent holiday in twenty years. There was a stricken look on Daniel's face when he related this, as though he still could not quite accept the horror of it. He had no other family. The trip he had made to accompany his parents' bodies back to France was the last one he had ever taken to Europe. He had stayed for nine months, and knew even then there was nothing left for him. He would never go back. In retrospect, Sara realized those were the only details of his personal life he had ever given her.

Occasionally he referred to Rondelais, the town in France in which he had grown up, and now and then he talked about his college days at Oxford. He had come to the United States shortly after graduation, and had lived here, on and off, the past twenty years. He told her she was marrying a poor man and a dreamer. She told him she didn't care.

There was a part of her that knew this was not the way adults entered into marriage. And there was the bigger part of her that didn't care.

In the delirium of the passion they both shared, neither of them talked much about their pasts. Sara had assumed they would have a lifetime to discover all of those details about each other.

But in fact, they had only three weeks before Daniel lost control of his new sports car—her wedding gift to him—during an ice storm, and plowed into a tree. Only after his death did Sara realize she had been married to a man she didn't even know.

The nightmare of sorting out his affairs—such as they were—across two continents had been overwhelming, and without Dixie's help Sara did not know how she would have navigated the mess. His publisher had put her in touch with a law firm in London that was apparently authorized to handle Daniel's estate, however little of it there might be. Daniel was as free with his money as he was with his heart, and he had left very little behind. Nonetheless, the British lawyers kept writing, e-mailing, and telephoning to remind her that, according to French laws of succession, she was obligated to settle Daniel's estate within a year. She managed to postpone the requests for a meeting until the most recent correspondence requested instructions as to how she wished to pay the taxes on Daniel's property in Rondelais. She knew she couldn't put it off any longer. She had to go to France, sign whatever papers the lawyers wanted her to sign, liquidate whatever small acquisitions Daniel had managed to hold on to, and hope that would be enough to pay the French taxes, which she had heard were outrageous.

And once that was done, the brief, glorious madness that had been her marriage to Daniel would be over, erased from time almost as surely as though it had never been. It wasn't that she didn't want to go to France.

It was that she didn't want to say good-bye.

In the Land of Make-Believe

· FOUR ·

Sara arrived at Charles de Gaulle airport feeling rumpled and disoriented, which was not unusual for a trans-Atlantic flight, but not the way one wanted to face Paris for the first time, either. Dixie had tried to persuade her to at least stay a day or two in the city, to see the Eiffel Tower and sit in a sidewalk café, but Sara overruled her. She had booked a room at a B&B in Rondelais, which Dixie had looked up on the Internet and told her was adorable, and the law firm had offered to have a car meet her at the airport, which simplified her life greatly. Sara did not want to try to negotiate the rail system by herself in a country in which she did not speak the language.

She had been married to a Frenchman and she didn't speak enough French even to get herself on a train. She felt like more of an imposter than ever.

Armed with her French phrase book, Sara had spent the

half hour in which the plane circled the airport practicing one of the two French sentences she knew: *Je voudrais aller a Rondelais*, just in case she did have to do battle with a French ticket seller. The other sentence was *Ou sont les toilettes?* And she practiced that, too, just in case.

She managed to make her way to baggage claim by scanning for the signs in English, and was just tugging her dark blue suitcase off the conveyor belt when a voice behind her said, "Pardonnez-moi, Madame Orsay?"

Sara turned as a hand swung her suitcase onto the floor, and faced a man in a dark suit and chauffeur's hat. He repeated, "Madame Orsay?"

It took her a moment to understand. No one had ever called her by Daniel's last name before, and it made her feel strange. "Um . . . Yes. I mean, *oui*." She smiled at him gratefully, cleared her throat, and said with casual, deliberate enunciation, *"Je voudrais aller a Rondelais, s'il vous plaît?"*

The driver relieved her of her carry-on bag, locked the extended handle of her rolling suitcase into place, and replied in impeccable English, "Of course, madame. If you'll just follow me, we'll be on our way."

"Right," she murmured, trying to look nonchalant as she kept the pace beside him. "Thank you."

The uniformed driver led her to a long black car parked just outside the doors. He opened the back door of the car for her. "You'll find the bar is nicely stocked," he said, "and I've opened a pleasant little Montrachet for you. There's also cheese and fruit, if you like. We have a two-hour drive to Rondelais, so plenty of time to relax after your trip."

"Oh . . ." replied Sara, trying not to show her surprise as she climbed into the backseat and settled down into the cushiony folds of buff leather. "Yes, umm . . . Thank you."

"Well, well," she murmured to herself when he closed the door. "This is what I call service."

She started to search her purse for her cell phone to call Dixie, but was distracted by what appeared to be a small refrigerator built into the seat in front of her. As promised, there was a china platter of cheese and fruit with flat crackers and squares of dark chocolate. There was a silver bucket padded with shredded raffia in which nestled a bottle of red wine and a crystal glass. She wondered how much the lawyers would pad her bill for these amenities, but then she tasted the Montrachet and she didn't care.

There was a privacy panel between the front seat and the back, soft classical music floating over hidden speakers, and her own temperature controls. The driver negotiated with expert skill the busy roads of the largest city in France, and the luxury car was so smooth and silent that Sara hardly noticed when they left the busy highways behind for the more leisurely pace of the secondary roads that led east, toward the valley of the Loire River.

Sara sat back, sipped wine, nibbled on cheese, fruit, and exquisite morsels of chocolate, and actually started to enjoy the trip as the French countryside rolled by. The only traveling Sara had done in her life was circumscribed by hotel rooms and boardrooms; the concept of a vacation was alien to her. But for the first time it occurred to her that Dixie might be right . . . simply getting away could be good for her. There was something a little exotic about the smell and feel and look of a foreign country, and it made her feel exotic, too. She felt different in these surroundings, as though the pain and discontent that weighed her down throughout the winter was still trying to catch up with this time zone. It was an odd feeling, and not entirely unwelcome.

The swatches of blue and green outside the window were like a gently undulating quilt whose symmetry was broken occasionally by the spire of a village church or the arches of a stone bridge. Rich, dark fields were turned in long, curving rows, and she turned to gaze wide-eyed at the almost military precision with which the carefully pruned and tied vines of the famous wine country were lined up along the hillside. It looked like a video from the Travel Channel.

She was starting on her second glass of wine—and third or fourth square of chocolate—when the car turned gently off of the paved road and onto a narrow lane lined with those tall, cone-shaped trees she had seen in Renaissance paintings. In fact the entire vista looked a lot like a painting—the deep green trees silhouetted against a pale sky, the glint of a deep crystal blue lake in the distance that was spanned by a charming wide planked bridge, and beyond that bridge, half obscured by a dip in the road, she got a glimpse of the tall towers and chimneys of what looked very much like one of the oft-photographed châteaux of France. It was then that she remembered, with chagrin, the camera Dixie had stuffed into her purse at the last minute. She had promised the boys—well, mostly Dixie—a full photographic essay, and she hadn't taken a picture of a single vineyard. Hopefully, a picture of a castle would make up for it.

To Sara's amazement and delight, the car crossed the bridge, and at the height of it the full château—or at least as much as the eye could see—came into view. The structure seemed to have been built around a pointed-roofed tower on the west side, so that it was as much round as square in appearance. It was constructed of a pale, rough gray stone, three stories high, with a darker stone accenting each of the multiple arched windows in an uneven, charmingly hand-hewn fan shape. There was a deep, shadowed entryway slightly asymmetrical to center with an arched portico that reached to the second story, and Sara counted six chimneys on the front side of the house alone. The sun, now long past its zenith, was aligned behind the ancient fortress in such a way that the entire structure seemed to glow with a silvery luminescence. It was everything she had ever expected from a fairy-tale castle, and more.

She stretched from window to window to try to take it all in at once—the glittering water, the sweep of emerald lawn that surrounded the castle, the wavy leaded glass windows, the small dark rectangles in the tower that Sara believed had once been used as battle stations in the time of bows and arrows. She snapped a dozen pictures through the windows, and the driver, who must have noticed her efforts, was kind enough to pull the car around the circular drive and stop in front of the castle. He got out and came around to open her door.

"Oh, thank you so much!" Sara exclaimed, climbing out. "Do you think it's okay if I take pictures? I mean, will anyone mind?"

"Certainly not, madame. As you wish."

"It's gorgeous," she said, backing up and checking her frame in the digital camera. "Just like Cinderella's castle, only older. And real," she added, snapping the shutter.

The timeworn stones were mossy in places, and she could see white patches where the mortar had been repaired. She felt small, and overcome with awe, at the thought of the centuries this place had witnessed, the hands that had carved and stacked these stones so long ago, the feet that had trod its halls. Suddenly she was glad she had come to France. There was nothing like standing in the shadow of an edifice that had been erected by people who had lived and died centuries before you were born to put your own small life into perspective.

Maybe she would make time to visit a few churches and museums after all.

She had wandered a dozen or so steps from the car in her enthusiastic photo-taking, and now she turned back. "Thanks again for . . ."

But she stopped. The driver had removed her bags from the car and was standing beside them, waiting patiently for her. Sara hurried over to him.

"Excuse me," she said, gesturing to her suitcases. "Is something wrong? Aren't you taking me to my hotel?"

He nodded. "*Oui*, madame. This is Château Rondelais."

"But . . ." She scrambled in her purse for the folded paper on which she had printed all her travel instructions. "I'm staying at—at the Rosalie, in the village."

"No, madame," he explained patiently. "There has been a change in your accommodations. Mr. Lindeman himself instructed that I am to make certain you are settled in the château."

"Oh," she said, trying not to show her astonishment. *Lindeman* was definitely the name on the letterhead she had received from the British law firm. And this was definitely a castle.

"But . . ." She looked around helplessly, but he gave her a reassuring nod and gestured her to precede him up the path.

The flagstone walkway was cracked with age and showing a few weeds here and there, shadowed in places by the giant, rounded boxwoods that dotted the lawn. The château loomed huge and silent as she approached, with absolutely no sign of life within. She had heard, of course, that many of the châteaux in the Loire Valley had been transformed into B&Bs, but she had never expected to actually spend the night in one.

The massive oak front door swung open just as they gained the top step, and a plump, uniformed maid receded into the shadows. Sara glanced uncertainly at the chauffeur, who smiled and nodded and, with his arms occupied with her luggage, gestured her to precede him. Sara stepped inside.

There she was struck dumb and motionless. Why had she expected a cold, dark stone foyer lined with suits of chain mail and battle-axes? This was France, after all, the land of opulence and fairy tales. The enormous hall in which she was standing was clad in gleaming, pink-veined marble, floor to two-story ceiling. A banister curved upward alongside a marble staircase that was wide enough for a giant and a couple of his drinking buddies to climb side by side. Overhead was a chandelier that was as big as the bathroom in her Chicago apartment, and every prism of it sent shards of light cascading off the polished surfaces below.

In the center of the room was a table with delicately curved legs, on which rested an enormous vase of flowers—nasturtiums, lilies, saucer-sized dahlias, stately yellow and pink gladiolus, and deep purple iris. There were mirrors in baroque frames, and a painting of a boy in knee pants with a greyhound that was taller than she was. Far beyond the crystal chandelier, the domed ceiling was painted a Renaissance blue, its panels edged in gold. The white marble floor beneath her feet shone like glass.

Granted, the banister was dark with age and the steps were worn. The silver arms of the chandelier showed signs of tarnish and the blue ceiling was faded, the gold leaf blackened in places and flaking. But the sheer enormity of the room, the vast quantity of all that marble, the glitter and gleam of polished surfaces, swallowed up insignificant details.

Sara was aware that she was gaping like Alice in Wonderland, but she couldn't help it. The big oak door swung slowly shut on heavy hinges, and the driver began speaking in rapid French to a woman in a crisp gray maid's uniform. In a moment he turned to her. "Madame, it has been a pleasure serving you. Madame Touron will show you to your room."

"Oh, uh, thank you." Sara pulled herself out of the spell of wonder that had entrapped her the moment she entered the house, and fumbled in her purse for a tip. She had no idea how much would be appropriate. "You've been wonderful."

He ignored her futile search for euros and instead gave

her a small bow. "Good day, madame. Enjoy your stay at Rondelais."

As he departed by the front door, the maid gestured toward the staircase in invitation. "Madame?"

Sara felt like royalty as she followed the woman up the broad, sweeping stairs, her soft-soled shoes squeaking against the polished marble. The stairway was lined with portraits of people in costumes from various centuries, some in stiff Elizabethan collars, some in floaty empire gowns, some in Victorian ballroom attire. The only thing that prevented Sara from grabbing her camera and snapping photos at every step was that she didn't want to seem like a typical American tourist to the maid. But she vowed to sneak down later and get some photographs—for Dixie, of course.

They reached the second floor, and turned down a wide hallway with a high medallioned ceiling and a faded, rather threadbare blue tapestry carpet that ran the length of the gleaming marble floor. It was a hallway in the sense that it was a corridor flanked on either side by rooms, but it was unlike any hall Sara had ever seen in America. It easily could have accommodated several apartments, complete with furniture, in its breadth and depth, and even though their footsteps were muffled by the carpet, every movement echoed. There were deep alcoves and high windows, elaborately carved wood moldings and panels, but almost no furnishings, which Sara thought was odd for a place as luxurious—and large—as this. At the far end, the corridor branched right and left, presumably leading to the separate wings, but before they got that far the maid stopped, and opened a door. Sara followed her inside.

"Oh . . . my . . . goodness," she said softly.

It was like a picture out of a coffee-table book entitled *World's Most Luxurious Suites*. The most prominent feature was the bed, raised on a dais and adorned with a puffy white silk comforter, blue silk pillows trimmed in gold fringe, and gold silk curtains, lined in blue, that dropped from a ceiling coronet and were pulled back in graceful drapes on either side of the tall, slim headposts. There was a marble fireplace with elaborately carved flowers, butterflies, and scrollwork, and a fire burned cheerily in the grate.

A blue velvet settee and matching Queen Anne chair were drawn up before the fire, and between them was a small, elegant table, on which was arranged a tiered dish of chocolate-dipped fruit. Beside the settee was a silver ice bucket on a stand, which held a bottle of champagne and a flute glass. In the center of the room a marble-topped table sported another enormous vase of flowers, this time lilacs and white roses. The room was filled with their fragrance.

She hardly knew where to look, it was all so overwhelming. Surely this was not all meant for her. How much must a room like this cost per night, anyway?

"Um . . ." She turned to the maid, who had already made it clear she did not speak English, but Sara wasn't sure what she would have said even if she could have made herself understood. *Do you have a smaller castle? Maybe there's a more affordable room in the gardener's shed?*

The maid opened a door and stood aside, her smile inviting Sara to look inside. Almost tiptoeing, Sara ventured to the door. She caught her breath at what she saw.

The bathroom was approximately the size of her bedroom in Dixie's basement. The ceiling was frescoed with cherubs and clouds, and trimmed with intricately carved moldings that were painted white and brushed with gold leaf. The room had its own fireplace, in which another fire danced and sparked. A plush white robe was draped over a velvet-cushioned stool, and an elaborately scrolled dressing table was topped by a baroque gold-framed mirror. A careful arrangement of lotions, oils, and toiletries was displayed in cut-glass bottles atop the table. But the centerpiece was a sunken marble bathtub as big as a child's swimming pool. A teardrop chandelier was centered over it, reflecting prisms of light off the aqua water that filled it and the gleaming marble steps that led into it. As Sara watched, slack-jawed, the maid opened one of the jars on the dressing table, and sprinkled a handful of red rose petals over the steaming water.

Sara pulled the French phrase book from her purse, frantically flipped a few pages, and finally came up with the words she wanted. *"Pour moi?"* She pointed at her chest. For me?

"Oui, madame." The maid proceeded to rattle off a litany of French, to which Sara merely smiled and nodded dumbly, feeling as dazed as she no doubt looked. Finally, with something that must have been her closing statement—Sara hoped it wasn't anything important—the woman gave a small bow of her head and left the room.

A marble bathtub. A marble bathtub filled with scented water and rose petals. In a castle. Sara debated for only another moment.

"I don't care how much it costs," Sara decided out loud. "I'm going to take a bath in a castle once before I die."

And so she did.

"And *then*," Sara said into her cell phone, swinging her feet up over the arm of the settee and adjusting the folds of the luxuriously soft robe around her knees, "I came out of the bathtub and all my clothes had been unpacked and put away! They had even been steam pressed! And my dirty clothes were gone, whisked away just like that to the magical laundry or wherever dirty clothes go. Even my shoes were polished! Can you imagine how many elves must have been working while I was in the bathtub? Dixie, are you *sure* you didn't have anything to do with this?"

"Are you kidding?" Her sister, an ocean away, sounded as though she could be in the next room. "I wish I'd thought of it! A castle," she repeated for what must have been the sixth time. "You're staying in a castle! Wait until I tell the boys!"

"The chauffeur said the law firm had changed my reservation. Why would they do that?"

"Maybe something went wrong at the other place," suggested Dixie. "A flood or something."

"Their loss, my gain." Sara bit into a lush, ripe strawberry coated in white chocolate and barely repressed a moan of delight. "Did I tell you about the towels? They were so fluffy it was like drying off with kitten fur. And they were heated with these flat stones that were packed in the bottom of the basket. And the whole room smells like roses. What's the name of that fairy tale, where the princess goes to this mysterious castle where food magically appears and the fireplace magically lights itself and beautiful gossamer garments are magically laid out for her?"

"You mean the one that was an animated classic and an international hit musical?"

"Yes, yes, that one."

"Here's a hint: Watch out for the Beast."

Sara paused in the act of reaching for a cherry dipped in dark chocolate. "Oh," she said. "*Beauty and the Beast*. Right."

"The downside of living a fairy tale," Dixie pointed out. "Sara, who's paying for all this?"

"I have a theory about that," Sara said, examining the label on the champagne bottle. It looked expensive, and on second thought, she decided not to open it. "The only thing I can guess is that the law firm must own this place—like a corporate retreat or something. And whenever they have clients from out of town, or out of the country, this is where they put them up. What I can't figure out is why I would rate a room in the castle."

"Don't ask too many questions," Dixie advised. "Enjoy yourself."

"Well, until the Beast shows up, anyway."

Dixie chuckled. "Just make sure they don't try to charge you for the champagne and flowers when you go to sign the settlement papers. Sara, it sounds like you're having a good time."

"Despite my best intentions," Sara admitted. She returned the champagne bottle to the ice bucket. "I only wish you could have come with me."

A continent and a lifetime away, a screen door slammed

and a clamor of shrieking voices filled the background. Dixie said, "What? And give up all this?" Then, sharply, "Boys! Mommy's on the telephone!"

Before Sara could succumb to the prickle of nostalgia she was starting to feel, there was a knock on her door. She swung her feet to the floor. "I have to go, Dixie, someone's at the door. Tell the boys I love them."

"We love you, too," replied Dixie, shouting a little to be heard over the ever increasing excitement level in the background. "Send photos!"

"I will. Bye, Dixie." She flipped the phone closed and swung open the door, expecting the maid with more food, wine, or flowers.

It wasn't the maid. It was a tall, blond man of about her age in a gray cashmere sweater and perfectly creased charcoal slacks that looked Italian, and custom-made. His features were patrician; his light hair was thick and wavy and worn just long enough to curl slightly around his ears. The sleeves of his sweater were stylishly pushed up to bare his forearms, and the shine on his oxblood loafers—which again looked Italian, and handmade—was a deep gloss. He had deep blue eyes and wore the beginnings of a polite smile. He looked like every American's idea of a European aristocrat, and was so perfectly suited for these surroundings that he might have been hired for the part.

Good God, she thought, a little dazed. *It's Prince Charming.*

But what she said was, "Um . . . you must be the Beast."

· FIVE ·

He replied smoothly, "That's a bit harsh, don't you think, on such short acquaintance?" His accent was British, his expression amused and slightly quizzical. "Which is not to say," he admitted with a small, considering tilt of his head, "that you won't yet be proven right."

"Lawyer," Sara amended quickly. "I meant lawyer. Owner, that is."

"Part owner," he corrected politely, and extended his hand. "I'm Ashton Lindeman. Welcome to Château Rondelais."

She was confused. That was the name of the law firm, which meant he was partner. Why would they send a partner all the way to France to meet her? Moreover, she was meeting him for the first time wearing nothing but a bathrobe.

She fumbled self-consciously with the open collar of her

robe, trying to pull the two pieces a little closer together. "But—I've been dealing with a Mr. Winkle."

He smiled. "I hope I won't disappoint."

She noticed his still-extended hand and took it quickly, still clutching the collar of her robe. "No, of course not. I'm Sara Graves. Sara Graves Orsay." The name sounded clumsy when she said it out loud, and she probably blushed a little, because he gave her an odd look.

"Yes," he murmured. He held her fingers another moment, still smiling, but regarding her with a strangely curious look on his face. Then he said, "It's the oddest thing. I don't suppose we might have met before."

She said, "I don't think so." He was still holding her hand, and it was beginning to make her a little uncomfortable. He must have noticed, because he released her fingers, and the puzzled expression on his face smoothed into easy courtesy.

"Forgive me," he said. "For a moment you must have reminded me of someone; I can't think who. At any rate, it's delightful to meet you, Sara. So sorry to disturb. I just popped by to make certain you were comfortable, and to place myself at your service."

"Oh. Yes, thank you." She felt foolish, clutching her robe together like a schoolgirl, so she dropped her hand and instead tightened her belt. "What I mean is, how could I not be?" She gestured backward into the opulent room. "This room is . . . unbelievable."

He nodded, smiling a little. "Yes, it is a bit over the top, isn't it? We had a wedding here some years back and the bride insisted on redoing the entire suite for her wedding night."

Sara's eyes widened. "For one night?"

"Indeed. No insult intended to the lovely bride, but there is a saying, I believe, about a fool and her money. Nonetheless, we made out rather well for it, wouldn't you say?"

That made her laugh a little. It occurred to Sara that he was far too charming to be a lawyer—or British, for that matter. He was not at all what she had expected. But then, neither was anything else about this trip.

"I would," she agreed. "And, whether it's thanks to her, or to you, I definitely appreciate the accommodations."

"My pleasure to arrange. I thought we'd dine in about an hour, if that suits. And they've set up drinks on the terrace, whenever you'd like to come down."

"Oh," she said, glad that she hadn't opened the champagne . . . and wishing she hadn't sampled quite so liberally from the cheese, fruit, and chocolate platters. She had forgotten the European tradition of dining late. "That sounds lovely."

"Shall I meet you downstairs, then?"

"It will only take me a minute," she assured him. "Thank you."

"Not at all." He started to turn away, but then turned back as she was closing the door, a forefinger raised as though in caution. "You weren't by chance thinking of blow-drying your hair, were you?"

Sara fingered the few damp strands of hair that had escaped from her top knot, wondering if that was a suggestion. "No, I don't think so."

"Excellent." He smiled. "See you downstairs, then."

She closed the door and rested against it for a bemused moment. This entire trip was turning out to be one puzzle after another, and she had quite a few questions for the elegant Mr. Lindeman.

But first, the big question. What did one wear to dinner and drinks with Prince Charming?

* * *

He was on the telephone when she descended the wide marble staircase a few minutes later. Sound carried perfectly in the vast hall, and she could see him leaning casually against the ancient, elaborately carved, and timeworn banister with a cellular phone to his ear. What she could not do was understand a word he was saying.

He murmured a few clipped and indecipherable words into the telephone when he saw her on the stairs, and disconnected. "A woman of her word," he observed, smiling as she reached him. "I admire that. And you look lovely."

Sara doubted that, since she had been far too anxious about keeping him waiting to spend much time fussing with her appearance. She had drawn her hair back from her face with a butterfly clip, hastily applied foundation and lipstick, and pulled on a white silk shirtwaist that Dixie had insisted she bring "just in case." She shrugged a little at the compliment.

"I wasn't sure what to wear to dinner at a castle," she said.

He chuckled. "My constant dilemma as well. We'll bring out the beaded cloaks and scepters another time, shall we? Since it's just the two of us tonight, I thought we'd keep it informal."

She said, "I didn't mean to eavesdrop, but was that Japanese you were speaking on the phone?"

"It was. I've always found it much easier to persuade someone around to your point of view if you actually speak their language. We're to the left, my dear."

He touched her shoulder lightly, guiding her toward a doorway at the far end of the enormous room. He brought with him the subtle scent of an expensive cologne when he moved close—or perhaps it was a hand-milled soap—that was mildly suggestive of citrus and leather.

The marble hall through which they had been walking was cool and churchlike, filled with nothing but the sound of their echoing footsteps. As he turned her easily through a doorway and into another massively proportioned—and completely empty—room, he added, "I thought I'd take you on a proper tour of the place tomorrow. It's not something you want to attempt on your first night in."

"How big is this place, anyway?" Sara inquired. She didn't even attempt to keep the awe out of her voice as she tried to take in everything at once—the buttressed ceiling, the paneled walls, the two fireplaces, each of them big enough to hold an entire tree and the truck that delivered it.

"Rondelais is one of the smaller châteaux in the valley," he replied. "Only forty-seven rooms."

She stared at him. "Forty-seven?"

"Of course, a good many of them are unrestored."

"Of course," she murmured.

They had reached a set of paned glass doors, and he opened one, stepping back for her to precede him. "Here we are."

Sara stepped out onto a wide flagstone terrace lined with geometrically sculpted topiaries in stone pots. There was a fountain on one corner, its water cascading musically into the half-moon pool below. Near it was a round table that appeared to be carved completely from a single piece of white limestone, with cushioned chairs drawn up around it. Teak furniture, looking oddly modern in this ancient setting, was arranged in comfortable conversation groups across the terrace. Beyond them, the Loire Valley spread out its rippling shades of emerald green, spring green, hunter green, indigo blue, and deep lavender. The angle of the sun was gentle, bathing the terrace in a golden glow and reflecting warmth from the pale stones underfoot. Sara inhaled a deep breath of honeysuckle-scented air.

"This," she said, somewhat overawed, "is magnificent."

"It is, rather." He stood beside her, and she noted the surprise in his voice. "I haven't been here in ages. I'd forgotten."

She glanced at him, and though there were a dozen questions battling for attention, what she said was, "I have to thank you for going to so much trouble to make me feel welcome here. The flowers, the champagne . . . it was really too generous. And completely unnecessary," she added. "I'm sure I would have been perfectly happy at the B&B in town."

The glow of the sun planed one side of his face in gold, and deepened his eyes as he looked down at her. "It was absolutely necessary," he assured her with a smile. "First impressions are everything, you know, and I wanted you to see the old girl at her best. "

Before she could respond to that, a frown creased his brow

and he brought his cell phone from his pocket to read the screen. "Forgive me," he said, but was already turning away. "I should attend to this."

She caught snatches of his conversation as he walked across the terrace: "Terribly sorry, but I thought we were clear on that . . . Those are the terms . . . Well, then, my darling, I suppose you will simply have to go back to your board with our counteroffer . . . No, it's quite firm, I'm afraid . . . Do let me know. But within twenty-four hours, yes? Ciao."

He returned to her with his hands turned palms up and an apologetic smile on his face. "A thousand pardons. Where were we?"

"I thought it was only rude Americans who couldn't bear to be parted from their cell phones," Sara observed.

He looked amused. "Actually, Europeans are decades ahead of you in that regard. It's because the technology is so much more advanced." But as he spoke, he removed his phone from his pocket and made a show of turning it off. "However, you're right. It's rude to ignore a guest and I am properly chastised. I forget sometimes there is such a thing as being too involved in one's work."

He smiled at her, the kind of smile that caused deep crinkles to form at the corners of his eyes, and Sara began to suspect that being charming was, quite simply, what he did for a living.

She said, "Why is it, again, that you are here rather than Mr. Winkle?"

And even as she spoke, a waiter appeared—or perhaps the correct term was *footman*—in black jacket and white gloves, bearing a large silver tray with a selection of decanters and hors d'oeuvres. He set the tray on the shaded stone table near the fountain, and Ash said, "I wasn't sure what you'd enjoy to drink; I should have asked. Will sherry do? I like a good Scotch before dinner, myself. Or I can send for something else."

"Oh," she said. "Oh, no, this is fine. Sherry is fine. Sherry is wonderful."

Ash spoke a few words of smooth, fluid French to the footman, who nodded a bow and departed.

"I thought we'd enjoy our wine with dinner," Ash said, pouring the drinks. "I've chosen a nice selection from some of the lesser-known vineyards that I thought you might appreciate while you're here."

Suddenly Sara was reminded of her corporate days: the grand hotels, the expensive wines, the smell of chafing dishes and rich cigars. The sharp deals, the slick pitches, the clash of triumph and desperation. There was a hollowness in the pit of her stomach that was at odds with the grandeur of her surroundings.

"You know," Sara said carefully, "I really didn't expect all of . . ." She made another vague gesture. "This. I'm starting to feel a little overwhelmed."

He handed her a glass of sherry. "I'm glad I didn't order the caviar, then." He indicated the tray, smiling. "The pâté is quite fine, though. The chef is one of the best in the valley, I'm told. We can look forward to a real feast tonight."

She repeated, "Chef?" And then she had to know. "Do you treat all your clients this . . ." She searched for the word. "Extravagantly?"

He said, "Actually, I hardly ever bring clients here. It's far too much bother, and the devil of an expense."

And that was enough. Her fingers tightened on her glass, and she said firmly, "Mr. Lindeman, why am I here? Why are *you* here?"

His brows drew together, and he dropped his gaze to the glass of whiskey in his hand. "Sara," he said, and then he glanced at her. "May I call you that?"

She nodded, and something about the sober expression on his face made her attention sharpen. His frown deepened briefly, and he looked uncomfortable, as though searching for words. She remained silent, and waited for him to continue.

He said, "I feel the perfect ass. I wanted to say something earlier." Again he dropped his gaze, and small, hard lines appeared at the edges of his mouth. "I was in Australia when I got the word about Daniel," he said. "I should have called. I know that. I'm no good at the bloody formalities. I didn't know what to say. I wanted to send a note. Started to write you more than once. But I couldn't. I'm sorry."

She stared at him for the longest time, not understanding. Her memory, dulled by jet lag and the reluctance to revisit the horror of the winter, reluctantly began to shuffle through details. Finally she said, remembering, "But . . . there was a note. Besides the letter from your firm about—about the estate, there was a lovely handwritten note. I remember."

He gave a brief, sharp shake of his head, shifting his gaze away. Every word seemed clipped, and forced. "My secretary wrote it. I asked her to sign my name. I meant to do more. I have no excuse. Daniel was my best friend. I should have done more." He forced out a breath, as though ridding himself of something unpleasant, and said shortly, "There. That's said."

And suddenly she understood. "Oh my God," she said softly. "Ash. You're Ash. Daniel's friend from school."

She turned away, her fingers coming to her lips, feeling a familiar surge of humiliation. She should have known that. That was something a wife should have known. How could she have been so oblivious?

"I'm so sorry," he said swiftly. "I didn't mean to upset you."

She had to swallow before she could speak. "No," she said. But she couldn't turn around to face him. "I'm the one who should apologize. I'm just so embarrassed. I should have realized who you were sooner."

"My fault entirely," he assured her. "I should have been more clear in my introduction."

She could tell by his voice that his brief discomfiture was gone. He was back in his element now, saying the right thing, knowing what to do, putting people at their ease. As she turned, he came over to her and made a small movement with his hand, as though to touch her, and then seemed to change his mind. "I understand," he said simply. "I do."

She had no doubt that he was sincere in his effort to make her feel better. And that was also exactly the right thing to say.

Sara tried to think of something to say. "How long did you know Daniel?"

He gestured her toward one of the teak chairs that was drawn up around a low table, and waited until she was seated to answer. "Since we were boys, off and on. His family did business with my father, and later, we were at Oxford together." He smiled as he leaned back in the chair opposite her and sipped his drink. "He was the most impractical fellow I've ever known, and probably the most fun. Life was a circus to him. It was almost as though . . ."

"As though he knew his time was short," Sara finished for him softly, "and he was determined to make the most of it."

Ash said simply, "Yes."

"So," she said, when she could speak again. "That explains why you took over from Mr. Winkle."

He looked a little uncomfortable. "Truth is, I should have done so from the beginning. Our firm has handled the Orsay affairs for generations, but estate law isn't really my specialty, and I thought you'd be better served by Winkle. I meant no disrespect."

"What is your specialty, Mr. Lindeman?" Sara asked, with interest. "I have to be honest, I always assumed Daniel's lawyers were, well, a small-time operation . . . you know, the type who do wills and trusts and not much else. I didn't expect one of them to speak Japanese."

He said, "Lindeman and Lindeman specializes in international law. Truth be told, we do very little estate work these days, but the Orsays, as I mentioned, are old friends of the family. For myself, I'm what you call in America a *closer*, I believe. I put together the impossible deals. When Coca-Cola wants to bottle Perrier, or McDonald's wants to franchise in China, my job is to make certain everything goes smoothly for everyone involved. And if Apple Computer wanted to buy Microsoft, for example, I would find a way to convince Mr. Gates that the deal is not only in his best interest, but that he simply cannot survive without it. I package proposals; I make them look irresistible; I make certain everyone comes away feeling he has won the game. It's really quite exhilarating."

Sara blew out a soft breath. "Why do I feel I need to call my stockbroker?"

Those lines about his eyes appeared again, and he tipped his glass to her. "The moment I hear from Apple, I'll be certain to give you a call."

"So," she said, "how did you end up with a castle in France?"

"A portion of a castle," he corrected her. And then he paused with his glass halfway to his lips, an odd expression coming over his face. "Don't you know?"

She shook her head, uncomfortable with the way he was looking at her. "Know what?"

Still he fixed her with that penetrating gaze, his whiskey untasted, as though he were seeing her for the first time. "Impossible," he muttered, almost to himself. And, aloud, "You do know who holds the controlling interest in Château Rondelais, don't you? What I mean to say is, Daniel did tell you that at least?"

She really didn't like the way he was looking at her, and his tone, so crisp and British and lawyerlike, made her bristle. But he was her host, and he had sent her flowers and champagne, so she was determined to be polite. "Okay, I give up," she said. "Who owns the other part of the castle?"

He leaned forward, his elbows resting on his knees, and fixed her with that watchful gaze. "As a matter of fact," he answered her carefully, "you do."

· SIX ·

Sara simply stared at him, without speaking, without blinking, without, it seemed, even breathing, for an intolerable moment. Ash sat back heavily in his chair. "Good Christ," he muttered. Then, lips tightening, "I'll have Winkle's scalp for this."

Sara set her glass very carefully on the small table beside her chair. She blotted her fingers on her skirt. She said, "Is this a joke?"

Ash lifted his glass, and took a drink. He said, "It is not."

Her expression was immobile, her gazed fixed on him. Clearly she was waiting for an explanation, but he hardly knew where to begin. He decided, at length, on the beginning.

"Château Rondelais has been in the Orsay family since 1715," he said, "when it was awarded to the marquis of the day for some service to the crown, or perhaps to pay off a gambling debt; no one has ever been clear on that part of the story. Family fortunes declined over the generations, as they've a tendency to do, and châteaux are expensive to maintain. Daniel's parents practically bankrupted themselves trying to put the place into the shape it is now, and sold most everything that was disposable to keep it up and pay the taxes. Unfortunately, a condition of Daniel's inheritance was that the property itself could not be sold, so when he needed money a few years back I managed to get around that encumbrance by offering to purchase an investment share. Which is how I came to own part of a castle and how you . . ." He took another drink. "Came to inherit one."

Sara stood up and walked across the terrace. He watched as she reached the stone wall and paused there for a moment, her hands resting lightly on it, gazing out over the valley. She stood stone still, her face in profile, the curve of her shoulder and the fall of her skirt in perfect alignment, and in the pinkish twilight she almost could have been a sculpture: a piece of modern art designed to complete the terrace, a part of it. *Woman Surveys the Future*, it would be called.

Ash took another drink to clear his head, and was surprised to find his glass almost empty.

She turned after a moment and walked back toward him. She was wearing sandals with a low heel, and her footsteps made almost no sound on the stone. She sat down again and picked up her glass, looked at it for a moment, then returned it to the table with very great care. He could see that her hand was unsteady.

"I see," was all she said.

"There's no excuse for your not having been told all of this from the start," Ash said, his voice harsh. "It was our job, as executors of the estate, to make certain that all the paperwork detailing your inheritance was clear and in order. Unpardonable that we shouldn't have done so. I assure you that there will be an accounting—"

She held up a hand to stop him. "No, don't. It wasn't your fault. It wasn't anyone's fault. I'm sure it was all explained perfectly . . . I just wasn't paying attention. I hardly read the letters your office sent. And all Daniel ever told me about his family home was that it was old and falling apart. I . . ." She stopped on a sharp inhalation of breath, pressing her fingers to eyes. "We were married for *three weeks*!" she cried. "Damn it!"

And suddenly she started to laugh, softly. She leaned back against her chair, shaking her head. "It *is* a joke," she said. "It's a great big twisted cosmic joke and I'm the punch line. I'm Cinderella trapped in a freakin' fairy tale that just doesn't know when to end. And what the *hell* am I supposed to do with a castle in France?" she demanded, turning on him. Her eyes glittered and her voice was beginning to take on a shrill edge. "Could you just tell me that, please?"

"I thought we could discuss your options after dinner," he said, watching her carefully. "I had hoped to get a couple of drinks into you first. Or perhaps a Valium?"

Sara looked down at the sherry glass on the table as though suddenly remembering it, then picked it up and downed the contents in a single swallow. When she spoke again her voice was matter-of-fact, almost flippant. "You must think I'm a complete idiot. That's okay. Because that's exactly what I feel like." She held up her empty glass. "Maybe I'll have another."

Ash did nothing but lift a glance toward a shadow somewhere beyond her shoulder, and a waiter appeared to refill her glass. This time she sipped more slowly.

"My father walked out on us when I was six," she said. "My mother—wasn't the kind of person who could recover from something like that. She was broken, I think, from the inside out. She started to drink, couldn't hold a job . . . I kind of took over for her, fixed the meals, made sure my little sister got to school on time and that we had clean clothes to wear . . . I lied about my age so I could get an after-school job at fourteen, and I kept telling myself if I worked really, really hard, I could get Dixie and myself out of there. And eventually I did. I got a scholarship, a degree, and a great job. It was all I wanted, all I'd ever wanted. Of course . . ."

She shrugged, and sipped her sherry. "All those years I threw myself into my work like that I really was still just a little girl trying to get out of that trailer park, but by the time I realized that, half my life had gone by. And when Daniel showed up—the most impossible, exotic, romantic fantasy any woman could ever imagine—I tried to make up for every dream I'd never let myself have all at once. I was ready to be swept away. I wanted the insanity. I'd lived the buttoned-down life for almost twenty years and I was ready to throw caution to the wind. It's not that I didn't know better. It's that I *wanted* to believe in the fairy-tale ending. My sister had it all, why couldn't I?" A small smile. "And of course, who could resist Daniel? I sometimes wonder whether he wasn't as caught up in my fantasy as I was."

As she spoke, twilight was deepening, bathing the terrace in rich blue shadows that seemed to encourage intimacy. In the background, silent figures moved, dropping a white linen cloth over the stone table, bringing out trays, lighting candles. With a gentle *whoosh*, a torchiere flared to light a half dozen feet away, smelling of butane and citrus, and in soft sequence—*whoosh, whoosh, whoosh*—more of them followed, encircling the terrace with a golden glow and casting dancing shadows across the stone. Ash watched her silently, and listened.

Sara took another sip of her drink. "I knew it wasn't real," she said. "I knew it couldn't last. I just didn't care. I guess, if I thought about it at all, I expected to just wake up one morning to find him gone, like my dad . . . but no, I didn't think about it. I just wanted to live the dream for as long as I could, because I had gone so many years without any dreams at all. I didn't expect him to *die*. I didn't expect him to die without telling me who his next of kin was or where his insurance papers were or if he even had a will . . ." Her voice tightened here, and she stared into her almost empty glass. "When the coroner released his body they wanted to know how I wished to dispose of the remains, and *I didn't know*. I was so angry at Daniel for that, for dying, for all the things he didn't tell me and all the things he left me to take care of. But mostly for just making it all so *real*, and messy and ugly."

She looked at Ash. "But eventually I got over that. I got

over the anger, I got over the disappointment, I was even starting to get over the pain. Now I find out my handsome prince has left me a four-hundred-year-old castle to remember him by, and how am I supposed to deal with that? What am I supposed to do now?"

Ash put his drink aside and stood, extending his hand to her. "Come to dinner," he said. Sara hesitated, then put her hand in his and allowed him to draw her to her feet. He placed his hand lightly on the back of her arm as they crossed toward the table, guiding her across the uneven flagstones. She said tiredly, by way of apology, "Too much information, huh?"

"Daniel," he said, "had an uncanny knack for complicating the lives of those who cared for him. Still, it's rather interesting, don't you think, that of all the things he could have left to a woman who never before had dreams of her own, a castle is the most fitting?"

She glanced at him, and smiled a little, though it was fleeting. "That was a nice thing to say," she said. "And I apologize for making you listen to all that. Are you married, Mr. Lindeman?"

He pulled out her chair and waited until she was seated to respond. "I was, briefly." He went around the table and took the chair opposite her. "To Daniel's cousin, actually. She is a viper." He compressed his lips in a brief gesture of distaste as he shook out his napkin. "I make it a point never to speak of her during meals."

Sara's tone was both surprised and dismayed. "I didn't know Daniel had any living relatives."

"The relationship is distant, to say the least," Ash assured her. "There was a breach between the two family branches in the 1800s, and they've barely been civil to each other since."

The table was beautifully set with fresh yellow flowers and candles flickering in a silver candelabra. She could smell the aroma of something cooked in wine and garlic, and warm fresh bread. A waiter poured wine, and Ash told her it was from a vineyard only a few kilometers away that was known for its aromatic wild clover hues and chocolate bottom notes, and she tried to look interested as she tasted it. It was good, but she did not taste any chocolate.

"I don't know much about wine," she admitted.

"You will, if your visit lasts more than a few days," he assured her. "You should try to get down to the village on market day. Many of the local wineries bring samples, and in November there's a delightful Beaujolais Neauvoux festival."

Sara said she might like to ship a case of wine home to her sister, and he said that would be easy to arrange, and they talked like that for a time, about unimportant things. Sara knew that he was doing what he did best—directing the conversation, putting her at ease, carefully choreographing the flow of the evening away from such disturbing topics as widowhood, legacies, and castles.

He reminded her of a certain type of CEO she had occasionally come into contact with in the course of her job . . . the ones who knew, from the day of their birth, that they would always be in the ninetieth percentile and who had followed a predictable path to that point. They had finishing school manners that were so impeccable they seemed genuine. They never told crude jokes or smoked cigars at board meetings. They were attentive and concerned hosts. When they entertained you on board their yachts they did not spend the day ogling your ass. Sometimes those men would ask Sara out, and sometimes she would accept. When they made love their hands were always cool.

The waiter served something delicious with leeks and crisp cabbage in a sweet red sauce, and a warm evening breeze made the torchlights sway and the candles sputter. The first course was replaced with a creamy soup. Sara caught the reflection of torchlight on dark water at the far end of the terrace, and she inquired, "What is that lake?"

Ash followed her gaze. "That's not a lake," he said. "It's the moat."

And there it was, the elephant in the room. The point of their meeting.

Sara put down her spoon, and sipped her wine. "Of course. We're in a castle, after all."

"It's an affectation, really," Ash said. "Châteaux of this era weren't built for defense."

"What were they built for?"

"Ostentation. Or, occasionally, summer homes for the court."

Sara said, "Ah."

The waiter poured white wine, and whisked away her empty glass of red. The soup was replaced with fish. Sara stared at it, her hands in her lap.

Ash lifted his fork and smiled at her. "The trick," he said, "is to take only a taste or two of each dish. There are four more courses on the way."

She said, "What are my options?"

Ash touched his napkin to his lips, sipped his wine, and leaned back in his chair. "The first, and perhaps simplest, would be to do nothing. Over time we could arrange for you to buy out my shares at a reasonable profit and you would take sole ownership. Once that's done you could proceed with the restoration, lease the land as a vineyard, open the place to tourists, whatever you like. A good many Americans have had excellent luck with similar projects."

"Do you mean . . . live here?"

"Not necessarily. You could hire a management firm."

"It sounds expensive. And complicated."

"It can be. But there are many variations on a theme. Winkle has prepared a very detailed report for you on several different scenarios. I suggest we review that together in the morning." He picked up his fork again.

"I'd rather you just tell me. Now."

He tasted the fish, chewed thoughtfully, and took his time reaching for his wineglass. "The other option, of course," he said, "would be for you to sell outright. You hold the controlling interest; you're within your rights to do so. You would buy out my investment with your profit, and walk away with a tidy sum."

Sara sank back in her chair, relieved. "Yes," she said. "I like that one. That's the one I think I'll do. How much—how much do you think it's worth?"

Ash's eyes were masked by the deep shadows, and a spark of candlelight glinted off his uplifted glass as he replied mildly, "Between six and ten million, appraised. Of course that doesn't necessarily determine what it would fetch."

He spoke the numbers easily, as though they were in his everyday vocabulary, which of course they were. The only time Sara had ever used the word *million* was in reference to someone else's money; never her own. She actually felt dizzy for a moment.

She took a drink of her wine without tasting it. The waiter came to remove the fish and gave her a disapproving look. She managed, "Would that be euros or dollars?"

"Euros. Of course, there is a lien against the property of something over a million."

"To you?"

"Correct. And any buyer would have to be advised that the cost of restoring the property would run something close to fifteen hundred euros per square meter."

She was still trying to convert euros to dollars in her head. "Is that a lot?"

"Only if you have three thousand square meters to restore."

She gave up on the math. "Bottom line?"

"It would cost very nearly as much to restore as it's worth. Private buyers with that kind of capital are few and far between. It could be on the market for quite some time. Meanwhile, you've still the exorbitant expense of maintenance."

Sara was beginning to wish the waiter had stopped refilling her wineglass after the first one. "Do you mean to tell me," she said carefully, "that I own a property worth millions of dollars, but could conceivably end up in debt?"

"I'm afraid so." His tone was sympathetic. "That's why so many of these old places pass out of the families that have owned them for centuries. They're simply impractical to maintain."

Sara thought about that for a time. Then she said, "I don't suppose you'd like to buy me out?"

He chuckled in the dark. "I'm afraid my holdings portfolio is already quite plump with châteaux in the Loire."

"Couldn't I just sell my share to someone else?"

He sipped his wine, his eyes still shadowed. "Inadvisable. There is, however, another alternative. We could form a partnership, you and I, and lease out the rights to the property on a long-term basis to a corporation—a hotelier for example— who planned to develop it over time. Or we could form an investment group and do the same ourselves. Either way, the venture would take the burden of maintenance off our shoulders and pay a very handsome annual return."

The waiter placed a plate of sliced lamb, redolent of rosemary and garlic, before her, and poured yet another glass of wine. She shook her head slowly. "I was in the business world for a long time. Long enough to know that's not how I want to spend the rest of my life."

"I would handle the entire matter for you," he assured her smoothly. "All you'd need do is cash the checks."

She picked up her wineglass, regarding him with barely disguised skepticism. "Said the spider to the fly."

He laughed softly, leaning forward into the light. "I have references," he assured her, "from only the most highly placed flies."

She released a weary breath. "And I have a headache."

"You see now why I wanted to wait until after dinner to discuss this. Do please at least taste the lamb, my dear, before I have an irate chef to deal with as well." He lifted his glass to her. "And tell me what you think of the cabernet. It's a bit peppery for my taste but it's quite popular in the region."

She sipped the wine. "Peppery," she said without inflection, and returned her glass carefully to the snowy tablecloth. Her head was swimming with facts and figures, and the dizzying plunge from multimillionaire to practically impoverished. What she really wanted to do was forget the entire conversation, but there was one thing she had to know first. "What," she asked, "did Daniel do with a million dollars? I mean, euros?"

Ash did not answer at once. It might have been because he didn't understand what the question referenced, or simply because he was swallowing the bite of lamb he had just taken. Sara knew his type well enough to suspect he was, in fact, trying to decide how to answer.

He placed his fork, tines down, on the edge of his plate, used his napkin, sipped his wine. His easy, forthright gaze, however, never left her. "Daniel, as you know, was somewhat improvident. The cash amount he received from my investment shares was considerably less than a million euros, but part of the contract was that I would continue to pay the taxes and other necessary expenses as they accrued. That has mounted up over the years. Of course we do what we can to offset the expenses by letting the place out now and again for special events—someone actually shot a film here last year, I believe it was—but the balance sheet is rarely even. The firm has kept a full accounting, naturally," he added, "which you'll want to have your own experts review before any documents are signed."

Sara was suddenly weary to the bone. All she wanted to do was finish her dinner, drink absolutely no more wine at all, and go to bed. She said with a sigh, "That sounds like a perfectly fine arrangement. Maybe we should just keep things as they are."

His smile was sympathetic. "Or perhaps you should give yourself a bit of time to get accustomed to the situation. This has all been a great deal to absorb at once. Things will look clearer to you in the morning, I'm positive."

Sara gave him a weak smile, and picked up her fork, at last, to taste the lamb. But by that time it was cold.

· SEVEN ·

Dawn arrived as a touch of gold on the windowsill, painted its way down the rough, white plaster wall, and began a slow, seeping flood across the floor. By the time it reached the puffy silk duvet under which Sara lay, she was fully awake. Yet she stayed there for another moment, sunk in feather bed luxury, listening to some strange bird chirp its heart out outside her window, and watching the ancient room slowly fill with muted light. Overhead, a canopy of gold silk. Beneath her, the gleam of sun-bathed marble. All around her, the fragrance of flowers. She thought, with an odd and wondrous contentment, *I am sleeping in a castle*. Then she thought, *Good God. I own a castle*.

She had called Dixie close to midnight the previous night, before she went to bed. She had said nothing about millions, and had described the charming Mr. Lindeman in only the vaguest of terms. "Slick," she had said, groggily, "but nice. And kind of cute, in a very British sort of way." Dixie had kept saying, "A castle? You own a *castle*?" And Sara, fighting the effects of too much wine and a throbbing headache, murmured something about taxes and entailments. Then Jeff got on the phone and wanted to know whether they should call her "your highness" from now on.

Afterward, she tumbled into a sleep that was completely untroubled by dreams, and awoke to find that what she thought she had dreamed was in fact a reality.

She pulled jeans and a cotton sweater from the wardrobe where the maid had hung them, thinking how forlorn her few possessions looked in such elegant surroundings. She quickly applied makeup, caught back her hair in a ponytail, and made her way downstairs. Following the route Ash had taken her last night, and with only a few wrong turns into dark and forbidding-looking rooms, she found the kitchen.

It was a big, windowless space that had been tiled in black-and-white marble and seemed to have been designed exclusively for catering. A butler's pantry covering most of one wall held what looked like a service for one hundred—bone-white china with a discreet silver rim, glasses of every size and description, serving platters and bowls. There were two old-fashioned-looking white refrigerators and a giant butcher's block in the center of the room. The industrial-sized stove had eight gas burners, and the fuel tank was mounted on the wall a few feet away. A mammoth collection of copper pots and pans was suspended from the ceiling. The space beneath the counter was covered with a plain linen curtain, and rather than built-in cabinets, there were tall wooden cupboards, like pieces of furniture, in which she found an array of canned and dry goods.

There was a bowl of fresh fruit on one of the worktables, and she found a round of cheese in a cloth-covered bowl on a shelf, and next to it a loaf of soft bread wrapped in a colorful linen towel. After some searching, she discovered a black metal contraption that might be an espresso machine, but try as she might she could not find any coffee.

"Try the freezer," suggested a voice behind her, and Sara whirled.

Ash Lindeman lounged in the doorway behind her, looking drowsy and slightly rumpled in jeans and an untucked shirt. He glanced up from examining the screen of his mobile phone to add, "For the coffee. You Americans are really quite helpless without your breakfasts, aren't you?"

A little annoyed, Sara opened the freezer compartment of one of the refrigerators and found a sack of coffee beans on the bottom shelf. "While you Brits, of course, can leap tall buildings in a single bound fueled on nothing but tea and determination." She examined the bag of coffee with a small frown.

He smiled and pocketed his phone. "So the story is told. The machine grinds the beans," he told her, taking the sack. She watched as he snapped together a few parts on the black contraption, poured the coffee beans, added water, and plugged the thing in. Within moments the room was filled with the sound of grinding and the aroma of rich, dark coffee.

"The staff won't be in until ten," he said, leaning against

the counter as the raucous rattle gave over to the hiss and gurgle of brewing coffee. "I didn't expect you up and about so early."

She said, "I didn't mean to wake you."

"You didn't. My habits are early ones, as long as I'm in a familiar time zone."

"Even though you were up most of the night catching up on your phone calls?"

He looked surprised, and then returned an endearingly abashed grin. "However did you guess?"

Sara found a small earthen pitcher of heavy cream, covered with an elastic-rimmed cloth cozy, in the refrigerator. "Let's just say I know your type."

He lifted an eyebrow. "I wasn't aware I had a type. I'm not certain I like that, actually."

Sara took a plate from the pantry and a knife from the wooden block on the counter, and began to slice fruit. The pears were as soft as butter, the apples crisp and tart. She said, "How old is the castle?"

"It dates from the 1600s, I believe. Rumor is that Louis XIV had it built for one of his mistresses, but there has never been any proof of it. Bad luck, that. Otherwise, we might be able to have it listed." He helped himself to a slice of apple and bit into it.

"Listed?" Sara took a mango from the bowl and, before cutting into it, brought it to her face to inhale the aroma. It smelled as clean as a tropical island, and her expression softened with the sheer pleasure of it. She was aware of Ash watching her, and she put the fruit on the plate and began to slice it. "What does that mean?"

"The government keeps a list of places with an especial historical significance, particularly those with ties to the monarchy. If a property qualifies, and only a few of them do, it would be eligible for a restoration grant."

She stopped slicing. "Do you mean the government might pay for restoring the castle?"

"A rather large 'might,' I'm afraid. The firm looked into the matter for Daniel's parents years ago. Very few properties qualify anymore, and for those that do, it can be a double-edged sword. The property owner is required to use the government's architects and craftsmen, which can double the time and expense, and to meet all manner of other pesky rules and regulations. At any rate, it doesn't apply to Rondelais, so there you are." He chose a slice of pear and bit into it.

He seemed more at ease in the early-morning kitchen, more casual and approachable. She found she preferred this version of his charm to the very careful and correct form he had shown the previous night. She returned to the pantry and brought two plates back to the table. "You've certainly done your research."

"It's my job. Not so very different from what you did at Martin and Indlebright when you were trying to impress a client, now, is it?"

She was surprised. "I don't remember telling you where I worked." Then, before he could answer, she accused, "You Googled me!"

He looked offended. "You needn't make me sound like a pervert. Besides, I didn't Google you; Winkle did. I merely read your file."

"I have a file?" Something about the mere sound of that filled her with dismay.

He took two cups from the pantry over to the coffee machine. "Information gathering is what we do, my dear. And it's not as though we sought anything that's not readily available to public access. Date of birth, marriage certificate, citizenship, length of residence, state of employment—these are all necessary to complete the forms for property ownership in France."

She continued to regard him suspiciously. "You certainly are . . . efficient."

He handed her a cup half filled with rich black coffee. "Of course. We are an extremely well-regarded firm. Careful with that," he advised her. "The French make their coffee strong."

She tasted the coffee and grimaced. He filled the remaining half of her cup with cream, then did the same to his own.

"I thought you'd drink tea." She tasted the creamy brew as she took one of the ladder-back chairs at the table. It was much more palatable now.

"There isn't a decent cup of tea to be had in all of France." He sat at the chair opposite her, and began to slice the bread she had set out. "Or Italy for that matter." He shrugged. "One learns to pick up native habits in a pinch." He transferred a slice of bread to her plate and unwrapped the cheese. "Tell me about North Carolina, Sara."

She told him about Dixie and Jeff and the kids, and the

bookstore, and the little island village that dozed the winter through and burst into a bustling, tropical-colored tourist town in the summer, about art festivals and concerts in the park and the sand that got simply everywhere. Even as she spoke, it all seemed so far away, almost as though she was describing a place she had read about, or seen on television, but had never really been. It was an odd feeling, which she didn't have a chance to analyze, because then he asked, in his easy conversational way, what had caused her to leave Chicago. She surprised herself by telling him.

"I thought I was happy," she concluded with a brief, puzzled shake of her head. Even now, she was baffled by how she could have been so wrong about who she was, and what she wanted. "Then I just woke up one morning and—I couldn't move."

When she glanced at Ash, he was frowning into his coffee. But the expression was instantly wiped away when he sensed her gaze on him. He sipped his coffee, his face pleasantly interested, and remarked only, "Happiness is a relative thing, I suppose."

Anxious to turn the conversation away from herself, she asked, "Who is the other Lindeman in Lindeman and Lindeman?"

"My father." He got up to refill his cup. "He passed on some years ago. His heart." When he turned, his eyebrows were drawn together once again, and his eyes looked past her. "He was only fifty-six. Not so much older than I am at the moment, come to think of it." Then he smiled quickly and resumed his seat, tipping more cream into his coffee. "Rather maudlin, that. You should ask me about my mother, who regularly beats me at snooker, and who once tried to poison the prime minister."

He made her laugh with stories about his family—his mother in Northampton, and his three sisters, all of them married with, as he described it, "a veritable slew of progeny." She ate two slices of soft white bread spread with the sweetest, buttery-textured cheese she had ever tasted, and Ash ate pears and drank coffee. She realized, with pleasant surprise, that she felt as comfortable here as she would have in Dixie's kitchen back home . . . perhaps even more so. Because this was actually *her* kitchen. This vast, marble-floored hall with its European coffeemaker and service for one hundred and its scarred wooden worktables belonged to her.

The thought, coming as it did from out of nowhere, made her heart beat faster.

She finished her coffee and sat back in her chair. "Mr. Lindeman . . ."

He gave her an admonishing look. "I had really hoped, now that we've shared our first breakfast together, you might call me Ash."

She drew in a breath, and returned a small smile of agreement. "All right, Ash. I have some questions. About my . . . situation."

"Of course you do. And I'll be pleased to answer them all. But first . . ." He put down his coffee cup and pushed back his chair. "I promised to take you on a tour, remember?"

She caught a small sound in her throat that was amuse-

ment mixed with amazement. "You really have this all orches-
trated, don't you?"

"To the last detail," he assured her, and his smile was
so charming she saw no point in arguing. "Give me a few
moments to return some phone calls . . . Upon my honor," he
assured her with an upraised hand, "it's the last time today."

She started gathering up the dishes.

"Please," he said, pulling out his phone as he moved
toward the door. "Leave the dishes for the staff."

"Staff," Sara repeated to herself, wonderingly. She carried
the dishes to the big stone farmer's sink. "I have a staff."

From the doorway, with his mobile phone already to his
ear, Ash lifted a cautionary finger. "*I* have a staff," he corrected. "You have a castle. Or part of one, to be precise."
Then, "Sébastien! *Comment allez-vous?*" His voice faded away
as he moved down the hall.

In retrospect, Sara would realize she had fallen in love
with the château the moment she got out of the car and
started taking photographs of its fairy-tale turrets and crumbling moss-covered walls. But that morning, as Ash took
her through room after ancient, majestic, marble-clad room,
what she felt was a kind of enchantment. She kept thinking, *Kings walked here.* Princes and cardinals and ladies of the
court in their silk panniers and powdered wigs almost seemed
to flit past them in the corridors, to disappear just before a
door was opened, to whisper their secrets around each corner
they passed. She placed her hand against a dark mahogany
panel and she thought, *Some craftsman carved this panel four*

hundred years ago, with tools that aren't even in existence today.
Ash pointed out a nick in the banister that he said was made
during a sword fight centuries ago and she caressed it with her
fingertips, feeling history rise to meet her.

There were seven reception rooms downstairs. Most were
empty. One housed a banquet table that could seat thirty-five
and, Ash told her, had actually been assembled inside the dining hall because it was too large to be otherwise moved there.
There was a library with soaring, arched bookshelves built of
cypress from Spain, and, high in the room, a six-foot stained-
glass window that depicted a young girl with flowers in her
hair feeding a unicorn. The bookshelves were empty except
for a few contemporary volumes from the 1970s and 1980s.

"The books were sold long ago," Ash said apologetically.
"So were the paintings. Although they were replaced with
some very good copies."

Sara flipped through a copy of something in French, and
replaced it on the shelf. "That's so sad," she said, and meant
it. All of those generations of treasures, guarded so carefully
over the years, now simply gone. No wonder Daniel had
never talked about his home. For him, there was nothing left.

He took her upstairs, through the vast warren of bedrooms
that comprised the second and third floors. To her surprise, a
few of them were furnished like midclass hotel rooms, with
plain industrial carpet covering the floor, standard-sized beds,
and inoffensive decor. Three or four others were slightly more
well-appointed, with antique furniture under dust covers, and
faded carpets, and dressing rooms attached to each. None of
them compared to the room in which she was staying. The

bathroom fixtures were dated; the pedestal sinks rusted and chipped in places and the toilets of the pull-chain kind, but Sara was in awe of the intricate tile work, the hand-painted patterns, and gold borders.

"Some of the suites were used by family members," Ash explained. "The others were made ready for special events with overnight guests. It doesn't happen often, but it's best to be prepared."

Sara opened another door and was momentarily taken aback to note that it was occupied. The tall four-poster bed was rumpled, the brocade draperies were half-closed, and a suitcase stood open on the valet. A laptop computer glowed on the cherry Queen Anne desk.

"I'm afraid I didn't make my bed," Ash apologized, but there was a twinkle in his eye when he said it. "The staff, you know."

Sara smiled and started to close the door, but something on the desk caught her eye. It was Daniel's book. She walked over and picked it up, feeling a familiar tightening in her chest as she did so. She glanced at Ash. "Did you read it?"

He came inside the room. "Yes."

She opened the book, touching the pages. "What did you think?"

He hesitated for only a moment. "I thought it was utter drivel."

Sara laughed softly, briefly. "So did he. But I liked it. I just wish . . ." But she stopped before finishing the thought, because now she didn't know what she wished. She replaced the book and looked at Ash. "What's next?"

He took her up a winding stone staircase into the attics, which were layered in dust and cobwebs. The floors were water-stained and the walls were streaked. Except for a few pieces of broken furniture, empty picture frames, and cracked mirrors, they were barren. They descended to the main sleeping floor again and Sara turned toward a set of arched wooden doors adjacent to the stairwell. When she tried to open them they wouldn't budge.

"Where does this go?" she asked. "It's locked."

Ash came over to her. "That leads to the west wing, and another set of empty rooms. It's been closed off as long as I can remember."

"Is there a key?"

His brow furrowed. "I really don't know. I could check for you. A complete inventory was done after Daniel's parents died. Come along." He touched her shoulder lightly. "There's one more thing I want to show you."

They descended the grand staircase again, through what Ash called "the small reception room," which had two fireplaces, three chandeliers, and four separate sitting areas under dust covers. Adjacent to it was perhaps one of Sara's favorite rooms, a small morning room with a bank of leaded glass windows that looked out onto a walled garden. It was into this garden, through a heavy glass-paned door, that Ash led her now.

"This is the shortest route," he explained. "Otherwise, we'd have to go clear around the central tower. The problem with these old places is that no one seems to have had a plan. Careful on the path, now." He touched her elbow to guide her.

The stone path was so old that the pavers were half-sunk into the ground, almost swallowed in places by the neatly mowed carpet of mixed grasses the garden had become. Though nothing grew there now but a few carefully kept miniature flowering trees, Sara could see the worn stone outlines of former flower beds, and imagined what the garden must have looked like when some woman loved it. Morning glories trailed up the sun-bleached limestone wall, and one whole section was covered with ivy. As she watched, a small blue lizard darted across the top of the wall for the safety of the ivy. She thought what a lovely spot this would be to place a table, chairs, perhaps a wicker settee for reading a book or drowsing in the sun.

Ash opened a wooden gate set into a hedge, and when he did the gate sagged and scraped against the stone. He shrugged and left the gate unlatched. Sara breathed deeply of an aroma so sweet she felt as though she had stepped into a perfume factory, and then looked around and realized that she had, in fact, walked into another enormous walled garden. This one was filled with riotous purple lavender.

"Oh my goodness," she said softly, turning around. She could see, by the occasional glimpses of bone-white stone on the ground, that there had once been a circular pattern to the plantings, but now it was simply an unfettered festival of color and scent.

Ash responded to her delight with a dismissive, "It certainly has grown wild, hasn't it?" He brushed aside a trailing vine that partially obscured another set of glass-paned doors and pushed them open with a creak. He stood aside, holding back the persistent vine, so that she could precede him.

Sara reluctantly left the fragrant garden and, ducking under the vine, stepped inside. There she could do nothing but stare.

She was standing in an enormous stone room, glass walled on three sides, and paned in glass overhead. The floor was a pale, faded brick; the first brick she had seen in the house. The glass was so thick with grime that it was almost opaque, and missing entirely in a few places, and the room smelled like a cave—old and damp and deserted. There were alcoves carved into the walls that held dark, mossy statues. And in the center of it all was a huge, open concrete pit.

"Unbelievable, isn't it?" Ash said behind her. His voice echoed in the empty space. "It was originally an orangery, when such things were popular. Someone in the 1920s, I believe, got the notion to install the swimming pool. Of course no one ever quite figured out how to heat it properly, and eventually it cracked and developed a leak that flooded this entire section of the house, and took out part of the hill beyond. If you'll look on the other side, there, you'll notice that the floor actually slopes several inches downward where they've tried to repair the brick."

"It's spooky," Sara said.

"To say the least. Outrageous and indulgent, to say the most. But that's rather typical of the Orsays . . . all of the old French families, actually. They simply couldn't envision a time when the party would end."

She glanced at him, but there was nothing on his face but a simple statement of fact. He touched her shoulder, turning her toward the door. "So there you have it, or most of it anyway. The pantries, service areas, and cellars are not particularly interesting, and frankly even spookier than the orangery. There's a kitchen garden out back but no one keeps it up."

Outside, Sara breathed deeply of the lavender air to clear her head of the smell of mildew. Ash led the way around the clumps of lavender toward the far end of the garden, where the wall had tumbled to create a view of the valley below. Sara noticed that there was rosemary planted around the circumference of the garden, and it stained her hands with its crisp fresh scent when she brushed against it.

Ash stood with his hands clasped beside his back, looking out at the valley below. A breeze lifted his hair away from his forehead and the morning sun narrowed his eyes, painting his face with a faint bronze hue. "This is your inheritance, Sara," he said when she came up behind him. "Fifteen hectares of the Loire Valley, almost all of it suitable for vines. The smart investor knows that God isn't making any more of that."

She gazed out over the terraces below. There must have been a hundred different shades of green. "Those look like boxwood," she said, pointing.

"Hmm. I think there were topiaries there once. Everyone of that era wanted his own Versailles. If they had planted vineyards instead, the château could have been self-supporting and *you*"—he gave her a wry smile—"would now be the proud owner of the Cézanne that used to hang in the front hall, instead of some anonymous Canadian."

Sara sat on the fallen wall, studying the view, the lavender garden, the grimy, overgrown glass roof of the orangery with its missing panes. She said, "How much would it cost, do you suppose, to plant a vineyard?"

He shook his head. "I haven't the foggiest. It's an extremely long-term investment, and those are not the kind that interest me."

She looked at him, surprised. "Why not?"

"I haven't the patience for them. Life is short, and I prefer my gratification a bit on the more immediate side."

"It sounds to me as though you have more in common with the Orsays than you might like to admit," Sara observed, and he looked startled.

Then he laughed, although it sounded a little less than genuine. "I suppose you're right. I'll be certain to be more careful where I cast aspersions from now on out."

A small butterfly sailed up from the grass and Sara held out her hand. It skittered across her fingers, then fluttered on, bobbing on the breeze. She said, "It would be completely ridiculous to consider living here."

"Full time? I can't imagine why anyone would want to." And then he suddenly seemed to realize what she was really saying, and he struggled to hide the alarm in his eyes. "Sara, you can't be serious. Most of the rooms aren't even heated, and the electrical wiring is so old it's a miracle the place hasn't gone up in blazes before now. There are only two functional WCs in the entire building and they don't work at the same time. The reason the west wing is closed off is because the roof began to collapse on that side years ago and it simply isn't safe. So to answer your question, it would be beyond ridiculous to consider living here. It would be an act of virtual madness."

"But," she continued reasonably, "last night you said one of my options was to stay here, and start a restoration, and gradually buy out your shares. So let's just say, for the sake of argument, that I wanted to do that. What would be the procedure?"

As he looked at her, she could see his brilliant, agile mind analyzing, projecting, rearranging, and drawing conclusions from an entirely new set of possibilities. "I did say that," he admitted. "I did not recommend it. And before I can do so I need to ask you a rather delicate question, one that I would never broach in any capacity other than as your advisor. So forgive me in advance, but . . . what sort of access do you have to your resources?"

At first she didn't understand. "What do you mean?"

Whatever discomfort he may have initially shown was now lost in his brisk lawyerly demeanor. "Of course, I realize you must have significant personal wealth, but if your means are currently tied up in other sound investments, I really can't suggest . . ."

Sara had to laugh. "What makes you think I have any kind of wealth at all?"

He gave a dismissive turn of his wrist, his thoughts clearly occupied with rapid calculations. "Well, for one thing, Daniel never would have—"

The words hit her like a cold fist in her solar plexus. Ash seemed to realize what he had said only an instant after the words were spoken, and the shock of regret flashed in his eyes. But it was covered smoothly with, "What I mean to say of course is that I know the reputation of Martin and

Indlebright, and their relationship with their executives has always been quite generous . . ."

She said, "You think Daniel married me for my money." She was surprised she could speak at all, because her entire core ached as though the breath had been knocked out of her. She stood slowly, and felt a fine tremor run down her legs. "My God."

She had to close her eyes for a minute to orient herself, and when she opened them again, the morning seemed less bright, the garden less fragrant. She felt cold. Ash simply stood there, his lips compressed, his eyes dark.

The sound that came from her throat was strange and high and bordered on something like a laugh. "Of course you think that! Why wouldn't you? Why wouldn't *he*? I bought him a sports car for a wedding gift! I live in a resort town with an ocean view. He met me at a party with *Sting*, for the love of God!"

Her mind was suddenly churning with truths she had never before considered, the obvious and the not so obvious . . . Daniel, the impoverished poet, so enchanted with all things American, the diamond necklace she used to wear, the Vera Wang gown, the credit cards she always had at the ready whenever they went out to dinner, or on a weekend trip. She felt sick. She actually thought she might throw up, and she pressed her fingers against her lips, hard.

Ash took a step toward her, his face wretched with apology. "I'm so sorry. That was a beastly thing to say. I don't know what came over me. It's simply that Daniel was known to associate with a certain crowd . . ."

"Rich American women," Sara said dully, staring at him. He should have denied it, but he didn't. And she saw in his eyes that, if he could have, he would have. She felt that fist in her stomach again.

"I made an assumption," he said simply. "I should not have done so. But whatever I may have implied has nothing to do with Daniel's motives toward you. I shouldn't wish you to think—"

She said shortly, "Your assumption was wrong." Repressed emotion made her voice tight and her skin hot. She could feel her teeth grinding together between utterances. "I'm not a rich American. I live in my sister's basement. The only resources I have are what's left of my settlement package from Martin and Indlebright and a retirement plan that's lost half its value over the past two years and that I can't touch for another ten years anyway. Maybe that was enough to make me attractive to Daniel but it's not enough to finance the restoration of a four-hundred-year-old castle, and I don't need you to tell me that."

By now her eyes were blazing and her voice was a cold reflection of the ice that was slowly seeping through her body—her fingertips, her toes, her lips. She closed her fists, digging her nails into her palms, simply so that she felt something. "What I do need you to tell me," she said, struggling to keep her teeth from chattering, "is exactly how much in U.S. dollars it would cost me to claim my so-called inheritance. That's all."

In a moment he replied stiffly, "You would owe the French government approximately forty-seven thousand dollars at property transfer. There would be an additional habitation tax payable at the end of the year, should you choose to reside here."

"Thank you." The pain that radiated from the cut of her nails on her palms was like the burn of dry ice, darting up her arms. "I believe you said Mr. Winkle had prepared a report with the details of my options on the property."

"Of course." He lifted his arm as though to usher her back to the house. "I'll be happy to go over that with you."

"Mr. Lindeman," she said coldly, stepping away from the potential of his touch. "I have a master's degree in business. I do not need you to go over anything with me. Just have one of your staff"—she practically bit out the word—"bring me the report. I'm sure you have phone calls to return."

He looked at her for a long moment, expressionless. And then he gave her a polite, distant nod of his head. "I'll drop the papers by your room," he said.

· EIGHT ·

Sara did not see Ash the remainder of the morning. When she returned to her room, she found her bed made, her worn nightshirt whisked away, the champagne and fruit from the night before removed, and the flowers freshened. And an important-looking blue folder with the words Lindeman and Lindeman inscribed in gold was centered on the Louis Quatorze table that was arranged before the fireplace. Sara took it downstairs to the terrace.

She tried to concentrate on the estimable Mr. Winkle's work. She went upstairs twice, once for sunglasses and once for a calculator from her purse. A smiling woman in a gray uniform brought her a tall, chilled glass of something that tasted like citrus and sunshine. She read the report without comprehending a word. Her mind drifted over and over the past year of her life with Daniel, and she felt like a commuter who, having traveled the same route to work for years, suddenly finds the landscape has been altered. It was familiar, but strange. She knew the road, but the terrain was different. She thought she would feel better if she could cry, but she was too wrung out inside for tears.

She made herself concentrate on the report. Appraisals, inventories, investment scenarios. She ran the figures: taxes, maintenance, transfer costs. By the time she was finished she hated Daniel, and Château Rondelais, and the entire family Orsay as far back as they were documented. And she loved them all with an equal ferocity. This magnificent place, brought to ruin through carelessness and neglect. Her own sad, lonely life, brought to ruin by a foolish middle-aged fantasy. Now, *that* was something to cry about. But she couldn't.

I have no more tears left for you, Daniel, she thought wearily, leaning her head back and closing her eyes. *I think it's really over.*

Ash came onto the terrace in the early afternoon. She saw his shadow, out of the corner of her half-closed eyes, before she saw him. He said, "You should get a sun hat. You're getting burned."

Sara glanced at the pinkening skin on her arms, and felt the flush on her face for the first time. "The sun feels nice," she said, and it was the best she could do by way of an apology for the way she had treated him earlier. "It's been a long winter."

He extended his hand to her. "Come along, then," he said briskly. "We're going on a picnic."

She turned her head slowly to look at him from behind her dark glasses, but she did not get up, and she did not take his hand. "Why?"

"Because," he replied, "you are much too beautiful to look so sad, and I'm much too charming to dine alone."

He coaxed her with a gentle smile. "You don't have to talk to me," he said. "You don't even have to eat anything. But you do have to stop sitting all alone, thinking about the past. I really can't bear any more." He turned his gaze toward the house behind them. "My window overlooks the terrace."

She thought about him, standing at his window and watching her throughout the morning. She put her hand in his and let him pull her to her feet.

He took her in a rowboat on the moat with a wicker basket between them. The sky was reflected a brilliant blue in the water and the sun glinted off his hair like gold. She could see the muscles of his shoulders and chest work beneath his shirt as he maneuvered the oars, edging the boat out of its mooring. Had she been wearing a filmy white dress with a ribboned hat instead of jeans that were almost a size too big for her, it would have been the picture of a perfect romantic fantasy—until Ash, having positioned the boat in the direction he wished it to go, politely handed her an oar. "It's just like paddling a canoe, my dear," he said.

That made her laugh, which she suspected he had intended, and after a few false starts they developed an easy rhythm, dipping their oars in and out, gliding the boat across the water. They saw swans, and sailed beneath the shimmering fronds of a weeping willow that dipped its branches into the water. "Walt Disney couldn't have done better," Sara murmured, and Ash smiled his agreement.

They brought the boat to rest in a stand of rushes where

the bank sloped gently upward to a small knoll. She could see the château in the background, not so far away, but partially obscured by a stand of trees. It was very quiet here, and cool.

Ash tied off the boat and she handed the picnic basket to him, and he helped her onto dry ground. He didn't release her hand until they had climbed a few steps up the slope; she wasn't sure why.

"I wanted you to see this place," he said. "It's the ruins of the old chapel. There was fire at the turn of the century, and since then the stones have started to tumble whenever there's a strong wind. But it's almost more interesting this way. And the view is magnificent."

They crested the hill just before her breath started to become labored from the climb, and she saw the four stone columns that marked the corners of the building, the walls—three with gaping holes, and one that had collapsed altogether—that soared toward the sky. The roof they had once supported was gone, and fallen stones littered the ground. There was something magnificent about coming upon this place, so stoic despite its collapse, all alone on the knoll. Once again, she started to think in terms of centuries, instead of months. She thought that might have been why Ash had brought her here.

She picked her way around the rubble to enter the building. Where the back wall had been there was now an open view of wide valleys and a small village below. She could see chimneys, rooftops, and colorful storefronts. Far in the distance, too far to be called neighbors, really, was the façade of another château, its gleaming white shape barely visible on the hillside.

A large stone slab, possibly a door lintel, or perhaps even

an altar, had fallen in such a way as to form a bench between the collapsed back wall and another boulder-sized stone. Ash placed the basket on it and stood close behind her. "There's something else I wanted you to see," he said.

She turned and he was taking his mobile phone from his pocket. She found the anachronism particularly exasperating in this ancient, once-holy place, and she said, "Oh for heaven's sake, can't you—"

"It's an e-mail from Daniel," he said. "It took me a while to find it." The phone gave a muted beep and a blue light emanated from the screen. He turned it toward her.

Sara wanted to refuse. The very mention of Daniel's name had made her throat go tight again. She wanted to turn away, to walk away. Instead she reached helplessly for the mobile, and read what was on the screen there.

To: Lindeman@Lindemancorp.uk.com
From: Americophile2000@yahoo.com
Subject: Congratulate Me!

I have married my American! I know you will say I am the fool, and I think you must be right because I'm quite mad about her. She makes my heart sing. Come to the States, or I will bring her to London. I want you to meet her. She will enchant you just as she has done me.

Daniel

She read it three times, and with each reading, she felt

a little bit of her hurt, and confusion, seep away. Finally, she pushed a button and watched the screen go blank. She returned the phone to Ash. "Thank you," she said.

"He loved you, Sara," he said, quietly.

"I know he did, in his way." She looked at him. "And I loved him. In my way." But it was only make-believe. She knew that now more clearly than she had before. She turned back to the view of the village, and stood there, lost in her thoughts, until ·Ash came back to her and placed a glass of wine in her hand. She had not heard him unpack the picnic basket, or open the bottle, and she accepted the glass with a little surprise. He sat on the half-fallen wall near her, his forearm resting on an upraised knee, and sipped his own wine, gazing out over the valley in silent contentment. She liked that he didn't speak. It was good to simply be there, and listen to the quiet, and not feel any demands from his companionship.

She was the one who broke the silence at last, turning to look at him. "You said you didn't come here often. To Rondelais, I mean. But you know it so well, it's almost as though you grew up here, instead of Daniel."

He lifted a shoulder in a small shrug. "I did, in a way. Daniel, a French boy in an English school, didn't have so many friends growing up, and it was my job to sort of look after him. By way of repayment, I suppose, his parents always insisted he bring me home with him for holidays, and I can't say I objected. It's a fascinating place for young boys to roam, and for older boys . . ." He smiled a little into his wine. "To meet the most interesting sort of society. Daniel's parents were not always on premises, you see, and, well . . ." He gave another shrug and let her imagine, from the twinkle in his eyes, the rest.

"Boys will be boys?" she suggested.

"Ah," he said, his eyes still dancing with mischievous memories, "I see you know us well."

She was curious. "What do you mean, it was your job to look after Daniel?"

He took a sip of wine, and some of the mirth left his expression. "The Orsays were clients of my father's, and of my grandfather's. It's one of those traditions, handed down through the ages, a bit of cultivated helplessness on the part of the French aristocracy, a rather heavy reliance on their sturdy British solicitors. I inherited Daniel. I was part of the tradition."

"That sounds a little cynical."

"Don't misunderstand," Ash said. "I was fond of Daniel. If I was his best friend, he was also mine for most of our youth. But our relationship was . . ." He seemed to search for the word. "Complicated."

He frowned then, and reached into his pocket for his phone. "Dreadfully sorry," he murmured, glancing at the screen. "It's my office. Do you mind?"

Without waiting for a reply, he walked away, and Sara, trying not to show her annoyance, turned back to the view and deliberately blocked out the sound of his voice.

"At any rate," he said, returning to her casually when he had finished his phone call, and resuming the conversation as though it had never been interrupted, "I have grown to think of the old place as something of a second home after all these years. Something to do with my enjoyment of history, I should suppose. It fascinates me to think of all the centuries these stones have seen, the deaths, the births, the bloodshed, the intrigue. Did you know, for example, that by one account Robespierre actually blessed a marriage in this very chapel? Completely unsubstantiated, unfortunately, but there's very good evidence for it having actually happened."

Sara turned to look at him as he resumed his seat on the bench, but her fascination turned to irritation when she saw that, as he spoke, he was also tapping out a text message on his phone. She waited until he was finished to inquire, "Do you mind if I ask you something?"

He pocketed the phone and looked up at her. "Not at all."

"What are you so afraid of?"

He looked surprised, as well he might. "Why, offhand, I can't think of a thing." He picked up his glass and added thoughtfully, "Unless, of course, you want to include the obvious. My mother springs to mind. And my secretary, Mrs. Harrison, can be quite fearsome at times. Why do you ask?"

Before she could answer he put down his glass and reached again for his phone. He glanced at the screen, and pocketed it again.

Sara looked deliberately at the pocket where he had placed the phone. "It's just that I couldn't help but notice, over the years, that people who can't stand to be disconnected from the outside world, even for a minute, are usually afraid of losing something . . . Control, maybe? Their own sense of self-importance?"

For just the briefest moment he seemed startled, and then he laughed softly. "You're right, of course. I've been rude again and I apologize." He took out his phone and turned it off, then returned it to his pocket. "There. I'm disconnected. And I confess, I do feel quite a bit less important. I hope that won't make a difference between us."

That made her laugh a little, unexpectedly. "I can see why Daniel liked you," she said, and then she was unaccountably embarrassed for having said it, and she quickly turned her attention to her wine, and took a sip.

He regarded her thoughtfully, the corners of his eyes gently upturned, and observed, "And I can see why he fell in love with you. You have an oddly engaging manner about you, don't you? And you say exactly what you mean. I can't imagine you let him get away with much."

Sara shrugged, but kept her gaze on her glass. "Well, no. I didn't. I spent too many years selling lies to waste any more time on them. Life is too short."

And then, before the memories could become too painful, she looked at him again, abruptly changing the subject. "What's your agenda, Ash?"

"Mine?" He spoke easily, without breaking his contemplation of the view. "Oh, I don't know. I think I'd like to buy a place in Portugal some day, or maybe the Côte d'Azur. I'd spend the winters lying in the sun, reading the classics. Perhaps I'd cultivate orchids."

Until the orchids, she had half thought he was serious. A corner of her lips turned down dryly. "Somehow I can't picture that."

"No? Did I forget to mention the housekeeper . . . twenty years old, drop-dead gorgeous, and whose standard working uniform is a bikini?"

That almost made her smile. "And they say the British have no sense of humor."

"Libelous villains." He leaned back against the wall, sipping his wine, looking completely relaxed for perhaps the first time since she had met him. "Actually, twenty-year-olds bore me. That's one of the advantages of having reached a certain point in life, isn't it? Not being forced to listen to the prattle of children. Perhaps I'll get a dog instead. A nice spaniel, I think, or a collie dog. Do you like collies, Sara?"

"You're better off with the housekeeper in the bikini. At least she can feed herself while you're off jet-setting around the globe."

"True enough," he allowed lazily. "I've always wanted to learn to sail. I might get a boat. Or I might do nothing at all but sit here and enjoy this lovely view with you."

Sara shook her head slowly. "No, you won't. For an afternoon maybe. But for longer than that? The only thing you really enjoy in life is your work."

"I'm stung." His features remained unchanged, pleasant and relaxed, though his eyes reflected a slight annoyance. "What, may I ask, is wrong with that?"

"Nothing. Not a thing."

"Ah," he said, and he lifted his glass to her in a small, mocking salute. "You're going to tell me about there being more to life than the workday."

"Isn't there?"

He appeared to consider that for a moment. "I think that worrying about those things is another pursuit that I, blessedly, left behind with my youth. Now it's enough to simply enjoy being who I am."

Sara regarded him thoughtfully. "You really do enjoy yourself, don't you?"

"It's not so difficult to do at this stage, now is it? All those dreadful struggles we had when we were younger—the ambitions, the deadlines, the goal-setting, the conflicts, the building, the learning, the failures and humiliations from which we thought we'd never recover . . . they're all behind us now. We've mastered the game by now, or near abouts. All there is to do is play it with gusto."

"Most of our opportunities are behind us, too," Sara pointed out, even though she didn't mean to.

"Nonsense," he replied crisply. "And you are the perfect example. I'll wager you never imagined when you were at the height of your career toiling away for Martin and Indlebright that, at this point in life, you'd own a castle in France. What more in the way of opportunity could you ask?"

She thought about that for a moment. "Well . . . I'll never be a ballerina."

"Now, that," he replied earnestly, "is indeed a tragic loss."

A corner of her lips turned down skeptically. "Do you really mean to tell me you wouldn't change anything if you could?"

A shadow passed over his face that was in such stark contrast to his customary demeanor that Sara was immediately alert. He said, looking into his glass, "Well, now. I don't suppose there's a man alive who doesn't have regrets." His smile seemed tight, and he didn't quite meet her eyes. "But, as the song says, 'then again, too few to mention.'"

She observed, "You like Sinatra."

"Actually," he countered, relaxing, "I like Whitesnake."

She chuckled. "And just when I thought you didn't have a dark side."

He met her eyes steadily and his eyes were smiling, but deep behind that crystal gaze was something as hard as steel. It both intrigued and frightened her a little, and she thought in that moment that she was meeting the real man for the first time. He said thoughtfully, "I think we, all of us, have shades of dark and light, don't you? The challenge is not to let the one overcome the other."

Sara said softly, curiously, "What is it that you regret, Ash?"

There was a flicker of something in his eyes—surprise, perhaps, to have let down his guard, however briefly—and then the façade was effortlessly back in place. He stood to retrieve the bottle of wine, and replied lightly, "For one thing, I regret having not spent more afternoons picnicking with beautiful women."

She lifted an eyebrow. "In bikinis?"

He smiled as he poured more wine into her glass, his face very close. "Learn to take a compliment, love."

That surprised her enough to make her blush, and the corners of his eyes deepened as he noticed it. He refilled his own glass.

"I think," she said, "you're avoiding my question."

"Indeed." He sipped his wine, watching her easily. "Which one might that be?"

"The one about agendas," she said, trying to be stern. "In particular, yours for this property. And please don't bother trying to deny it, because I know you have one."

He tilted his head, considering, his gaze never wavering. "Well, you'd be right about that, of course. I suppose you want a straightforward answer."

"If you can manage it."

"Straightforward answers are not my strong suit," he admitted.

"So I've noticed."

"But for you, I'll try. My agenda," he told her, without further reservation, "is the same as it is for any other client: to negotiate the best possible outcome for you *and* your partner."

She blinked, momentarily confused. Then she said, "My partner. You."

"Correct."

She sipped her wine. "Go on."

His eyes, masked by the glint of sun off the water, were as blue as a still lake, but she could sense debate in his brief hesitance, and then decision. He said, "You recall I mentioned Daniel's cousin Michele."

"Your ex-wife," she said, alert now.

He nodded. "She has an unreasoning obsession with this place. She is about to make you an offer, I think, for your share, which is much less than it's worth. That would be bad for you, and very bad for me. So my agenda, as you put it, is to make certain that you don't lose sight of reason and accept her offer in a moment of desperation just to be shed of the place."

Sara watched him thoughtfully. "When all else fails, tell the truth," she observed.

He dropped his eyes briefly to his glass, and his smile was wry. "Quite." He placed his hand lightly on her shoulder—not the one nearest to him, but resting his arm across her back in a brief embrace as he gestured her toward the stone slab where he had unpacked the picnic. "Let's have a bite before the wine goes to our heads, shall we? I think I saw white asparagus. And there's some of that cheese you liked so much this morning."

He had spread a red and black checked blanket over the stone and unwrapped a baguette and a round of cheese. There were purple grapes and covered bowls, and real china plates. It was all very L.L.Bean Does Europe, and it made Sara smile.

She said, a little wistfully, "You know, I really can't afford to keep the place. I wish I could, but . . ."

He said, "No, you don't, not really. You might be enchanted by the fairy tale now, but it would drive you into madness—and bankruptcy—before year's end. Fortunately, there's a better option."

He was back into his lawyer mode, brisk and commanding, and as he spoke he dropped his hand from her shoulder. She was glad, because his touch suddenly felt less comforting than purposeful. She supplied, with just a touch of dryness, "The hotel deal?"

"Precisely."

"Why do I think you already have a particular corporation in mind?"

He met her eyes steadily, without shame. "This is what I do for a living, Sara. I've put together a very attractive deal that will pay us both a handsome return with virtually no effort on our parts. All you need do is sign the papers."

"Which you just happen to have in your briefcase."

"Don't be absurd. But I can have my office fax them within the hour."

She started to laugh, softly. "You really are a force of nature, aren't you?"

"I'll take that as a compliment—which I do know how to accept, thank you very much." He gestured her to be seated on the stone bench, and, in a moment, she complied.

"I'd want to see the complete prospectus," she said. "And have my own lawyer look over your contracts."

"Of course." He showed neither surprise nor pleasure at her decision, as naturally he would not. He was accustomed to having other people see things his way, and accepted the fact that she had done so as simply inevitable. "If you have a financial team, I'd suggest you bring them in as well. If not, I'll be happy to recommend someone, either here or in the U.S."

As he spoke, he placed grapes and cheese on a plate, along with chilled white asparagus and red peppers in an herb marinade, and a portion of some kind of tart with black olives and thinly sliced potatoes arranged in a swirling pattern on top. He handed her the plate and a roll of heavy silverware wrapped in a napkin.

She ate a grape and looked around the peaceful ruin, thinking about what he had said. How could she have imagined a year ago, or two, that today she would be sitting on the altar of her own medieval chapel, gazing at her own château in the distance? How many more surprises like that could there possibly be in her lifetime? How many more chances to reinvent herself, how many more impossible dreams? She felt a small ache of longing to think that this might be her last chance at adventure, and that she was letting it pass her by.

But what choice did she have? Besides, if nothing else, the past year's impulses had proven she was not very good at adventure.

She said, "What will they do with the château? The hotel company, I mean."

He broke off an end of the baguette and placed it on her plate, then, straddling the bench across from her, placed tart and asparagus and bread on his own plate. "Under the terms of the agreement, the acquiring company will own the actual building, and a ninety-nine-year lease on the ground on which it stands and all attached property. They're required to bring in architects who specialize in this sort of thing, to stabilize the structure and do what's necessary to keep the building from continuing to deteriorate. After that, I imagine they'll seal it off until the renovations are complete."

"How long will that take?"

He shrugged. "Years, most likely. As few as five, as many as twenty, depending upon their plans for expansion in the valley. But it makes no difference to us because we will be paid the same rate of return whether the property is in use or not, and of course their investment will continue to grow."

"What about the land?"

"That will be up to them. I would imagine they'll use part of it for the grounds—swimming pools, tennis courts, gardens, and parking—and sublet the remainder. Again, we share in the return."

Sara frowned a little. She knew it was a good plan, and surely the most sensible thing to do, and that much the same was being done with castles all over Europe. But something in her recoiled at thinking of this beautiful old place being turned into a Holiday Inn.

Sensing her uncertainty, Ash reminded her, "It's a lifetime income for you, Sara, and for your nephews beyond. Far beyond that, as soon as the place opens you'll be able to come back here and stay anytime you wish at no charge."

"I suppose." She shrugged a little and picked up her glass. "But I probably won't."

"Why not?"

"Oh, I don't know. I'm not much of a world traveler."

Ash, in the process of cutting a slice of asparagus with his knife and fork, slowed. "What will you do, then, when you return to North Carolina?"

She plucked another grape, lost in thought. Dixie, the kids, North Carolina seemed a lifetime away. She could hardly even picture herself there anymore. "My brother-in-law, Jeff, had an idea about fixing up a little house on the beach for me."

"Well, you'll certainly be able to afford it now."

She said, "It was the house that Daniel and I lived in right after we got married."

He put down his fork, the asparagus untasted. "But what will you *do*?"

She looked at her wine, but didn't taste it. "My sister has a bookstore. I used to help her out."

He said absolutely nothing.

She felt defensive. "I liked it. It's good work."

He picked up his fork again.

"What?" she demanded irritably.

"Nothing," he replied. "Not a thing."

She scowled briefly, recognizing the cavalier reply she had given him earlier. "You disapprove."

"Why ever should I disapprove?" he returned blandly. "A house on the water, a quaint little bookstore . . . it all sounds perfectly lovely. For an afternoon."

He lifted his glass to her in a small salute, his eyes revealing nothing except the clear blue color of the water below them, and she struggled to hide her smile. "I think we're very different people, Ash."

"And I think we're more alike than you care to admit," he returned easily. "But either way, I predict you'll soon grow bored in your tiny island bookstore."

She hesitated, wanting to argue with him, but in the end simply said, lightly, "There are worse things."

"Can't think of any, myself."

And then he hesitated, the casualness leaving his face, and his tone. He glanced briefly into the distance, and then looked back at her. He said quietly, "No one remains broken forever, Sara. You either heal, or you die. And you are not going to die."

She wanted to say something, but she couldn't. She felt her throat grow tight again, and she could not be certain whether it was from sorrow or gratitude. Ash gave her no time to dwell on it. He resumed his easy demeanor, and broke off a piece of bread.

"Have you ever been to Carcassonne? It's only an hour's drive. Talking of some marvelous examples of restored châteaux . . ."

She slowly relaxed as they finished their picnic, and he took her effortlessly from one harmless, entertaining topic of conversation to another. It had been a long time since she had been so comfortable with someone she didn't know. Even with Daniel, there had always been that underlying sense of urgency, of purpose and intent, that was as exciting as it was exhausting. She had never really felt comfortable with Daniel. There was too much passion, too much that was larger-than-life, and simply being in his presence would leave a person breathless, more often than not. Ash, as insincere as he no doubt was, knew how to offer exactly what was needed, no more and no less, to make whomever he was conversing with feel at ease. It was a rare talent, almost a gift. And what made it even more impressive was that he actually seemed to enjoy the process as much as she did.

It was late afternoon when they packed up the picnic basket and made their way back down the knoll to the boat. The bottle of wine was empty, and Sara held on to the arm he offered along the slippery parts of the slope. She said, "I hope the chef hasn't prepared another feast for tonight, because I don't think I can eat another bite."

He chuckled. "Sorry, the chef's banquet was for one night only. That very nice housekeeper—Madame Touron—tells me the remainders are all nicely put away in the fridge, though, if you get hungry later on. Careful, now. Don't get your feet wet. I'll go first."

He placed the basket on the bottom of the boat and climbed inside, loosening the rope from the shrub around which he had looped it and then grasping her arms to swing her inside. She caught her foot against the rim of the boat and landed hard, causing the boat to rock violently. He scooped her against him, possibly to steady her, possibly to keep from falling himself, and when she looked up at him, half laughing, half gasping, his face was only inches from hers and she thought, *This is classic*.

She could see the pores of his skin and the soft, deep surprise in his eyes. She felt the heat of his thighs and his hands on her back and the warmth of his wine-scented breath across her lips, and she thought, distantly, that she must have had more to drink than she had realized because she did not pull away. His face moved, just fractionally, closer to hers and then he stopped, his eyes dark on hers, and he murmured, softly, almost to himself, "Now, that would be completely inappropriate, wouldn't it?"

Sara swallowed hard and broke his gaze, flooded suddenly with guilt and confusion. For a moment—just that moment when she was captured in his eyes—she had forgotten about Daniel. She had forgotten her grief, her loss, her emptiness.

She had felt almost normal, for just a moment. How could that have happened? She was a widow. How could he have made her forget that?

His hands slid to her waist, lightly steadying her, and then to her arms as he guided her to the plank seat. By the time he took his place in the bow and handed her an oar, his smile was easy and his demeanor relaxed, and she could almost believe the moment hadn't occurred at all.

· N I N E ·

They parted in the entry hall of the castle, Ash to check his
e-mail and Sara to retrieve the papers she had left on the
terrace. After the warmth of the sun, the marble interior felt
cool, and gooseflesh prickled on Sarah's sun-rouged arms. She
said, "Thank you for the afternoon, Ash—and for not turning
on your phone again. Don't think I didn't notice."

There was again that familiar crinkle at the corners of his
eyes; she was surprised to realize how much she enjoyed making him smile. "Actually, I rather enjoyed it myself. It's not
often I get a holiday."

She said, "I know it was hard for you to get away from your
work, and I appreciate your coming here in person. But now
that everything's settled, I'm going to try to get a flight back
tomorrow. And you can get back to your life."

He looked surprised. "I thought you planned to stay the weekend."

"I did . . ." She shrugged, feeling suddenly self-conscious. "But there's no reason to, is there? I mean, everything can be handled by mail from now on out, can't it?"

"I suppose, if that's what you prefer." And then he said, "But I wish you'd stay."

He seemed as surprised to have said that as she was to hear it, and, almost as though to cover, he made a small grimace. "The truth is, I'm in France by way of avoiding one of my mother's dreadful house parties, and if you leave, I shall have no more excuses."

She laughed. "How bad can your mother's party be?"

"My dear," he said sincerely, "you simply cannot imagine. I beg of you, don't make me return to England this weekend. Stay a little longer."

She considered this for a moment, trying not to show her amusement as she studied him. "Maybe," she agreed. "On one condition."

He winced. "Why do I think this has something to do with my mobile?"

She lifted one shoulder negligently. "I'm sure your mother won't mind at all if you check your messages every thirty seconds."

His eyes narrowed marginally. "Lord preserve me from clever women. You sounded remarkably like my secretary just then."

She chuckled. "Now, that's a compliment I can take. Do we have a deal?"

He thought for a moment. "Mobile telephone hours are from ten p.m. until ten a.m. Otherwise the bloody thing remains locked in my desk."

"Fair enough," she agreed. "You're not going to go into withdrawal, are you?"

He grinned and playfully tapped her nose with his forefinger. "We shall see, my dear, we shall see. I hope I don't live to regret this."

And Sara thought, but did not say, *Me, too.*

* * *

Over the next few days Sara got to know a part of Ash that she never would have imagined existed before. "When I first met him," Sara told Dixie when she called two days before her flight home, "I had a hard time picturing him as Daniel's best friend. He was nice enough, but you know Daniel—he never had a feeling he didn't express, or an impulse he didn't act on . . . Ash was so well rehearsed, so well thought out. He made it look easy, of course, but I have to say he seems a lot more real this way. And a lot easier to be around."

They walked down to the village on market day, and Ash bought her a baseball cap to protect her face from the sun, because he could not find a sun hat. They filled cotton bags with fresh produce and cheese and slim baguettes, and brown farm eggs that were practically still warm from the hen. They laughed when they discovered neither one of them knew how to cook well enough to turn the bounty into an actual meal, and dined instead on cheese and fruit and wine and watched the sunset from the terrace.

Ash's Armani gave way to jeans and short-sleeved cotton shirts that buttoned midway up the chest, and, for their day trip to Carcassonne and a hike through the hills, Bermuda shorts and hiking shoes. He had the whitest legs Sara had ever seen, and when she had teased him about it he devised a deadpan thirty-minute lecture on the dangers of sun over-exposure to peoples of, as he put it, "extreme Northern descent," that had her holding her sides with laughter before he was finished.

"He drove a Fiat," she told Dixie about the trip to Carcassonne, "with the top down. I didn't even know he could drive. But I guess he rented the Fiat in Paris and drove it down here. I never even knew it was here."

They had hiked in the morning and paused at the top of a steep trail overlooking the ancient city to catch their breaths. He had put his arm around her shoulders for no reason at all, and she had leaned against him companionably. She did not tell Dixie about that. They visited a marvelous château that was open to the public and she snapped photographs like a tourist while Ash pretended not to know her. They had a two-hour lunch at an outdoor café, then strolled the streets, sampling the local wines and visiting the boutiques. Whenever Ash found a wine he liked, he ordered a case. Whenever Sara commented favorably on a wine she tasted, he ordered a case for her. She tried to warn Dixie about all the wine that would shortly be arriving on her doorstep.

"He's teaching me French," Sara said. "Well, a little anyway. I guess it will take more than a couple of days to learn. He speaks five languages."

He took her to visit a local cathedral and spoke with easy expertise on the architecture and history of the place. On another afternoon he arranged to take her to a reception at the château she had seen on the hillside across from the chapel, which wasn't as intimidating as she had thought it would be, because he knew the hosts personally, and there were four other American couples there.

"And get this," Sara told Dixie, "they've *all* bought and restored ruins—that's what they call these broken-down old French mansions. None of them is as elaborate as Château Rondelais—they were all so jealous when they heard I'd inherited it—but they love living here in the valley. Apparently, everything we've heard about the French hating Americans doesn't apply when you pour tons of money into preserving their culture and settle down among them. Oh, and you should have *seen* the château! It was like something from a Hollywood set. It sits right smack in the middle of a vineyard, and everything smells like grapes. Of course, it was more of a palace than a château—big and white with lots of rooms and tall windows. Rondelais has a lot more character. All the Americans invited me to come visit them at their homes," she added, and a touch of wistfulness in her voice surprised even her, "to see how they've restored them. But I won't be here long enough."

"Why not?" Dixie demanded. "What do you have to rush back for? It sounds like you're enjoying yourself."

"I am," she admitted. "But I'm a little homesick, too. Besides, Ash has gone out of his way to make sure I had a good time. It won't be nearly as much fun without him."

There was a note of teasing in Dixie's voice as she observed, "It sounds like you might have the teensiest bit of a crush on this guy."

Sara's cheeks flamed, even though there was no one there to see it. "Don't be ridiculous." Her voice was a little too sharp. "He's just being nice, that's all. Besides, I haven't even been widowed a year. What kind of person would I be if I could get interested in another man, just like that?"

"A human one," said Dixie sincerely. "A *living* one."

Sara scowled, extremely uncomfortable now. "This is a stupid conversation. I know the difference between charm and sincerity. He's not the kind of person I would ever get involved with. We're business partners, that's all."

Dixie hesitated. "Sara . . . you're *sure* you trust him? That this deal he's set up is legitimate?"

Sara laughed, on easier ground now. "For heaven's sake, Dixie, you're the one who looked him up on the Internet! Didn't you say there was a picture of him at a White House dinner?"

"It was during the previous administration," replied Dixie archly, "which doesn't necessarily prove anything at all about his character." And then she added, somewhat reluctantly, "But you were right. He is cute."

"And I'm not stupid. I'm not signing anything without checking it out first. But it's going to be a solid deal. He doesn't do any other kind. And this is the best thing to do with the property. I'm sure of it." Then she sighed a little. "I might not like it, but I'm sure."

"Well, we miss you, honey. Jeff went to look at the Peterson property for you. He says now that you're going to be rich, you can really afford to do it up right."

Sara laughed, sitting on the bed to towel dry her hair. As much as she loved the marble bathtub, she had soon discovered there was an impractical side. There was no attached shower, and she had almost drowned trying to wash her hair. "I guess that could be almost as much fun as restoring a château."

"A lot more practical, anyway."

Sara reconfirmed her flight information and arrival times for Dixie, and even as she did so she was surprised to feel a stab of nostalgia. As reluctant as she had been to come here, that was how sorry she would be to leave. Secretly she was beginning to fear Ash might be right . . . that she was already beginning to outgrow Little John Island and everything on it. And if that were true, what was left for her?

The two sisters talked a little while longer, until Dixie pointed out in alarm how much Sara was spending on international phone calls. She said good-bye, and went to finish drying her hair. She plugged in her blow-dryer, careful as always to use the adapter to European wattage that Dixie had insisted she bring, and the minute she pushed the switch the room was plunged into darkness.

Sara stumbled from the bathroom into the bedroom area, feeling her way along the walls. Though there might have been a faint twilight remaining outside, the draperies were drawn across the huge window that overlooked the valley and the room was as dark as the inside of a tomb. "Great," she muttered, holding on to the doorjamb and desperately trying to orient herself. "Just great."

There was a knock on the door. "Sara? Are you all right?"

She almost went limp with relief. "Ash?"

"Stay where you are. I have a torch."

He opened the door and swept the room with a beam of light. She winced and shielded her eyes when it found her. His tone was dry. "You just had to plug in the blow-dryer, didn't you?"

She said defensively, "I've used it before, and the lights didn't go out."

He crossed to her, keeping the flashlight beam low. "Hold this for a moment," he said, handing it to her. "Shine it toward the bed."

She followed him with the flashlight beam as he crossed the room. "I used the adapter," she insisted.

"You have an adapter for a seventeenth-century château? Well-done, then."

She noted that he had changed from the jeans he had worn in the afternoon to soft gray trousers and a pale shirt that was closed only by one button at the chest, clinging to his wet skin in dark patches. His hair was damp, and it occurred to her she had roused him from the shower as well. As she made these observations the flashlight beam wandered; he collided with a piece of furniture and exclaimed, "Damn!"

She quickly corrected the beam. "Sorry."

He rummaged in a drawer in the delicate little bedside table, then turned a key on one of the sconces that flanked the bed. There was a hissing sound, and he lifted the glass globe and struck a match. With a soft sucking sound, the sconce flared to light. He skirted the bed and repeated the procedure with the other lamp. The room was filled with a shadowed, golden glow. "Gas lights," he explained, shaking out the match. "It was all the château had until the 1970s. All in all, more reliable than electricity to this day."

She switched off the flashlight. "Are the lights off all over the castle?"

"I'm afraid so. I'll get someone up from the village in the morning."

She crossed the room—carefully, because the shadows were still deep—and returned the flashlight to him. "I'm sorry," she said. "And thanks for rescuing me."

He smiled. She could see the moisture on his face and the dampness of his collar where his hair had dripped. "My pleasure."

She was wearing a nightshirt that did not quite reach her knees, but she refused to be embarrassed about it. His eyes swept her briefly, from wet hair to bare feet, and he said, surprising her, "You smell wonderful."

Now she was embarrassed, or at least a little flustered. She pushed self-consciously at her limp wet hair, and gestured vaguely toward the bathroom. "It's the shampoo . . . or the soap. It came with the castle."

The creases at the corners of his eyes deepened. "I shall have to discover the supplier." He held her eyes a little longer, smiling, and then, just before the moment became uncomfortable, he turned to place the flashlight on her night table. "I'll leave this with you, then. Will you be all right? Do you need anything else?"

"No," she said. "I'm fine. Or at least I will be, as soon as I figure out what people did with their hair before blow-dryers were invented."

"When you find out, let me know, eh? Good night, Sara." He touched her arm in a brief, companionable gesture, and turned toward the door.

His eyes fell on her suitcase, open on the bed. He looked back at her. "You're packing already?"

She moved to the bed and closed the suitcase, foolishly feeling the need to hide her underwear from him. "I thought I'd get a head start. I've bought so much since I've been here— presents for the boys, and all—I wasn't sure how I would fit it all in."

"We can ship some of it back for you, if you like."

When she straightened up, he was closer than she had realized, so that she would have to edge around him to step away from the bed. His face was bronzed by the lamplight, and his eyes a deep indigo. The small line between his eyes seemed puzzled. "Odd," he said. "I don't think I realized how close the time was to your leaving." He lifted his hand, lightly pushed back a strand of damp hair that tickled her cheek, and dropped it again. "I'm going to miss you, you know. You're very fine company."

She could smell the citrusy soap, and the dampness of his shower. She said, "You are, too. I've had a great time these last few days. And you were as good as your word about the phone."

He smiled. "It was no hardship, actually. I only wish . . ." But he didn't finish. In another moment he gave a small nod of his head, as though punctuating the unfinished sentence, and took a step past her toward the door. "Well, then. Good night."

She said, "Good night, Ash."

He turned back to her, that puzzled, contemplative line reappearing between his brows, and he said, "Actually, there is just one thing . . ."

He stepped into her and gently pushed back her hair again, with both hands. He drew in a breath as though to finish his sentence but instead his lips covered hers, tenderly at first, a gentle good-bye, and then simply melting into her, swallowing her, consuming her whole.

It was the kind of shock in which all the senses seem to explode at once and then freeze, like separate particles of brilliantly colored light, for a single suspended moment. It was as though she had never been kissed before. And perhaps she hadn't, not like this, not so unexpectedly, not so thoroughly, so sensually, so completely; not by someone who wasn't Daniel. It took her breath away.

All the blood in her body surged to her skin, to the brief, sharp flash of sensation in her nerve endings, and her knees buckled. She lifted her hands to his arms to support herself but it did no good; she sank to the bed and he followed, his hand on her hip atop the thin fabric of her nightshirt, now sliding to her waist, now pressing downward to her bare thigh. His hands were warm, deft, and where he touched fever flared. She let herself be touched. She tasted his tongue against hers, and she let the weight of her head fall back against the support of his strong fingers. She let herself be kissed; she drank him in. There was a part of her that couldn't believe she was doing this, another part that seemed to have simply been waiting for it all along.

He kissed the curve of her jaw, her ear, her collarbone. She pressed her hands against his chest, feeling the heat of him, the dampness of his shirt. She was light-headed, breathless, all of her senses singing with pleasure. She turned her mouth to his again, and then, with a very great effort, she pulled away.

"Ash," she whispered. She could barely hear her own voice for the thrumming rush of her heartbeat in her ears. She closed her fingers around his biceps, clinging to the strength of them. "I'm not going to have sex with you."

"Oh, thank God," he murmured. He pushed her hair away from her neck and placed a deep kiss there, tracing the throb of her pulse with his tongue. "For a moment I was in danger of . . ." And then he stopped, and lifted his face. His skin was flushed and his eyes were dark, pupils dilated with desire. But there was something else in his eyes, a kind of surprise mixed with confusion, and he finished softly, "Falling quite utterly for you."

He lowered his lashes, shading his eyes from her, and placed his forefinger lightly across her lips. "I am an idiot," he said. "Forgive me."

He stood, and crossed to the door. When he opened the door he hesitated and her heart caught, because she did not know what she would do if he came back to her. She honestly didn't know.

But he didn't come back. He simply gave a single apologetic shake of his head and repeated, "A complete idiot."

And he left, closing the door firmly behind him.

* * *

Sara's sleep was, not surprisingly, restless, and she awoke later than usual to find there was no hot water—which was only logical, since there was no electricity either. She splashed cold water on her face and did the best she could with her makeup in the dim bathroom. She dressed quickly, pulled her hair back into a braid, and made her way downstairs, hoping that the housekeeper might have arrived early and that she knew how to change a European fuse.

The kitchen was dark and deserted when she entered, and when she rather optimistically pushed the button on the coffeemaker, nothing happened. Typically, Ash spent the morning hours catching up on business and allowing her to enjoy her "American breakfast habit" as he called it, alone, although he usually joined her for coffee on the terrace at midmorning. And this morning, of all mornings, she did not want to face him without her first cup of coffee. She began to search the kitchen, the pantry, the small laundry area, and even the spooky, stone-walled storage closet for anything that looked like a fuse box.

It finally occurred to her that a building that had been retrofitted with electricity would probably have located the electrical box on an outside wall, and she opened the back door—just in time to see a man crawling out of the rosemary bush. She gasped and quickly stepped back, shielding herself with the door, but he called cheerfully, *"Buon giorno, signorina!"*

He appeared to be in his twenties, olive skinned, with thick black hair and merry black eyes. He was accompanied by an older, sour-looking man in baggy brown trousers with a cigarette hanging from one lip who carried a wooden ladder. The younger man came toward her and she tightened her grip on the door, but didn't entirely close it.

"You will be the beautiful American who owns the palazzo, *sì?*" he declared, grinning at her. "The *signor*, he says, the *signorina* she must have her coffee, so I come quick to bring you the light. Do you know Brad Pitt?"

Sara shook her head. *Italian*, she realized slowly. He was Italian. And what was he doing rummaging around in a French herb garden before nine o'clock in the morning? "Um . . . who are you?"

He shrugged. "It is no matter. I will make you the coffee, yes?"

He made as though to step inside, and, alarmed, she started to slam the door shut when suddenly she understood. "Light!" she exclaimed. "You're the electrician!" She opened the door wide. "Yes, come in, please."

He strode confidently inside, accompanied by the man with the stepladder. "I am Pietro," he told her. "I come many times to make the repairs. This is my papa, the finest builder in all of Lugano. He no speak *inglese* but you got something broke, he make it right."

As he spoke, he helped his father unfold the stepladder, and climbed toward the ceiling. Sara, clasping her arms across her chest against the morning chill of the kitchen, stepped back carefully out of the way, and watched as Pietro pushed aside a ceiling panel and reached his hand inside. He found a lever, pulled it with a snap, and exclaimed, "Voilà! Eh?" as the refrigerators hummed to life.

Sara laughed out loud, both with relief at having the electricity restored, and at the sheer outrageousness of having an electrical panel hidden inside the ceiling and discovered by a French-speaking Italian in a four-hundred-year-old castle.

"*Bueno!*" she declared, clapping her hands. "Is that right? Is that Italian?"

Ash said behind her, "Close enough, I think. *Buon giorno*, Pietro, Signor Contandino. *Grazie!*"

He was wearing loafers with no socks, rumpled khakis, and a blue silk robe. He went on in a rapid, easy stream of Italian as he took some bills from his pants pocket and paid the men, but that was all Sara understood. She quickly occupied herself with making the coffee, trying to appear at ease and un-self-conscious, trying not to look at Ash.

Pietro conversed easily with Ash while his father packed up the ladder and dropped cigarette ashes on the kitchen floor. Then he came over to her. "Do you know Tom Cruise?" he asked.

Sara, turning, found him much too close for comfort. She braced her hands against the counter and leaned back to give herself some breathing room, smiling uncertainly. "No, I'm afraid not."

He shrugged. "Ah well, it is no matter." He smiled at her.

"You need fixing again, you ask for Pietro. I come . . ." He snapped his fingers twice in quick succession. "Like that."

Sara, her bright smile frozen in place, replied, "Yes, I will. Thank you."

She didn't completely exhale until they both had left the kitchen, and the door was firmly closed behind them. "Wow," she said. "He's . . . larger-than-life, isn't he?" And she glanced at Ash. "An Italian family of handymen living in the Loire Valley?"

"It's a long story," Ash replied. "Suffice it to say, every small town has its eccentrics, whether they be in America or a village on the Loire. And by the way," he added with a raised forefinger, "do *not* call Pietro. He is a walking Italian cliché, and will try to bed you quicker than . . ." He broke off with a sudden realization, staring at her, then gave a soft, embarrassed exhalation and a shake of his head. He turned to leave. "I think I'll go upstairs and finish the shower I started last night."

Sara said, without knowing why, "It will take a while for the water to heat."

He hesitated, and turned back to her. "So it will." The coffeemaker began to gurgle and hiss. "Would it be all right, do you suppose, if I joined you for breakfast?"

She said, "Let's eat on the terrace."

She busied herself with gathering fruit and cheese and hard rolls from the bread box and jams from the cupboard and a fresh round of butter—which had survived the lack of electrical cooling just fine in the insulated refrigerator—surprised at how familiar she had grown with this kitchen in such a short time. She could hardly remember the layout of Dixie's kitchen. When she returned home, would she constantly be turning to the left instead of to the right to look for silverware?

She thought she should probably make an offer on the Peterson house as soon as she set foot on North Carolina soil. And yet, whenever she made up her mind to do that, she kept hearing Ash's voice, demanding, But what will you *do*?

Damn him, anyway.

They carried the tray of food and coffee to the terrace, and Ash went out of his way to be helpful. He never ate breakfast. He could only tolerate coffee if it was mostly cream. This morning-after encounter was, predictably, awkward.

Finally they sat at the stone table with plates filled and coffee poured and Ash said, his eyes calm and steady, "Sara, do I need to say anything?"

She burst out almost before he was finished, "I really wish you wouldn't."

"Because it seems as though there are things that need to be—"

"No, there aren't. Honestly."

"All right, then." He hesitated, his gaze unflinching, seeing far too much as he looked at her. "You're Daniel's widow," he said. "I respect that. I wouldn't want you to think I would ever take advantage."

She felt heat creep into her cheeks, and she had to shift her gaze away. "I don't," she said. "I mean, I would never . . ." She foundered, feeling flustered and confused and oddly guilty, even though she had done nothing to feel guilty about.

She sighed and looked at him apologetically, her face still hot. "I've had a wonderful time these past few days," she said. "But . . . it's probably a good thing I'm leaving now."

He nodded, and then he shifted his gaze away.

She brought her cup to her lips with both hands and sipped the strong black coffee without meeting his eyes again. He buttered a roll, and left it on his plate. She reached for a tangerine at the same time he did; he withdrew quickly and her hand fluttered to her lap. It was all too much a 1940s romantic comedy and, despite herself, she smiled. Almost as though reading her mind, he did, too, and just like that, the tension between them was gone.

He said, "Halves?"

She nodded and he took up a fruit knife and sliced the tangerine. "What time is your flight tomorrow? Shall we drive in together?"

"That would be nice. My flight's at two."

"Excellent." He placed half the fruit on her plate. "I can get a 1:45 back to London. What a pity you didn't plan time to stay over in Paris. I would have enjoyed showing you around."

She said, smearing jam on her roll, "You know you don't have any more time to spend showing me around."

"I could make time." He looked momentarily wistful. "It's been years since I was a tourist in Paris."

She was tempted, for one wild moment, to cancel her flight and take him up on his offer. But it was just for a moment. "You know the world of international law is falling apart without you, and my guess is that if you had to spend even one more day relaxing, you would do yourself serious harm."

He laughed. "No doubt you're right." He peeled the fruit. "So what would you like to do with your last day in France?"

Her last day in France. There was a little catch in her chest when he said that, and she thought how incredibly predictable it was, that she should have fallen so completely under the spell of this place. She wondered if she would be another cliché, weeping all the way home on her flight back to the United States.

"Let's go down to the village." She bit into her roll. "Maybe I'll see Pietro there."

At first he seemed startled, and then he laughed. He said something in French that she did not understand and he refused to translate, and she threw the remainder of her roll at him.

It was a good morning, after all.

They took the car so that Sara could box up and send home the items that wouldn't fit in her suitcase. They visited some of her favorite shops and had lunch at an outdoor café. Some of the vendors were beginning to recognize them, and smiled at Sara and waved her over to show her their latest merchandise when she walked by. "You've been here less than a week," Ash teased her, "and already you're their best customer. That's what we all love about Americans."

He held her hand as they strolled the streets, and it seemed completely natural.

It was midafternoon when they returned to the château, and there was a black Citroën parked in the circular drive. When Sara glanced at Ash, his answer was a shrug, and he looked as puzzled as she was.

The woman who turned to meet them in the bright marble hall was slim, fiery-haired, and dressed in a deceptively simple jade green couturier dress that hugged her body like a second skin. Even before she turned, even before she felt Ash stiffen beside her, Sara knew who she was.

"Michele," Ash said coolly. "What are you doing here?"

She smiled beatifically and spread her hands, palms up. "*Mon cher*, is that any sort of greeting? And after I have made a special trip just to meet your . . ." Her eyes were fixed on Sara and her smile didn't waver as she seemed to search for the word. "Friend."

Inexplicably, Sara felt a flush creep up her neck. She wasn't certain whether it was because the way Michele said the word made it sound dirty, or because, next to her, Sara—with her braided hair and cotton sundress and comfortable flats—felt dull and frumpy and completely American.

Ash said flatly, "Michele, may I present Sara Orsay. Sara, Michele Dupuis. Now, what are you doing here?"

There was in the distance the clattering sound of small running feet, and like a whirlwind, a little girl burst around the corner and raced toward Ash with open arms. "*Petit-papa! Je suis arrivé!*"

Ash looked as stunned as though someone had struck him, yet he automatically bent and scooped up the child, resting her on his hip and kissing her hair. "Alyssa, *ma petite chou!*" he exclaimed softly. "*Comment ça va? Quel joli ruban!*" He tugged at her hair ribbon and smiled, although his eyes still held nothing but shock, and they were fixed on Michele's.

The child couldn't have been more than five or six, and

she was adorable, with curly black hair tied back with a red ribbon, and big dark eyes. She wore a plaid skirt and kneesocks, like a school uniform. She chattered on in a stream of sweet, high-pitched French, playing with the buttons on Ash's shirt, and then she said, "But my English, she is very goodly, yes?"

Ash laughed, though it sounded strained, and he said, "Very goodly indeed, little one. "

Sara couldn't stay silent any longer. She said, smiling at the little girl, "Ash, you didn't tell me you had a daughter." She didn't know why this should hurt her, but it did a little. She had told him all of her secrets, and he hadn't even mentioned his offspring to her. "She's darling."

Michele came forward, her laughter light and tinkling. "*Mais chérie*, Alyssa is not Ash's child." She looked at Sara with malicious amusement tightening the corners of her otherwise flawless eyes. "She is Daniel's."

· TEN ·

There are certain moments in every life in which a curtain seems to be drawn, forever separating what was from what will never be again. One of those moments had occurred when a police officer had stood dripping icy rain in the dark on Sara's porch. Another such moment was now.

It was now.

The air in the great hall didn't really suddenly evaporate; time wasn't really frozen, and the silence that echoed after those words didn't really last a lifetime. But it felt like that to Sara. She couldn't move; she couldn't breathe. All she could do was stare at Ash, and at the child he held in his arms.

Ash murmured several swift, light-sounding sentences to the little girl, then set her on her feet and spoke in the same deceptively pleasant tone to Michele. The words were in French, and his eyes, when he looked at her, could have frozen salt water. He finished in English, perhaps for the child's sake, but very politely, "Or I will wring your bloody neck."

There was a flare of anger in Michele's eyes and a quirk of temper about her lips, which she purposefully subdued with a cool smile. She took Alyssa's hand with a shrug, and said, *"Très bien, ma petite, viens avec moi."*

And she led her off, at a deliberately casual pace, toward the kitchen.

Sara said the only thing she could manage, at that moment. "She called you 'papa.'"

"It's a nickname." Ash's face was tight, the muscle in his jaw knotted. "It means . . . it doesn't matter what it means."

"Were you going to tell me?" Now her breath was coming back and her voice began to rise as she closed her hands into fists. "Were you *ever* going to tell me? Don't you think that's the kind of thing I might have been the tiniest bit interested in knowing? I mean, did you think it wasn't important enough to mention? Are you kidding me? For the love of God, Daniel had a *child?*"

By this time she was practically screaming at him, and, with a quick glance around, Ash grasped her arm and pulled her into one of the empty reception rooms. It was a display room, furnished in horsehair settees and Queen Anne chairs upholstered in ivory and gold damask with delicate tables and china clocks. It was as big as a hotel lobby, and the only light came from two tall, velvet-draped windows at either end of the room. Motes of dust, disturbed by their entrance, were captured in the thin rays of sunlight that penetrated the thick glass.

Sara wrenched her arm away as soon as he closed the door. "How dare you?" she demanded lowly. Every muscle in her body was tensed with outrage and her words echoed about the vast, cold room. "How the hell *dare* you?" But even as she spoke she knew her anger wasn't at Ash, but at Daniel. *Daniel* hadn't told her. And there was no way for her to know whether he ever would have.

Ash drew in a sharp breath. "Listen to me. The reason I didn't tell you was because it's not true. Alyssa is not legally Daniel's child."

Sara stared at him, hardly believing her ears. *"Legally?"*

He thrust a hand through his hair, his eyes a storm of anger and apology and regret and bitterness. "God, it's such a sordid story." Another breath. "A woman contacted Daniel some years back with a two-year-old she claimed he had fathered when he last was in France. Daniel was adamant the child was not his and sent her away rather abruptly. I advised him to take a paternity test, just to circumvent any further complications, but he refused. He insisted he wasn't even in France at the time of the child's conception, and that the whole thing was just a scheme to get money."

He compressed his lips tightly, gathering his thoughts, or perhaps unwilling to speak them. "And within the week the woman, the mother of the child . . ." He paused here, and turned away from her, his gaze fixed on the far window. "She committed suicide, I'm afraid."

Sara sat down abruptly in one of the stiff, uncomfortable chairs.

It was a long time before he spoke again, and then his

voice was heavy, flat and stiff and deliberately devoid of emotion. "It was all simply ghastly. There were no relatives, and
the police found the child, Alyssa, with her mother's body,
trying to wake her up."

Sara pressed her fingers tightly against her lips.

"Daniel felt—well, you can imagine how Daniel felt. It
knocked him off his feet. He thought he was responsible. And
when he realized there was no one to care for the child, he
wanted to set up a trust for her."

Sara thought, a little hysterically, He *thought* he was
responsible? He *thought*?

She had married a man who had fathered a child and
refused to acknowledge her. She had married a man who was
responsible for another woman's death. She had done that.
She had done that and she had never known, had never
guessed, had never even imagined . . .

Somehow, in the spinning, sucking vortex of her wild
thoughts, Ash's voice came through, anchoring her.

"That's when he came to me for money, and I offered to
buy shares in the château. The trust is enough to keep her in
good schools with room and board and on to university, and
perhaps to set her up in a small place afterward. Since Daniel
lived abroad, the law firm—well, I, actually—assumed legal
guardianship, in case of a medical emergency or such as that.
We managed to place her in a very nice school in Lyon. There
are so very few of them that take children her age. Whenever
I'm in France I visit her, and send her gifts for the holidays—
that's why she calls me her *petit-papa*. Her almost-father."

It was a long time before Sara could speak. But she thought,

I can deal with this. I can. I've had to deal with so much . . . I can do this. When she spoke at last her voice was hoarse but almost steady. And the question she asked was not really what she wanted to know at all. It was simply all she could think of. "Why—would you do that? Any of it? Give him money, assume guardianship of a child who was a stranger to you, visit her at school . . . why would you do that?"

Through the entire speech his gaze had remained fixed on the window, his face in profile to her. Now he looked back at her. The corners of his eyes tightened just a little, but his expression was otherwise unreadable. He replied simply, "It's what we do, Sara. The Lindemans have been taking care of the Orsays for generations—straightening out their finances, managing their estates, cleaning up their messes. It's what we do."

He spoke of a world she did not know, and didn't want to know. For the first time she felt the full foreignness of this place—this culture, the man she had married, the man with whom she had just spent a fairy-tale week in a castle. She had never known any of them.

"But . . ." She foundered, still trying to find something to cling to, struggling to make her voice work. "You're telling me that Daniel . . . that you . . . did all this, mortgaged his inheritance, set up the trust, found the best school—all for a child who wasn't his?"

Ash's eyes were weary, and his expression sad. "There was never any proof of paternity," he said. "But if I have to be honest . . . I can't say whether Daniel ever knew for certain."

Sara thought dimly, *I never knew him. I never knew him at all.*

From the doorway, Michele said lazily, "Don't be absurd, *mon cher*, of course he knew. Daniel was many things, but he was no fool. He must have been convinced the child was his long before he invested money in her."

Ash turned on her, every ounce of his being radiating disdain. His tone was glacial. "This is beneath contempt, Michele, even for you. Where is Alyssa?"

Michele shrugged and responded in French, but he cut her off.

"Speak English, goddamn it."

Hatred darkened Michele's eyes and Sara stared at Ash. The smooth Prince Charming to whom she had grown accustomed was gone, and in his place was a man she barely recognized. This man did not play games, or mince words, or make allowances. This was the man who made multimillion-dollar deals happen with a single phone call, who crushed his competition without a qualm, and who never looked back. She had always known, of course, that man was there, just beneath the surface. She had simply not expected to feel so dismayed when she met him face-to-face.

Michele turned to Sara and gave a slow, exceedingly polite nod of her head. "The child is with Cook, having a sweet. She is happy as a bird." She even managed a smile for Sara, and strolled over to sit on the little settee across from her. She took out a cigarette and tapped it on the back of her hand. "The château is a marvelous place for a little one to play. I remember how much I enjoyed it as a child."

Ash said, "Don't smoke in here."

Glaring at him, Michele thumbed the wheel on her

small silver lighter. In a single stride, Ash snatched the cigarette from her and ground it beneath his heel on the marble floor. Michele surged to her feet with eyes flaming and Sara exclaimed, "Oh, for God's sake!" She stood as well, and pushed past the two of them. "Do I have to be here for this?"

It was with a visible effort that Ash rearranged his features into something almost resembling civility, and he glanced at Sara. "I'm sorry," he said stiffly. "You're right. This is no way for adults to behave."

He turned back to Michele. "How did you get her out of school?"

She seemed to hesitate a moment before deciding that her own interests could best be served by controlling her temper, and then she shrugged. "It is no matter," she murmured, smiling a little. "Soon I shall smoke wherever I want, *cher*, and then I will be grinding *you* under *my* heel."

She settled back on the settee, crossing her long legs and stretching one arm out over the back so that her breasts pushed firmly against the silky green fabric. She answered Ash's question with another little shrug. "It was not so difficult. The school, it is on spring holiday, as any proper guardian would know. When I identified myself as Mrs. Lindeman, wife of the sweet child's guardian . . ."

"I am going to have every person at that school sacked," Ash said tightly. "You are not Mrs. Lindeman, and you are not her guardian. They had no right to release her to you."

Michele just smiled. "Now, that is where you are wrong . . . or soon will be, I think. You see, as Daniel's only living relative, I think it is only right that I assume . . . what is that word? *Custodianship*, yes, that is it. Custodianship of his child."

A heartbeat passed, no more than that.

"And of her property." Ash's voice was soft, and tinged with something like relief—or perhaps it was a touch of admiration. "So that's your scheme."

Sara felt as though she had stumbled, somehow, into a bad play. All she wanted to do was get away from them both, from the ugliness that seemed to emanate from them and taint the very air of the room. She reached for the door.

"Sara, wait," Ash said, though he barely glanced at her when he said it, as though he was cautious about taking his eyes off Michele. "This concerns you."

"No, it doesn't," she said flatly, and she left the room.

*   *   *

Ash found Sara less than an hour later sitting on the grassy bank beside the moat, her arms encircling her updrawn knees, absently tossing stones into the clear blue water. Three swans floated in effortless circles in the distance, watching her incuriously.

He was, not surprisingly, on the phone even as he walked down the hill toward her, but he finished his conversation abruptly and pocketed the phone before he reached her. He was wearing sunglasses that reflected the lake and the sky, but she could see the grim lines of his mouth and the set of his jaw.

"Sara," he said without preamble. "I need to be in Paris before seven to meet with the French *avocat*, and I'll be flying back to London tonight. It's all very complex, but basically the problem is this: According to the French laws of succession, the claims of a child, even an illegitimate one, supersede the claim of a spouse on a deceased's estate. The only way Michele can file a claim on Alyssa's behalf is to file a petition for custody. She seems determined to do that and unless I can preempt her this could get very ugly indeed."

Sara tossed another pebble into the water. One of the swans noticed the splash and began to glide from the center of the lake toward it. "She's the child's only living relative."

"She's not a relative," he returned impatiently. "And even if she were, an alley cat's a better mother than she would be. She has no chance of gaining custody and she knows that. But she also knows if she challenges the estate, we won't be able to dispose of it until the courts clear it—which could take years in France. That's why I have to take care of this right away."

Another pebble. The swan circled the ripples.

"I don't think there's anything for you to worry about at this point," he went on, "but I'll need you to sign the settlement papers as soon as possible. My office will have them waiting for you when you arrive home, and you'll fax them right back to me, yes?"

She said lowly, without looking at him, "I hate that you've done this. I hate that you've ruined my memories of this place. And of Daniel."

He seemed startled, perhaps even hurt, and even as she said it she knew she was being unfair. It wasn't his fault her husband had had a child and neglected to tell her about it.

It wasn't his fault that the innocence had been stripped away from everything she believed about her marriage. She knew that. But she didn't know who else to blame.

Sunlight glinted off his dark glasses as he glanced back at the castle, and then, quickly, at his watch. She could sense his frustration. He said, "I've ordered a car to take you to the airport tomorrow. Michele is leaving. Will you be all right here tonight by yourself?"

She didn't bother to answer.

He started to lean down as though to—what? Touch her? Kiss her?—and then he changed his mind. "I'm so sorry it ended like this, Sara," he said quietly.

She replied, without looking at him, "So am I."

Still, he hesitated. "I tried to protect you from this. I'm still trying to protect you. But I have to leave."

She did not look up.

He lingered for only a moment longer. "I'll be in touch."

She didn't answer, and he walked briskly back up the hill.

She waited until the sound of the Fiat's engine had completely faded away before she got up and walked back to the château. The black Citroën was still in the drive, and to avoid an encounter with Michele she walked around the walled gardens toward the back terrace. By the time she smelled the cigarette smoke, it was too late. Michele, stretched out on one of the teak loungers like an exotic lizard luxuriating in the sun, turned a lazy gaze on her.

Sara hesitated at the edge of the terrace, and then, feeling like a fool for allowing this stranger to intimidate her, she moved on toward the door at a determined pace. Michele turned her gaze back to the view, inhaling cigarette smoke, ignoring her. It wasn't until Sara drew abreast of her that Michele spoke.

"It truly is magnificent, isn't it? To think of the generations of my family who have trod these halls, who have gazed upon this valley . . . it truly can take the breath away." And she glanced at Sara. "You have nothing like this in America. You cannot imagine the feelings it stirs."

Sara said flatly, "No. I can't imagine." She turned to go inside.

Michele drew again on the cigarette and exhaled a graceful stream of smoke. "My Ashton, he is so very clever. Too clever for his own good sometimes, I think. This agreement he has reached with the hotel . . . did he tell you he had been attempting to persuade Daniel of the same thing for years?"

Sara turned slowly to look at her.

"I wonder why Daniel would have refused?" Michele continued, pretending not to notice Sara's surprise. "It could have made him a rich man, and he did, after all, have a family to support." She smiled then and glanced at Sara. "But I am being indelicate, no?"

Good God, thought Sara distantly, and with something that felt like amazement creeping into the repulsion she was beginning to feel toward this woman. *All she needs is a basket of poisoned apples.*

Michele blew a thin stream of cigarette smoke into the air. Sara found herself unable to look away, unable to stop listening. "Here is something you must know about my Ashton," she said. "He is fascinated by all things Orsay. It is like a sickness with him. I think it is because, for all that he has acquired, there is something he can never be, and the Orsays—the last of the grand French aristocracy—are that. And so he is obsessed with what is Orsay. This château, me, Daniel . . ." She slanted a look at Sara. "Daniel's wife. Why do you think he worked so hard to find a way to own shares of this property? He could have given Daniel the money; he has it to spare. Or loaned it to him on other terms. And even now the contract he negotiates with the hotel is not for sale, it is for lease. He remains in control." She took one last draw on the cigarette, gave an elaborate shrug, and blew out the smoke. "I tell you this only so that you do not imagine this inheritance of yours will ever be truly yours. He is very clever, and he will not give it up."

She sat up and swung her legs to the ground, tossing the cigarette away. "You mustn't feel badly, *chérie*," she said, rising. "This game of seduction, it is what Ashton does. It is what he knows. You take my advice, you forgive, and you move on. It is a—how do you say—a lesson of life. I only wonder . . ." She regarded Sara speculatively. "Has the seduction gone beyond the business yet? No? How very peculiar. He is generally so much quicker in such matters. But never mind. It will come. And then, *chérie* . . ."

She crossed slowly to Sara and stood near her, smiling. "You have a treat in store. Ashton is very good in bed," she confided. "After all, I taught him everything he knows."

Michele moved past her, laughing softly, brushing Sara's arm with her silk sleeve. For a moment Sara didn't move. And then she turned sharply on her heel.

"Michele," she said.

The other woman turned.

"You're wasting your time with me." Sara's voice was strong, and even, and for that she was very proud. "I don't want your husband, your château, or your advice. I don't want anything that has been or ever will be yours. All I want is to go home."

Another time, she might have appreciated the slight wavering of the certainty in Michele's eyes, even though her steely smile did not fade. But as Sara jerked open the heavy door and moved quickly into the house, she didn't even notice. She walked calmly up the stairs with her shoulders square and her head high, and she closed her door quietly. Then she crawled up onto the enormous, silk-clad bed, buried her face in one of the tufted pillows, and sobbed out her fury, her disappointment, her bitter, bitter loss until she had nothing left.

Nothing at all.

* * *

She awoke to the sound of her own weeping with burning, puffy eyes and a throat that felt gummy. The room was dark, and the pillow beneath her cheek stiff with the salt of dried tears. The weeping wouldn't go away. And as Sara rolled over groggily, trying to focus in the dark, she gradually realized the weeping was not hers.

She sat up, rubbing her hands over her itchy, swollen face, and fumbled for the switch on the bedside lamp. The soft glow of light stabbed pain through her eyes and she squeezed them closed briefly. There it was again, muffled but unmistakable. Someone crying. She got up and stumbled to the door.

The corridor outside her room was dark. Ash was the one who knew where all the light switches were and he was not here. The sound was not in her imagination; it was in fact clearer now, and it was coming from somewhere in the dark. It made her flesh prickle. She ran her hand along the wall for a moment, looking for a light switch, and then remembered the flashlight that Ash had left in her room the night before. Had it been only last night? Or a lifetime ago?

She returned to the corridor, sweeping the beam across the vast space, every muscle in her body tensed for the sound . . . and there it was again. A heartbroken, hiccupping sob that made Sara's breath catch and her blood go cold. It was not a ghost. It was not an hallucination. It was a child.

She followed the sound with her heart racing and the flashlight beam bouncing as she increased her pace to a desperate jog. She opened one door, and then another. The third door she opened revealed a small huddled figure crouched against a massive, sheet-draped piece of furniture, sobbing as though her heart would break.

"Oh my God," Sara whispered. "Alyssa?"

Her hair was tangled and her face was dirty and tear streaked. She had lost her hair ribbon and had torn her white shirt. When she saw the light she stretched out her arms to Sara, and wailed.

It took only half an indrawn breath for Sara to recover from her shock and rush toward the little girl. "Oh, sweetie! Oh, baby, it's okay. Are you all right? Are you hurt?"

She dropped to the floor and Alyssa flung herself into her embrace, wrapping her arms around Sara's neck so tightly that it was difficult to breathe. Sara tried quickly to check her for injuries, but soon gave up and simply held her, rocking back and forth on the floor, murmuring softly to her while Alyssa, her thin arms like a vise, sobbed wetly into her shoulder and her little heart beat like a wild bird's against Sara's breast. *"J'ai peur, j'ai peur!"* she kept saying, and Sara just patted her back helplessly, rocking her.

"You're going to have to speak English, sweetie. I can't understand you."

And Alyssa whispered brokenly, "Afraid!"

Everything inside of Sara seemed to break in two. They had left her. The only adults she knew, the ones responsible for her care, the grown-ups she trusted had simply walked away and forgotten her, leaving her alone and terrified in a dark castle to fend for herself. Had she gotten lost exploring? Had she exhausted herself with playing make-believe and fallen asleep, only to awake in a cold dark place with no one in the whole world knowing where she was? When Sara thought of what might have happened—the stairs, the moat, the empty swimming pool; the dark passages that led nowhere, the unsafe garden walls, the kitchen filled with knives and matches—her throat convulsed and she could hardly breathe. They had left her. *They had left her.*

Sara closed her eyes and hugged Alyssa tightly, as though the simple force of her embrace could protect her, could take away the terror of this night, could assure her that she would never, ever be abandoned again. She hugged her so fiercely that she didn't even notice that Alyssa had stopped crying, and only when she began to squirm in protest did Sara loosen her grip.

Alyssa sniffed, wiped her runny nose with the back of her hand, and inquired solemnly, *"Ou sont les toilettes?"*

Sara smiled in spite of herself. *"That* I understand." She set Alyssa on her feet and took her hand, picking up the flashlight. "Come along."

After attending to the little girl's personal needs, Sara managed to find enough light switches to illuminate their way to the kitchen. By this time Alyssa, overawed by the splendor of Sara's bedroom and with the unique resilience of children, had recovered from her fright and regained her sense of adventure. She surprised Sara by chattering all the way to the kitchen—not in French, but in English.

"I do well to speak the *anglais,*" she assured Sara happily. "I know many of the words. Shall I tell you to them? Lamp," she said, pointing to the grand chandelier as it blossomed in the hall. "Stairs. Boy." She pointed to the portrait in the entry way. "Table. The flower is on the table. I am called Alyssa. I be five years of age. What is you called?"

"My name is Sara," Sara told her, smiling down at her. "And I'm a lot older than that. I wish I could speak French as well as you speak English."

"I teach you," Alyssa volunteered generously. "My English is very goodly."

And even though it was the last thing she felt like doing, Sara laughed.

She spread jam on a thick slice of bread and poured a

glass of milk for Alyssa, and while the little girl ate, Sara took out her cell phone and, smiling disingenuously, stabbed out the telephone number she had found on the letterhead of Lindeman and Lindeman. A recorded voice informed her, "The hours of Lindeman and Lindeman are Monday through Friday, nine to six . . ."

She resisted the urge to throw the cell phone against the wall.

"Plate," said Alyssa, pointing. "The bread is on the plate."

Sara sat beside her, smiling as she wiped a smear of jam off her face with a napkin. "Do you like to swim, Alyssa?"

Apparently Alyssa was not quite certain what those words meant, because she simply munched another bite from her jam sandwich and gazed at Sara with those big brown eyes. Eyes that went straight to Sara's heart.

Eyes that looked just like Daniel's.

Sara struggled not to let her smile falter, and she smoothed back one of Alyssa's tangled curls with her fingers. "Well, never mind. You're going to like my bathtub. Where have you been playing, anyway? In the dungeon?"

"*Qu'est-ce que c'est dungeon?*" inquired Alyssa with interest, and Sara spent the rest of the brief meal trying to define English words for an inexhaustible French-speaking five-year-old.

Sara washed out Alyssa's filthy school uniform in the sink and watched while Alyssa splashed and played in the giant bathtub. And even through the terror that gripped her chest whenever she thought about what might have happened, and the rage that flamed through her body when she thought about what *had* happened, she couldn't help laughing at the innocence of a child's play, and the ease with which she immersed herself in the moment. Sara scrubbed her down with the expensive-smelling soap and washed her hair with the expensive-smelling shampoo, then towel dried her and swaddled the little girl in one of her own cotton nightshirts. It dragged the floor when she walked, and Sara showed her how to hold it up in front like a court gown so that she wouldn't trip, with a train trailing behind.

She wished she had not already shipped home the toys she had bought for the boys, and she searched around for something to keep a five-year-old entertained. All she could find was a book of photographs of the Loire Valley that she had bought for Dixie, and she settled Alyssa atop the big bed with the picture book.

"Now you stay right here," she told her, "and look at the pretty pictures. I've got to go try to find a way to call your . . ." What had she called him? Something papa. "Your papa. He'll be worried about you."

Alyssa regarded her solemnly. "I have no papa. *Je suis un bâtard.*"

Sara stared at her. She did not have to understand French to know that word. *Bastard.*

"*Ma maman,*" she went on matter-of-factly, "she is *morte.* There is a cat at *l'école.* Now he is *mort.*" She turned a picture in the book, and her face lit up. "Voilà!" she exclaimed, pointing to a photograph of a château with round turrets and a drawbridge. "I am here! She is my *maison!*"

Sara hesitated, then sat down on the bed beside her, looking at the picture. "Yes," she agreed. "It looks very much like your house. But it's not. Your house is called Château Rondelais." She settled back against the pillows and pulled Alyssa close. "Let's see if there's a picture of it in this book, okay?"

She turned the pages of the book, reading the captions and pointing to the photographs, until she could see the little girl's eyelids begin to droop. She closed the book and tucked Alyssa under the covers, kissing her forehead lightly.

"Close your eyes now, sweetie. Time for sleep."

Alyssa gazed drowsily at the gold and blue canopy over-head, the satiny curtains surrounding her. "C'est très belle," she murmured.

Sara smiled. "Fit for a princess."

She started to get up, hoping against hope that Ash had left something in his room, or elsewhere in the castle—a business card, a list of emergency numbers—something, anything, that would tell her what to do now. She didn't even speak enough French to contact the local authorities, or to try to find the housekeeper who had come in so reliably every day . . . but who would not be here tomorrow because, of course, she thought the château was empty.

She slid off the bed, but before she could take a step toward the door a small, fierce hand gripped her sleeve. Sara looked back at Alyssa. She was practically lost in the giant bed, a tiny doll with big, frightened, shimmering eyes. As Sara watched, a tear spilled from one of those eyes and splashed fatly on the starched white pillowcase. She said nothing. She did not have to. The dread in her eyes spoke it all.

Once again Sara felt her heart rend, quite simply, in two. She climbed back up on the bed, and lay down with her cheek on the pillow next to Alyssa's. "Of course I'll stay," she said softly. She held Alyssa's hand. "Don't be afraid. I'm here." She smiled, and another tear slid down Alyssa's plump cheek. Sara wiped it away. "Would you like to hear a story?"

Alyssa nodded uncertainly, still-damp curls bouncing, and Sara suspected the little girl was not entirely sure what a story was.

"Okay. But you must be very quiet, and close your eyes, and cuddle in close."

Obediently, Alyssa squeezed her eyes closed and snuggled close to Sara, holding on to her hand, tucking her head underneath Sara's chin. Sara closed her eyes, too, and in a moment she began, softly, "Once upon a time, there was a beautiful fairy princess who lived in a castle . . ."

Fairy-Tale Endings

· ELEVEN ·

The flight from London to Paris was just over an hour long, even when one had access to a chartered jet and a private helicopter to Heathrow. The drive from Paris to Rondelais, at top speed, was an hour and a half. There was a one-hour time difference between Paris and London. At 9:07, London time, Mrs. Harrison interrupted Ash's meeting with a rather grim look on her face and handed him a folded note. At 12:52, Paris time, Ash pulled his rented Peugot into the circular drive in front of the château and got out. Approximately thirty seconds later, when he heard the sound of childish laughter, his heart, which had been frozen in his chest since he had read the note, started beating again.

He followed the sound around the perimeter of the castle to the long walled garden that overlooked the moat. Daniel's grandparents had put a croquet court in the center of it, and

Ash and Daniel had practiced soccer there on the weekends they came down. Around the perimeter there once had been flower beds and fountains and pergolas where elegantly clad guests would sip drinks and watch the croquet players and chat about nothing at all.

Little remained now but a few rusty benches and stone tables, empty fountain basins and cracked statues. But the grass had been recently mown, and the maze of boxwood shrubs that hid statues of frogs and pelicans and cherubs, the flat stone steps that led from one level to another, the stepping-stones and gazing balls, all made for an imaginative child's playground paradise. Alyssa, in her plaid school skirt and white blouse from yesterday, was holding Sara's hands as she jumped from one of the stepping-stones to another, both of them laughing when she teetered on the edge and clapping when she landed center. Sara's hair was pulled up high on her head in a ponytail, and she wore no makeup. In baggy shorts that reached to her knees and a mismatched T-shirt that barely skimmed the top of her shorts, she looked about twelve years old. Every time she lifted Alyssa high over the grass between the stepping-stones the T-shirt would ride up to expose several inches of her slender waist, and watching them, in those first few moments before they knew he was there, Ash felt something odd and sweet catch in his chest. He actually hesitated before opening the gate, just for a second, because he knew that once he stepped inside their world the laughter would stop.

Alyssa shrieked with delight when she saw him, and he scooped her up, hugging her hard, kissing her hair and her cheek. *"Chérie, chérie!"* he exclaimed, and made himself loosen his grip because he didn't want to alarm her. He spoke to her in French. "How pretty you look today! Have you had a lovely visit with Auntie Sara? Were you a very good girl? Of course you were!"

She settled herself in the crook of his arm and filled his ears with the details of her adventure, of swimming in the giant bathtub and sleeping in the princess bed, and making her own toast for *petit-déjeuner* and boiling eggs and learning to turn cartwheels in the grass. And all the while Sara stood a few yards away, her face expressionless, watching him.

At last Alyssa wriggled from his arms and exclaimed, "*Regarde-moi! Regarde!*" And he applauded her roundly for two clumsy cartwheels and called out to her in French, "Be careful!" And then there was nothing to do but walk over to Sara, and face her.

He began, "Sara, I am so desperately sorry."

She replied, "If this had happened in North Carolina, you would be in jail by now."

The cool contempt in her eyes stabbed at him almost more sharply than the truth of her words. He breathed out, "I know." He pushed at his hair. "I specifically told Michele to take Alyssa back to school before the offices closed yesterday. Apparently, when it came time to go and she couldn't find her, she thought I had taken her myself." He drew in another breath and gave one slow shake of his head. "I believe her. I don't think even Michele would do something like this deliberately . . . mostly because she's botched any chance she ever had of gaining custody."

Sara looked at him with an awful mixture of amazement, outrage, and pity. It made his blood run cold.

She said distinctly, "You forgot her. You are her guardian, the only father figure she knows. She trusted you to take
care of her and you *forgot* her because you were so damn busy
taking care of your deals and schemes and *yourself* that you
couldn't be bothered. Do you have any idea what could have
happened to a five-year-old girl wandering around on her own
in a place like this? Do you? Do you know how she felt when
she got lost in the dark in a *castle* and no one came when she
cried? Can you even imagine that, Ash, *can you?*"

Her breathing was rapid and her eyes were flaming and
her hands were in fists. He wanted to reach for her but he
couldn't. He couldn't even meet her eyes. He said, roughly,
"For the love of God, Sara, nothing you can say will make me
feel any more wretched than I do."

Silence pulsed between them. And then, from a few
yards away, Alyssa called excitedly, "Sara! *Regardez-vous! Un
crapaud!*"

The fury on Sara's face faded like magic into affection as
she turned toward the child. "Wonderful!" she exclaimed,
and under her breath to Ash, "What is—"

"A toad," he responded. And they both called at once, he
in French and she in English, "Don't touch it!"

That made him smile a little, but her expression showed
no such concession. He said, sobering, "You're going to miss
your flight. I'll be happy to arrange . . ."

She said, "Don't worry about it. I've canceled the flight."

Every sense in his body prickled to alertness, because he
knew there was more. And nothing he could do would make
her tell him before she was ready. She turned and started

to stroll toward the croquet mall, keeping a careful eye on Alyssa. He fell into step beside her, his hands clasped behind his back.

She said, after a time, "I've had some time to think."

He waited, keeping pace with her.

"The other day, at the picnic . . . you were right about me. I've been broken. I really couldn't trust my own judgment, as I think some of my actions have proven. But no one stays broken forever. You were right about that, too."

She glanced at him. "Michele told me that you've been working on this deal with the hotel company for some time, and that you offered it to Daniel. And he refused."

Ash felt heat at the back of his neck. He responded evenly, "That's right. As I may have mentioned before, Daniel was an exceedingly impractical fellow. I offered him a way to make money from his property without violating the terms of his inheritance. And he refused. He didn't want the château commercialized."

Sara nodded, almost as though in approval . . . almost as though she were wondering whether he'd tell the truth. He scowled at that.

Ash said, "What else did Michele tell you?"

"She said you're very good in bed."

He cast her a sidelong glance, but her face remained implacable. "I should send her a thank-you note."

"And that she taught you everything you know."

He muttered, "No jury in the world would convict me."

Sara said, "As I understand the situation, Michele feels, for whatever reason, that the property should pass to her as the last Orsay heir—however distantly removed. And that she plans to do with it exactly what you do—to make as much money as she can, whatever it takes to do it."

She seemed to be waiting for a reply, so Ash agreed cautiously, "More or less."

"And that the only way she can do that is to file a claim on behalf of Alyssa that names herself as conservator, or whatever they're called in France."

"She's no chance of that now. I will crush her in court."

"You probably will," agreed Sara amicably. "But that could take months, or years, and in the end she would only come back with something else. It seems to me the fastest way to discourage someone like that is to remove her motivation."

He looked at her, interested and impressed. This was an entirely different side of Sara than he had known before, one that was completely incongruous with her bouncy ponytail and baggy shorts, but he was intrigued.

"To that end," she went on, "I've decided to take possession of my inheritance, and execute my right to buy out your shares over twenty years at a rate of eight percent per annum. I've also made arrangements to put the entire château and its proceeds into a trust for Alyssa, with myself as sole conservator. Since Michele's only legal grounds for challenging the estate are the interests of Alyssa, and since I've already taken steps to make sure everything is in Alyssa's name, that should solve the problem, don't you think?"

Rarely was Ash caught off guard. But this he had not seen coming. It took him a moment to rearrange his thoughts, his plans, his world according to this new information. This new

Sara. He actually faltered in his step, but quickly recovered. He murmured, watching her with new alertness, "It would appear I'm not the only one who knows how to use a mobile phone. You've been busy."

She smiled without humor. "Busier than you know. There's a six-hour time difference between here and the U.S."

He agreed, watching her. "So there is."

"Which can be inconvenient when you're trying to transfer funds."

He stopped walking, stepping in front of her to block her passage. "Sara, you can't be serious."

She replied, without blinking, "Oh, but I am."

His eyes went over her—hair, eyes, lips, hands, torso, legs, and feet—in a single, brief, reassessing glance, as though seeing her for the first time, or trying to find the person he thought he knew. He said carefully, "It sounds as though you've been receiving some very astute legal advice in the past few hours. Might I have the pleasure of knowing with whom I'll be negotiating in the future?"

She informed him easily, "Mr. Theodore Winkle, Esquire. After all, he's represented me quite well throughout this whole ordeal. I couldn't think of anyone better qualified to help me now."

She was not joking. It took him a moment to realize that, which was a moment longer than it should have. "Excellent." He laughed softly. "Brilliant, in fact. Using my own people against me."

"Is there a problem?"

"None at all. Winkle is a good man; otherwise I should

never have employed him. He may also, of course, be looking for a job tomorrow."

She stepped around him impatiently. "Don't even try it. Alyssa! Don't eat the grass!"

He followed her gaze, and repeated the command in French. Alyssa, who had prepared a lovely serving of grass, leaves, and flower petals on the stone table, regarded them both with pouty lips for a moment. Then, distracted by a butterfly, she clambered down from the table to chase it.

Ash said, "You're being reactionary. You can't have thought this through. Why in the world didn't you talk to me about this first?"

She cast him a single incredulous look. "Why in the world should I have?"

He shook his head sharply, still hardly believing what she had done. "This is the road to financial ruin. You can't afford this château and you have no need for it. And Winkle, if he has any sense at all, will have advised you that placing the whole lot in Alyssa's name does not in any way free you from liability for its maintenance, taxes, or other expenses—in fact, it only makes the burden harsher. Furthermore"—he had to say it—"with no proof whatsoever that Alyssa is a legal heir, you have no grounds for a conservancy, and the French courts will never name you, an American, as trustee."

Sara started walking again, her gaze on Alyssa and the butterfly. "Did you know Daniel had dual citizenship?"

His tone was impatient. "Of course I did."

"Which means that Alyssa, as the child of a naturalized U.S. citizen born on foreign soil, is an American. And that means . . ." She swooped her hand down to casually pluck off the head of a tall stem of summer grass, scatterings its seeds to the wind. "I have a stronger claim to her guardianship than you do, or even Michele. I'm her stepmother."

He was silent for a step. When he spoke again his voice had an edge. "Very clever. Well-done. Of course, with no proof that Daniel is Alyssa's father, you have nothing—no conservatorship, no claim as trustee."

She said conversationally, "Please don't think you can use your legal tricks on me, Ash. Because you know how you were going to crush Michele in court? Those are the exact same strategies I'm going to use against you to gain custody of Alyssa if I have to."

He stared at her. "Good God, I half think you're serious. What in the world would you do with a five-year-old French child you've known less than twenty-four hours?"

"A lot more than you have," she shot back furiously. "You parked her in a boarding school for three years! You let her fellow students call her a bastard! How she's grown up as sweet and cheerful as she has is beyond me. And don't forget." Her eyes narrowed coldly. "You abandoned her last night, the same as Michele did. And you were legally responsible."

He stared her down for a long moment. "Very well," he said at last, calmly. "I think you've made your position clear. But enough. This is madness. There are easier ways to manage this."

"Let me explain something to you, Ash," she said, and purposefully resumed her easy, pleasant tone. "You are not managing anything. Not anymore. I am, until proven otherwise, Daniel's only legal heir. I will do with his estate what I please."

He said harshly, "You won't get away with this, Sara. I won't allow it."

He was distracted by a muffled buzzing. He reached into his pocket for his phone, but it was Sara who took her own mobile from the capacious pocket of her shorts. She flipped open the screen and read the message there. "Oops," she said, flashing him a brief, false smile. "Too late. I believe my certified check for $47,000 in taxes just made the transfer of ownership official. Sorry."

It took him a moment, just a moment, to understand what she had done. He said flatly, "Until the courts determine otherwise—which could take years, by the way—I will remain Alyssa's guardian. Even if you manage to put the château into a conservatorship, I can block any move you try to make for the next sixteen years."

"You can," she agreed easily, "but you won't. Do you know why? Because you have a serious conflict of interest here, Ash. And if word should ever get out that you tried to sabotage a client's interests for your own financial gain . . . well, let's just put it this way. People in your position rely on their reputation for integrity, discretion, and efficiency. Once that reputation's gone, you've got nothing. And . . ." She turned to look at him, her expression deceptively placid. "If there's one thing I know, it's how to run a media campaign."

He felt ice creep into his veins, his eyes, his voice. Without intending it, his eyes narrowed in challenge. "You don't have the resources to take me on."

And she replied, her own gaze like granite, "You don't want me to try."

This was fast getting out of hand. He searched for some way to smooth matters over, to level the playing field once again, but all he could do was stare at her. "Who are you?" he said softly. "I don't even know you."

"Don't you?" She lifted her eyebrows in elaborate surprise. "Then you haven't been paying attention. Let me help you out. I'm the woman who took care of her alcoholic mother from the time she was six years old, who raised her little sister all alone, who put herself and her sister through college, who got a job with a firm so prestigious even you've heard about them, and who managed the accounts of the very same corporations whose deals you brokered. And I am the woman who is going to kick your ass if you get in my way."

"Good God," he murmured, and forced a small, mirthless smile. "I think I'm in love."

She was not amused. "It's over, Ash," she said. "You lose."

She turned and walked away from him. He wanted to grab her and shake her hard. He wanted to hold her, just hold her, heart against heart, hands in her hair, lips on her skin, until the pain went away . . . her pain, and his pain. How had it come to this? How had *he* come to this? In all his life, there had never been anything he could not make right, given time. How had this gone so terribly wrong?

"Sara," he said harshly, without moving, "listen to me. It's not going to happen. I know what you're feeling. Honestly I do. But I can't allow you to go through with this."

She whirled on him, her color high, her hands in fists. The

anguish in her eyes tore at him. "You don't have any *idea* what I'm feeling. I spent my whole life chasing a dream I didn't even want. I was married to a monster and I never knew it. I have nothing—*nothing*—to show for my time here on earth. But now . . ." She drew a deep breath, calming herself. Her fingers unclasped, deliberately. "Now I have a chance to make a very big wrong right again. And you're not going to stop me. No one is going to stop me. Is that clear?"

He thrust his hands into his pockets, mostly to stop them from reaching for her. He said, "What if she's not Daniel's child?"

"Oh, for God's sake, Ash, look at her! Look at her eyes, her hair, her smile. She's Daniel's child."

"She has beautiful French eyes," Ash replied evenly, "and a lovely French smile. That doesn't necessarily mean anything at all."

Alyssa, who had been happily jumping off a small step a few feet away, chose that moment to run up to them, and wrap her arms around Sara's legs in a brief hug. The tension in Sara's face vanished into tenderness as she bent down and scooped Alyssa up before she could scamper away again. She swung the little girl through the air until she giggled and squealed with delight, and then carried her over to a rusty iron bench where she set Alyssa on her lap and began to retie her shoes.

In a moment, Ash came and sat beside them.

"You're going to ruin that suit," Sara said, without looking up.

Alyssa wriggled out of Sara's lap and climbed onto his, and surprised him by kissing his cheek. "Why are you so sad, *petit-papa?*" she asked in French.

He slipped an arm around her and replied gently, in the same language, "I'm sad because I have to tell Aunt Sara something she doesn't want to hear."

"And then she will be sad also?"

Ash looked at Sara, who almost seemed to understand what they were saying. "Yes. I'm afraid so."

Alyssa patted his cheek solemnly. "Don't make Tante Sara sad."

Ash smiled at her and set her on the ground. "Go, play, *chérie*. But stay close."

When she was out of earshot, Sara said, "What?"

His gaze followed Alyssa across the lawn. "I have to request a posthumous DNA test." He set his jaw, took a breath, and looked at her. "If I don't, the court will."

Sara lost a little color around her lips, and her eyes tightened. "You don't mean . . . exhumation?"

"Yes. That's what I mean."

She brought her hand to her throat, as though to massage away an ache, and then let it flutter to her lap. She, too, focused her eyes across the lawn where Alyssa played. Her voice was small, and distant. "I was going to have him cremated. But he told me once he was raised Catholic. A very badly lapsed Catholic, he said. Still . . . I thought a Christian burial was what he would want."

Ash reached for her hand, and covered it with his own. She did not pull away. He thought perhaps because she was in shock.

He said quietly, "Leave this alone, Sara. Let everything go back to the way it was. Alyssa's trust will take care of her. I can handle Michele. There's no reason to do this. Just let it go."

"I can't." Her voice was thick, and when she pulled her hand from his it was to wipe the corner of her eye.

"Why not?" he insisted, growing frustrated.

"Because," she said. She swallowed hard, and drew in a breath, and seemed to compose herself. "Because Daniel accompanied his parents' bodies back to France in October of 2002 and he stayed until November 2003. When was Alyssa born?"

Ash said, without looking at her, "June 2004."

"Daniel was in France when Alyssa was conceived, Ash, and you knew that all along."

Ash said stiffly, "Daniel was in Europe in 2003. I have no way of knowing where he was when Alyssa was conceived."

Sara nodded slowly, but without satisfaction or accusation, as though she had expected nothing more of him. "Every princess deserves a castle," she said softly.

She lifted her chin, set her jaw. "Do it."

"Good Christ, Sara." His tone was fierce, but then he looked at her, and he saw the firm and quiet resolution in her eyes, and he didn't know what to say. He could not, in recent history, remember when that had ever happened to him before. So he simply repeated, softly, "Christ."

"Tante Sara!" called Alyssa, waving to them. *"Voici! Voici les petits oiseaux!"*

She had uncovered a collection of cracked concrete statues, a mother duck and ducklings. Sara called, "That's great, Alyssa!" And to Ash, "What do I say?"

"*Très belle.*"

"*Très belle!*" she repeated. "*Très belle*, Alyssa!"

They watched her until she grew tired of chattering to the ducks and moved on to another game. Ash's frustration eased, almost without his having realized it, and so did Sara's sorrow.

Sara said, after a time, "You can't send her back to that boarding school."

"No, I suppose not." He frowned a little, watching Alyssa as she returned to her game of jumping off the steps. "I don't know what else can be done on this short notice. I could take her back to London with me, look for something there, I suppose. Mrs. Harrison could probably find a nurse for the short term. But it will take a while to get her documents in order."

Sara said, "Leave her with me."

He looked at her, startled, and she seemed as surprised as he was, as though she hadn't quite intended to say that. But even as he met her eyes, she seemed to come to a decision. "Yes," she said. "That's the best thing, I think."

"Sara, you can't mean to stay here."

Stubbornness darkened her eyes. "Why shouldn't I?"

"You don't even speak the language!"

She said stiffly, "I'll learn."

"You don't have a car, a European driver's license. What will you do with yourself up here all alone? For heaven's sake, be sensible!"

"I won't be alone," she replied doggedly. "I'll have Alyssa."

"You can't take care of this place by yourself, and the cost of keeping help for a house this size is beyond reasonable. This is absurd, Sara. I can't be a party to it."

She lifted her chin fractionally, her eyes narrowing. "What are your choices?"

He opened his mouth to reply, and said absolutely nothing. Scowling, he jerked his gaze away. "You are the most exasperating woman."

She called, "Alyssa, be careful!"

"*Soyez prudent.*"

"*Soyez prudent!*" she repeated, and Alyssa, shrugging, lost interest in jumping two steps at a time and went to find another game.

Ash said, "I can't just leave her with you. I'm her legal guardian."

"And I'm her stepmother."

Once again, what he wanted to reply died in his throat. He pinched the bridge of his nose, trying to forestall the headache that was starting there. "I suppose I could try to get a nanny up from the village."

"I don't need a nanny." Her tone was impatient. "I know how to take care of a little girl."

"Sara, there are procedures," he began, as patiently as he could manage, and then, meeting the obstinacy in her face, he finished under his breath, "Oh, bugger it."

Sara's expression softened, just a little. "It's only temporary," she said. "I know that. I'll be here for a while. Let her stay until you find another school."

He tried to think of alternatives, or even just one sound argument, and came up empty. He said, "The schools are unlikely to accept new applicants until fall term."

She didn't blink. "I'll be here."

She was staying the summer. That made him illogically pleased.

And worried.

Ash stood up, and walked over to Alyssa. Kneeling beside her, he said in French, "*Chérie*, would you like to stay here, with Tante Sara? Or do you want to go back to *l'école* and see your friends?"

But almost before he finished speaking she was shaking her head, curls whipping furiously. "*Pas d'école!*" she said adamantly. *No school.* She continued in the same language, "I will stay here, at my house. Tante Sara, she likes me. She thinks I am beautiful!"

Ash smiled at her, and tweaked her chin. "I think you are beautiful, too, *chérie*."

He started to rise, but she caught his sleeve. "Will you stay here, too, *petit-papa?*"

He shot a quick, almost imperceptible glance toward Sara, who was watching them. "No," he told Alyssa gently. "But I'll come visit often. And you will be very good for your Tante Sara, and do whatever she says, yes?"

Alyssa nodded solemnly. "I am a good girl."

He ruffled her curls affectionately, and returned to Sara. She rose from the bench to meet him, her posture careful and her eyes wary, as though greeting an adversary.

He said, "I think we can work something out, on a temporary basis." He reached into his inside coat pocket and removed a business card, and a pen, scrawling something on the back. "This," he said, thrusting the card to her, "is my mobile number. Don't lose it. What's yours?"

She said, "I'm going to have telephones installed in the château."

"Yes, well, good luck with that," he muttered. "France Telecom may have you hooked up by the next century. In the meantime . . ." He waited with pen poised on the back of another business card until she drew out her cell phone and brought up the number.

"Keep your mobile turned on and on your person at all times," he instructed her. "If you have any difficulties, anything at all, call me, and if I am out of range, call my office. Mrs. Harrison knows how to reach me, and if she can't reach me, it doesn't matter because she knows everything I know at any rate. In the storage pantry off the kitchen, taped inside the cupboard door that holds the linens, is a list of all the support personnel—the housekeeper, the caterers, the groundsmen, the repairmen, and also emergency numbers for fire and police. Now, from your mobile, you will have to dial a six-digit exchange . . ."

Her eyes widened purposefully as she listened to him. "Ash," she said, "I'm an American, not an imbecile. I can figure it out."

He compressed his lips briefly, glancing beyond her, searching for words, not even knowing what he wanted to say. "This—unpleasant business," he said at last, "may take some time. If you need anything . . ."

She lifted her chin a little. "I'm prepared to stay. Mr. Winkle is helping me set up bank accounts here, and get a visa when my passport expires. I think I can manage."

"I want you to get help from the village."

"I don't need any help. I can—"

"For God's sake, Sara, you can't even cook! I'm sending someone up."

She glared at him and he reminded her sharply, "Alyssa is my ward. I won't have her starving to death. And you don't even know how to work a European washing machine."

"How hard can it be?"

"I'm not going to argue with you."

"Three days a week. And she has to speak English."

"Every morning, six days a week. Learn French."

A smile, very tiny and almost indistinguishable, twitched at her lips. "I'll manage, Ash," she said.

He blew out a breath. "I well imagine you will. Sara . . ." How much easier this would have been if he could have touched her, drawn her into his embrace, stroked her hair. As it was he could only stand there awkwardly, offering an uncertain gift with the most earnest intent, knowing it was unlikely to be received. "I don't want you to think of Daniel as a monster," he said quietly. "He came from a different culture, with values that were different from those you and I might hold. If you stay here, you will be part of that culture. I just want you to know that."

Her lashes shadowed her cheek, and he saw her throat convulse. She looked suddenly frail, and vulnerable, and he hated that he had done that to her. Or that Daniel had done that do her.

"And by the way," he added, his tone hardening, "your offer is rejected."

Her head jerked up. She stared at him. "What?"

"By the terms of my contract with Daniel," he informed her flatly, "which is transferable to his heirs and assigns, my shares in the château may be purchased with accrued interest at current market value in cash. No allowances are made for payments over time—that was merely a suggestion I made to you on a day I was feeling generous. I am feeling slightly less generous today, so unless you have approximately 3.7 million in ready U.S. dollars, we have no deal. I will of course make certain you are reimbursed for the amount you've paid in taxes. I assume Winkle has your bank account information."

Her expression hardened. "Mr. Winkle said you might pull something like this."

"Good for him. I hope he also pointed out that you'll thank me for this someday."

"You're not going to get away with this."

"I already have," he assured her. "You're not going to kick my ass, and I'm not going to kiss yours. This is a compromise. Take it or leave it."

"You son of a bitch."

He smiled. "*Bonjour, chérie.* And *bonne aventure.* I'll be in touch."

Before he left, he scooped Alyssa up into the air, and kissed her soundly on both cheeks. "Take care of your aunt Sara," he whispered to her before he set her on her feet again. "She needs you very much."

· TWELVE ·

Ash let himself into Michele's Paris apartment, tossed his blazer over the back of her sofa, poured a Scotch, and made himself comfortable in one of her Louis Vuitton leather chairs. The room was decorator perfect, with art pieces collected from each of her previous three husbands. Ash's contribution was a framed copy of a letter supposedly written to Louis XIV from the mistress for whom he built Rondelais, which he had purchased from Daniel's father for two hundred pounds, back when he was first falling under the dark spell of Michele's enchantment. It wasn't worth that, since it had already been proven to be a nineteenth-century copy of a seventeenth-century document that may or may not have ever existed, but its language was explicit, if not downright erotic, and Ash had thought it would amuse her. After the divorce, he had offered to buy it back from her for a thousand pounds, simply because it annoyed him that she should have it. She of course had laughed at him.

He wandered around the apartment for a time, smoked one of her cigarettes—which reminded him immediately why he had abandoned the habit years ago—and eventually returned to the chair by the window. He sipped the whiskey slowly and listened to the muffled sounds from the busy streets below, watching the sun set over one of the most magnificent cities in the world. Michele kept excellent Scotch, and he was almost sorry when he heard her key turn in the door before he was even half finished.

Her heels were three inches high and her skirt about three inches too short, but like most Frenchwomen, even at her age, she could pull it off. If she was startled to see him sitting there in the twilight, she did not show it.

"And so, *mon chéri*," she murmured, dropping her packages on the table by the door, "at last you have come to your senses." She came over to him in a drift of musky perfume, rouged lips upturned in a practiced vixen's smile, her fingertips threading through the back of his hair.

"Indeed I have." He let his eyes examine what she offered: the swell of an ivory breast, the curve of a silk-clad hip. "I've come to understand, my love, that subtlety is lost on you. So I will be explicit." He took one last sip of the Scotch and stood. She was so close that their thighs brushed and his face was mere inches from hers. He took her chin between the fingers of his hand and he said, softly, "You will withdraw your petition for custody before nine o'clock in the morning or at five after I will have you charged with abduction and child endangerment, is that quite clear?"

Her brows drew together in an annoyed moue and she tried to turn her face away, but he held it firm. "And you will never—please understand me, Michele, I said *never*—molest either Sara or Alyssa again under any pretense whatsoever. You have seen what I do to people who get in my way. You don't want to be one of them."

She struggled to pull her face away from his grip. "You're hurting me."

"Good."

But he released her abruptly and she took a half-stumbling step back, rubbing the red marks his fingers had left on her chin. Her eyes were smoldering green embers in the dim room, but her voice was deliberately casual. "I am no fool, my love. The silly petition has been already withdrawn. But the damage, she is already done, *n'est-ce pas?*"

He looked at her without compassion. "It's over, Michele. This time you've finally gone too far."

He started to move past her, but she stopped him with a hand flat on his chest. Those eyes, those hard, dark gems, moved back and forth over his face, as if collecting his secrets, tasting his thoughts. "When will you abandon this foolishness?" Her breath, hot and sweetly perfumed, fanned across his mouth, her fingers closing slowly around the fabric of his shirt. "When will you stop chasing something you are not? You think your American would not have you if she knew you inside, and you are right. But I know you, Ashton." Her breasts tantalized his chest and her nails closed on his skin, stinging, bringing fire. "I know you," she whispered, her mouth against his now. "I know you because inside you *are* me."

He felt her heat, and it was a fever in his own skin. The taste of her breath, the sharp, hot caress of her nails, caused his heart to pound and his throat to grow dry. He reached for her hands, his fingers closing tight around hers. He stepped away.

"No," he told her. "I'm not."

He released her hands with a motion so abrupt that she stumbled a little on her high heels, and he pushed past her and out of the door without another word.

Yet into the hallway, into the street, into the taxi, and all the way to the airport, her words clung to him like the scent of her perfume. He couldn't get them out of his head. And what troubled him most was that deep inside there was a part of him that was afraid she was right.

*   *   *

Ash left sixteen messages on Sara's voice mail over a period of half as many days. The first was when his check for five hundred euros, along with a very nice note from Mrs. Harrison instructing Sara to use the money to purchase whatever Alyssa needed for the summer, was returned without comment. He then requested that Mrs. Harrison go out and secure an assortment of "dresses and playclothes and underthings and such as that" for a five-year-old girl, along with a selection of toys and picture books, to be boxed up and sent to Rondelais posthaste. When that box, too, was returned unopened, he left a perfectly polite message asking Sara to call him. The next message was not so polite. Nor was the next one.

She did not return any of his calls. She did, however call his office and leave a message with Mrs. Harrison explaining that she had already taken Alyssa shopping and there was no need for him to send any more boxes.

He was annoyed. "Impossible. There's nothing in the village but T-shirts and sundries. The only clothing Alyssa has are school uniforms. She'll need shoes and—"

"I believe Ms. Graves said something about Lyon, sir."

"She took her to Lyon?" Ash didn't know why that surprised him so. "How?"

"There is a train," Mrs. Harrison pointed out.

Ash muttered, "Yes, I suppose there is."

"Apparently she needed some things to make their stay more comfortable," Mrs. Harrison went on, "since the château is not set up for young visitors. She asked if I could recommend a supplier of children's furniture, so I rang up Mr. Finnish and asked him to send her a catalogue. I trust that was appropriate."

He looked at her suspiciously. "It sounds as though you had a lovely chat."

"She seems a pleasant enough person. Quite attached to the little one."

"She'd be a lot more pleasant," replied Ash irritably, "if she'd return my calls."

The next voice mail he left pointed out that as Alyssa's guardian and administrator of her trust, it was his responsibility to supply her basic necessities and Sara was not to return any more of his checks. Furthermore, he reminded her in no uncertain terms that part of their agreement was that she would keep her mobile phone turned on and with her at all times. The next several messages pointed out that she was in unquestionable violation of her part of the bargain and that there were consequences—he stopped short of spelling out what they might be—for her behavior.

She sent a message, via Mrs. Harrison, to remind him that she had agreed to keep her phone turned on and on her person and that she had done so. But that did not mean, "And I quote, sir," said Mrs. Harrison, "'that I have to answer every time the fool thing rings.'"

Ash glared at her. "Did she say anything else?"

"Yes, sir. She wondered if I thought teal would be a suitable color for draperies in a little girl's room."

Ash considered and rejected a number of pithy remarks—none of which would be suitable for Mrs. Harrison's ears—and finally decided on, "Oh, bloody hell. Get Argentina on the telephone for me."

To which she replied, "The entire country, sir, or is there someone in particular you had in mind?"

He decided then and there that he did not approve of Sara's relationship with Mrs. Harrison. She was definitely exerting a bad influence.

*   *   *

Dixie said, sounding alarmed, "Wait a minute. Are you telling me you're moving to *France*? Right now? Without talking to anyone or packing or . . ."

"No," Sara said. "I mean, yes. What I mean is, not exactly." She blew out a breath and sank down on the floor, leaning her head back against the wall. "I don't know." She closed her eyes briefly. "God, Dixie, it all happened so fast. I didn't have time to think. I just had to do something, and if I hadn't done it quickly, I mean, within a matter of hours, that crazy woman, that ex-wife of Ash's, would have filed a suit that could have kept the estate tied up in court for years. I couldn't have cared less, personally, but the little girl, Alyssa . . . she's an orphan. This is all she has. I couldn't let someone steal it from her like that."

"But . . ." Sara could sense Dixie's frantic effort to try to make sense of all the things she had learned—so outrageously, so unexpectedly—in the past few minutes. "Didn't you say you still don't have clear title to the estate? Why wouldn't Ash let you buy out his shares?"

"Because he's an ass," returned Sara shortly. Then, in an effort to be fair, she added, "He did say he would clear the title if I could come up with the cash. Frankly, I think he just wants to hold something over me—or maybe over Daniel. Maybe that crazy Michele is right about him. He's obsessed with this place. Maybe he just doesn't want to give up control."

"And he's the little girl's guardian?"

Sara sighed. "That's what makes it complicated."

"Sara . . ." Dixie sounded worried. "You don't think that he and his ex-wife are in on this together, do you? To try to cheat you out of the estate?"

Sara rubbed her eyes wearily. "God, I don't know what to

think. My instincts say Ash is an honest man . . . or as honest as a lawyer can be, anyway. And I think he really cares about Alyssa, and any man who's that good with children has to have *some* redeeming characteristics. But I thought Daniel was honorable, too. So all that proves is that I have lousy judgment where men are concerned."

"Oh, Sara," Dixie said softly. "I'm so sorry."

Sara swallowed hard, and couldn't speak for a moment. "I don't know if I can ever forgive Daniel," she managed after a time, in a low voice, "or myself, for believing in him. But when I look at her . . ." A smile made its way to the surface, and the tension left Sara's shoulders and neck. "She's such a miracle, Dixie. I look at her and I feel like I'm in a Hallmark commercial. I'm just blown away by what a human being can be, you know? By how bright and perfect and innocent and funny and full of unmitigated potential we all start out. And she's so smart! She already knows more English words that I know French ones.

"Yesterday . . ." Sara's voice picked up energy as she spoke, and she even laughed as little, remembering. "I was moving some furniture—it's a long story but you wouldn't believe what a job I've had, trying to turn a castle into a home for a little girl—and I dropped a dresser drawer on my foot and it really hurt. I guess I said a few words I'm glad she didn't understand in English, and I sat down on the floor and took off my shoe and was rocking back and forth, you know, and she ran up and dropped down on the floor and kissed my toe! And then she put her little hands on my face and looked at me really solemn-like, and she said, '*Je t'aime*, Tante Sara.' That means 'I love you' in French."

By now Sara was misty-eyed, simply from relating the incident, and she pushed at the tears with the heel of her hand. "Oh, I know, I'm a total sucker. But she's got me by the heartstrings. I'm crazy about her. And sometimes I think . . ." She drew in a breath. "I made a choice, you know, between having a family, and having a career. And for years I was okay with that. Then I wasn't. Now I think that maybe . . . if there's any good that's come from marrying Daniel, it wasn't inheriting this château, no matter how much it's worth. It was in finding Alyssa."

There was a mother's warmth in Dixie's voice as she said softly, "I understand. And I'm so happy for you. But . . ." There was always a *but*. "I don't know what this means. If she has a guardian already, what does that make you?"

Sara sighed. "Right now, her temporary babysitter."

Dixie hesitated. "And . . . later?"

"I think . . ." Another careful, almost wondering, breath. "I want to adopt her."

Dixie didn't say anything for the length of time it took several heartbeats to cross an ocean. And then, "Wow."

Sara rushed on, "Of course, it's not going to be that easy, with a ten-million-dollar estate hanging in the balance and that crazy Michele trying to do whatever she can to get her hands on it and Ash refusing to cooperate, but once the paternity test comes back I'll have a much stronger case. That's why it's so important to do this, do you see?"

"Oh Sara," Dixie said softly. "This is big. This is huge."

And Sara agreed, "I know."

"I hope you know what you're doing."

"Did you?" challenged Sara. "When you finally got pregnant with the twins?"

Dixie laughed softly. After twelve years of failed attempts, fertility treatments, and in vitro fertilization procedures, Dixie would be the first to admit that what had seemed like the answer to a lifetime of prayers had turned out to be nothing like she had expected. "All right," she said. "All right. What can I do to help?"

"Just send me the things I asked for. As soon as my laptop gets here, I'll e-mail you. Ash has got to have an Internet connection installed here somewhere; I just haven't been able to find it yet. I can't be wasting any more money on international phone calls now that I'm a homeowner . . . castle owner. You've got the list, right?"

"Right here. Computer, books, summer clothes, tennis shoes . . . No winter coats?" she prompted, only half teasing.

Sara hesitated. "I'll let you know."

Dixie said fervently, "I hope everything works out the way you want it to, Sara. But if it doesn't . . . you know where home is."

Sara smiled softly, almost to herself, and closed her eyes. "Yeah," she said. "I do."

When Dixie hung up the kitchen phone, Jeff said, "When is she coming home?"

Dixie sighed. "I don't know."

"How's she doing?"

Dixie turned to him, her expression helpless and concerned, and admitted, "I don't know."

* * *

One of the few pleasures Ash had allowed himself throughout this entire interminable debacle was the moment he called the inestimable Mr. Winkle into his office. Theodore Winkle was twenty-eight years old, had graduated top of his class, and was good-looking enough to model underwear for Calvin Klein. Ash found himself hoping, rather absently, that Sara never had cause to meet with her solicitor in person.

And that surprised him.

However, that uneasiness was offset by the satisfaction he took in the fine film of perspiration he could see beginning to form at Winkle's hairline as he held him there in the uncomfortable lime green chair, in silence, for one minute; two. It was going on three minutes when Winkle finally burst out, "Sir, I know why you've called me here. In my defense, I should like to say that I joined this firm out of the greatest regard for its reputation of integrity and high moral standards, two qualities which are sadly lacking in today's world of international commerce, wouldn't you agree, sir?"

Ash nodded, slowly, tipping the Montblanc in careful balance between the forefingers of two hands, watching him.

Winkle straightened his shoulders. The perspiration was beginning to sheen his upper lip now. "When you assigned me the Rondelais matter, I resolved to carry it through with the same unwavering dedication to the client's best interests that you have always impressed upon me as being tantamount to the corporate creed of Lindeman and Lindeman. I felt a particular responsibility in this respect, since the party in question was the widow of a personal friend of yours—and my abject sympathies, on his passing, which I may not have properly expressed before—and since you, yourself, sir, had a personal financial stake in the matter. I believe I handled everything according to form until the young lady approached me with certain . . ." He hesitated, and cleared his throat. "New information, and a proposal for resolving the matter which, if I may say so sir, even I could not have come up with on such short notice. I then acted as I presumed you would wish me to act on behalf of the client. If this has inconvenienced you in any way, I apologize but . . ." And he set his jaw in a very Sir Galahad fashion and declared, "I stand by the letter of the law, and I believe I have acted accordingly."

Ash said, "Well-done."

The satisfaction was in seeing every well-formed muscle in Theodore Winkle's body sag in relief. "Sir?"

"I said, well-done. You've acted exactly as I would expect a representative of this organization to do. I shall count upon you in the future to continue to hold high the standard of Lindeman and Lindeman, without fear or compromise."

"Sir, I—thank you, sir." Winkle simply sat there, looking stunned and deflated.

Ash said, "You expected something more?"

"To be honest," he admitted, "I rather expected to be sacked . . . or if not, to be transferred to Bulgaria."

Ash's lips twitched. "Fortunately for you, our offices in Bulgaria are fully staffed." And he sobered. "But you're right.

My involvement in this situation, both from a personal and financial perspective, makes it imperative that you represent your client's interest with vigor and dedication. What Sara wants, Sara gets, if at all feasible within the law. Are we clear on that, Mr. Winkle?"

Winkle blinked, several times. "Absolutely, sir. Absolutely."

"Excellent. You may expect a twenty percent bonus in this period's pay, if that's acceptable."

"Yes, sir." Winkle scrambled to his feet. "Thank you, sir."

Ash dismissed him, and he couldn't help smiling as he watched the younger man go. There were, after all, distinct advantages to a twenty-year seniority. One of them was, of course, being the boss.

He buzzed Mrs. Harrison, feeling lucky today. "Ring up Sara in France, if you'd be so kind."

"On her mobile, sir?"

He scowled. "Since she has no other means of communication, yes, on her mobile, if it's no trouble."

"One moment, then, sir."

Several moments later, Mrs. Harrison appeared in his office, her expression as always implacable. "Ms. Graves regrets that since she is currently engaged in putting Miss Alyssa down for her nap, she cannot take your call at the moment, and suggests that, if you have anything of import to say, you leave a message."

His temper surged, and he stood up from behind his desk, lending power to his words. "You may inform Ms. Graves for me . . ."

"Excuse me, sir," interrupted Mrs. Harrison with only slightly raised eyebrows, "but are we ten?"

He scowled at her. "What?"

"It merely occurs to me," she replied calmly, "that whatever difficulties you are having in communicating with Ms. Graves might be resolved if you attempted to do so in person."

He stared at her for the longest time. "Yes, of course," he said, moving briskly from behind the desk. "Excellent suggestion. I'm going to Rondelais."

"Actually, sir," Mrs. Harrison reminded him gently, "You're going to Amsterdam."

He stared at her for another frustrated, disbelieving minute. But in the end, he went to Amsterdam.

He also went to Singapore, Milan, and Salzburg over the next three weeks. He had dinner with a woman in Austria whom he had been seeing, off and on, for more than a year whenever he was in town. She seemed surprised when he declined her invitation to finish their evening together, as was customary, at her apartment. So was he.

He stopped leaving voice messages for Sara and started texting her instead. This worked only to the extent that he would occasionally receive a one-word reply from her. "Is Alyssa well or shall I send the gendarmerie?" received a simple "Well" from her. And, "In Rome. Do you need anything?" was met with "No." And, perhaps most infuriating of all, when he sent a simple "Weekend?" her reply was "Busy."

And to top it all off, the bloody stupid dream had returned, sometimes waking him in the middle of the night, always leaving him feeling shaken and empty and aching for something he could never have.

He surprised his mother with a middle-of-the-week visit for no reason at all.

Shortly after his father's death, his mother had sold their London townhome and retired to the country manse of a former squire in Northampton, where she became a scion of her own sort of society. She was, at seventy-two, still vigorous and still beautiful, with a flawless English complexion and platinum hair that she often wore swept up in a fetching Gibson girl, or occasionally, particularly when jumping her horses, in a shamelessly youthful braid over one shoulder. She headed the Society for the Enrichment of British Social Customs, the Ladies for a Better Tomorrow, and was the chapter president of the United Kingdom Kennel Club—despite the fact that she did not actually own a dog. She knew everyone worth knowing, and, perhaps most important, didn't particularly care.

"It was all rather lovely," she recounted now, "until Lady Willingsley's poodle lifted his leg on the cake. Fortunately, no one noticed but me, so I simply cut that part away and served it anyway."

Ash, who had been gazing distractedly out the misty window, stopped with his Scotch halfway to his lips. "Mother, you didn't."

"No, of course not." She sipped her own whiskey complacently. "I merely wished to see if you were paying attention."

He gave her a weak, apologetic smile. "Your pardon. I suppose I have been rather inattentive."

"You're a horrid guest," she informed him. "I really wish you wouldn't come at all if you can't manage to do better."

He made a visible effort to focus. "I've some good news. I think we may soon be signing on the Dejonge family."

His mother, who was top-notch when it came to all things business, raised an eyebrow. "Now, that is impressive. Your father tried to collect them in 1973."

"They've always been very peculiar about keeping all of their associations in-country. And of course they can dictate whatever terms they wish since they've held a monopoly on the South African diamond trade for over a hundred years. However . . ." He allowed himself a small smile of satisfaction into the Scotch. "I've good reason to believe all that is about to change."

"You'll be a part of history, then, my dear. It all must be terribly exciting for you."

"It is, rather."

But he did not seem particularly excited, and soon fell into a brooding silence again.

"You look tired, Ash," his mother observed, after a time.

He admitted, "I haven't been sleeping, to tell the truth."

"You should take more exercise."

"Perhaps."

"A bit of fresh air wouldn't hurt."

"No doubt." His brow furrowed briefly as he gazed into his Scotch. "Mother, do you happen to remember when I was a boy—perhaps on holiday—an occasion when we had an outing in a meadow by a river, and children tossed a red ball back and forth. There was a woman with a big hat . . . could it have been you?"

"Good heavens!" She gave him an astonished look. "I never wear hats, look hideous in them. And how should I recall what color ball your schoolmates might have tossed some forty years ago?"

"Good God," he said softly. "Has it been that long?" He sipped his drink. "Ah well, never mind. It was just a foolishness that crossed my mind the other day."

She held his gaze for a moment, and then returned to her drink.

"I've heard from your sister Margaret."

"Indeed. How is she doing?"

"They've another one the way."

"Good Lord." His tone was absent. "How many does that make? Seven?"

"Four."

"Perhaps I'll pop in to see her when I'm in Scotland next."

"Well, I do certainly hope you're more entertaining by then than you are now."

"Mother," Ash said abruptly, "you know those Americans, the Bostarts, don't you? They bought that ruin outside of Lyon a few years back."

"I believe so, yes. He was in bonds, or something boring like that, wasn't he?"

"I saw them at a party when I was in France last month. They inquired after you."

"Did they? How lovely. I shall have to send a note. It's been some time."

"When you do, I wonder if you might suggest they call on Sara sometime. It must be difficult for her, all alone in a strange country. She'd enjoy a visit from her fellow countrymen."

His mother noted, with great interest but without comment, that, in the past hour they had sat together this was no less than the seventh time he had brought up the subject of Daniel's widow.

She said, "I understood you to say she had the child with her. An odd arrangement, that."

He frowned a little. "There's nothing odd about it. It was very generous of her."

"To be sure," his mother murmured, sipping her whiskey.

"At any rate, I'd like to think she isn't simply pining away out there."

"Very likely she's far too busy to pine, my dear, with a five-year-old to take care of and that monstrous place on her hands. What on earth does she intend to do with it, anyway?"

Ash tossed back the remainder of his Scotch. "I don't know."

"I would sell, if I were she."

"So would I." Ash set down his empty glass with a rather impolite clack against the marble-topped side table.

"No one can afford those old places anymore except the Saudis."

"Yes, I know. Mother, if you would just . . ."

"Don't worry." His mother gave a dismissing wave of her hand. "I'll make certain your little American isn't wanting for company while she's in France. I'm really quite good at this sort of thing, you know."

He smiled, and for the first time it seemed genuine. "Yes, actually, you are." He stood and crossed to her chair. "Now I must rush. I've a dinner tonight." He bent and kissed her cheek. "I love you, Mother."

"What a very peculiar thing to say." She pretended to shrug him off, trying to hide her pleasure with a scowl. "You might demonstrate it by visiting more often—and by being far better company when you do."

He merely grinned at her and blew her a kiss from the doorway on his way out.

When he was gone, she took up pen and paper. But she wrote, not to the Bostarts, but to Rondelais. Having given the matter some thought, she had decided that there was nothing much going on in the country this time of year and that she was curious, all in all, as to what type of woman could so befuddle her son as to cause him to visit his mother in the middle of the week for no reason at all.

And there was really no better way to find out than to investigate the matter in person.

· THIRTEEN ·

For the first couple of days after Ash left, Sara was horrified by what she had done. She had taken responsibility for a child whose language she didn't even speak. She had virtually moved to a foreign country with no preparation, no background, and only one change of clean underwear left. She still used the currency converter and couldn't recognize coins. And inside the belly of this vast, ancient structure all alone on the hill she and Alyssa were as tiny, and as defenseless, as baby robins in a nest.

She didn't answer Ash's voice mails because she didn't want him to hear in her voice how uncertain she was, and she didn't want him rushing back in to fix things. He had left her with an ache in her core so profound it felt as though vital organs had been ripped out, and she did not want to be around him now. It took all of the strength she had to focus on Alyssa, keeping her clean and safe and well fed and entertained and making certain that the little girl never guessed the person she depended on for all of those things was, in fact, scared to death.

But she soon learned that necessity trumps fear every time, and if she had made a horrible mistake by staying here—and by volunteering to care for Alyssa—it was definitely too late to regret the decision now. There was no time to be baffled by language, currency, or train schedules when Alyssa needed clothes and other necessities. There was no time to feel sorry for herself when every waking moment was spent making sure Alyssa didn't tumble down the stairs or fall into the moat or paint herself, from head to toe, in mud. Her entire conscious being was consumed with all things five-year-old, and it was exhausting. For the most part Alyssa was a happy, energetic, and sweetly affectionate child. But she knew how to throw a tantrum when she was thwarted, and a child's endless stream of "Why?" and "What's that?" took on an entirely new dimension when the answers had to be given in two languages.

Most nights, if she managed to get Alyssa bathed and into bed by eight, Sara was dozing by eight thirty. But sometimes, with her back aching from lifting Alyssa and her muscles sore from dragging furniture from one room to the next, her thoughts racing with things she had to get done before Alyssa awoke the next day, she would sneak down to the terrace and sit with a glass of wine she was almost too tired to sip, watching the sun set over the layered greens and purples of the valley. That was when she missed Ash. She missed his crisp British accent and his lazy humor. She missed the thoughtful blue of his eyes and the way he held himself, with such easy, elegant confidence. She missed the way he looked at her when she was talking, completely absorbed in what she had to say. She missed the way he could be such an unexpected smart-ass, and make her laugh. But mostly she missed the fantasy he had created for her here, that sense of living in a timeless fairy tale where all things were possible and nothing bad ever happened. And she hated that the fantasy was gone forever.

At first she had been furious with him. Furious that he dared to play games with her over something this important, furious that he thought he could win, furious that, just when she had started to relax her guard around him again, he had shown his true colors. But most of all she was furious, hurt, and deeply disappointed that Michele had been right about him. That he was so predictable.

And that he was not, after all, Prince Charming.

After dissecting in minute detail the forty-eight pages of settlement documents she had insisted that Mr. Winkle fax to her immediately, the logical businesswoman in Sara was forced to admit that the compromise he offered was a good one, and if she tried to fight him, she would only be hurting herself, and, by default, Alyssa. Until the question of Alyssa's parentage was resolved, neither one of them would have full legal rights to the property, and by continuing to pay the taxes, Ash had forestalled a potential financial crisis for her. And for himself, of course, he had kept the door open to a potential financial windfall in the future.

The truth was that he had acted in the only way that,

being Ash, he could act. So after a few days of fuming every time she thought about him, she stopped being angry at him. It was just too much hard work, and she needed every ounce of energy she had to keep up with Alyssa. She stopped being angry. But she didn't stop being disappointed.

And sometimes, late at night when she was too tired to even sleep, or when she sat on the terrace and ached with loneliness for what might have been, she would take a deeply secret and guilty pleasure in playing back his messages on her phone, just to hear the sound of his voice. The way her name, *Sara*, rolled off his tongue with all soft vowels and a resonant *r*. His drawled *my dear*, and the crisp consonants of his impatience. She remembered the way he had kissed Alyssa's hair and swung her up into his arms, and how stricken he had looked when he had come for her that day, realizing Michele had abandoned her, and how desperately he had embraced the little girl then. She thought about how Alyssa adored him, and then persuaded herself that it could not have been very hard for him to win a five-year-old's heart; after all, look how easily he had captured her own.

She thought about the way he had kissed her, that one unguarded night that seemed like a lifetime ago, and when she did a flush started in her core and spread outward through her skin until her fingertips were hot and her chest ached. Until she could taste him.

The emotions left her feeling foolish and confused. She was barely a year widowed. Even though Daniel had betrayed her with his secrets and his lies, even though the marriage she thought she had had never really existed, it felt wrong, somehow, to have been so quickly drawn into another man's charm. It was wrong, it was foolish . . . but she missed Ash. And she took comfort in the sound of his voice, even if it was only a recorded playback.

*   *   *

When Sara discovered that Marie—the plump, cheerful woman who came up from the village every morning to clean their rooms and do their laundry and leave the refrigerator filled with scrumptious covered dishes and the cupboard filled with homemade jams and sweet soft breads—had a grand-daughter close to Alyssa's age, life at Rondelais improved dramatically. At least four mornings a week Marie brought her granddaughter to play with Alyssa, and the two girls became fast friends. A huge burden was lifted from Sara's shoulders just knowing that Alyssa was not lonely, and that she was doing the kinds of things a five-year-old should do—even if she did live in a castle.

On fair days, Sara worked in the gardens—trying to bring the lavender and rosemary under control, trimming back the wild shrubs, sorting out what remained of the kitchen garden—while the girls raced and tumbled across the lawn nearby. Or they would bring their baby dolls and coloring books inside and Sara would set them up in one of the mostly empty upstairs rooms that she had designated as a playroom, and while they were immersed in their world of make-believe, she would return to one of her projects.

It all started when Sara decided to move out of the elegant blue and gold suite and into one of the hotel-type rooms where less damage could be done by sticky little fingers and muddy shoes, because, even with her choice of rooms in which to sleep and with an entire castle in which to play, Alyssa always ended up in Sara's room. Sara hated the new room, which reminded her of sleeping in a conference center, and Alyssa pouted over the loss of the "princess room," as she called it. Who had ever had the idea of painting real wood panels— four-hundred-year-old wood panels—such an ugly shade of taupe? And covering marble floors with Berber carpeting?

The fact of the matter was that Ash had been right: The castle was not particularly livable at all, especially with a child thrown into the mix, and after the first couple of weeks of novelty had worn off, Sara began to see that. The rooms upstairs were too large and linear and the rooms downstairs were too cold and empty. And while Alyssa had a wonderful time skating along the marble hallways in her socks and knocking down plastic bowling pins with a plastic bowling ball in an empty reception room, this was hardly a home. She couldn't picture Daniel as having grown up here. She couldn't imagine any child growing up here, but dozens of them had, for generation after generation after generation.

Tentatively she had started to explore the other rooms, gently tugging dust covers off antique furniture, polishing grime off of windows and tarnish off of metal. When Ash had taken her on her first brisk tour of the castle he had done so as part estate agent, part museum curator. He'd pointed out the things he thought would interest her—number of bathrooms and beds, fireplaces, hand-painted tiles, imported fixtures, square footage, connections to history, practical usages. It had all blended together for her in a kind of daze of disbelief. But now, on her own, she slowly began to uncover a way of life that made sense to her.

There was an entire apartment located on the second floor, far removed from the showy Queen's Chamber and the bland taupe hotel rooms, and it was in these rooms that a family had lived. The bedrooms were elaborate, to be sure, with tall four-posters and separate sitting areas and heavy carpets, now rolled up and stored under canvas. There were separate dressing rooms with empty clothing racks and shelves, and crystal chandeliers, and tall-ceilinged, elegant bathrooms, which did not appear to have functional plumbing. But there was also a cozy central sitting room with comfortable, modern furniture, and even a television set, and a small, bright, red-tiled kitchen whose plumbing, once again, did not work. Sara felt like a burglar as she went through these private rooms, because so much of the family—Daniel's family—was left behind. A book on a nightstand. A carved wooden truck that she almost crunched underfoot. It had to have been Daniel's toy when he was a child. The ghosts of those who belonged here were everywhere, and she was careful to touch nothing, to disturb nothing, because she was, after all, the intruder.

She wasn't comfortable opening up that section of the house again, but she had to find a way to make her stay here—and Alyssa's—more functional. That was when she decided that, if four-hundred-year-old walls could be painted taupe, they could also be painted vanilla; that carpet could be ripped up and soft floral rugs placed in their stead; that stiff brown industrial draperies could be replaced with floaty sheers and easy-care bedding could be upgraded to something slightly more luxurious. And that the toilets—all of them— needed to work.

To that end, she called Pietro, who came with his silent, grumpy father and his trail of cigarette smoke to examine the situation. "*Sì, signorina,*" he assured her cheerfully. "We will make for you the most beautiful WC in all the valley, we will build it *magnifico, sì?* Do you know Britney Spears?"

Sara regretfully admitted that she did not, and reminded him that she really didn't need an entirely new bathroom built; all she wanted was for the existing ones to work. He assured her that all would be well, and returned the next morning with hammers and crowbars and lengths of pipe— and Papa—and the reconstruction began.

Her life from that point on took on the rhythm of hammers and buzz saws and high-speed Italian shouted at full volume. She stopped wincing at the sound of crashing tile. She resisted the urge to peek behind the carefully hung tarps when Pietro and his father left every evening. She learned to be unsurprised when she turned on a tap and nothing came out.

She moved the furniture out, opened a can of vanilla-colored paint, and started painting the bedrooms. She gave Alyssa a paintbrush, and she painted, too. She pored over the catalogue Mrs. Harrison had sent her, and soon trucks began to arrive. A bed with rails that needed to be assembled. Draperies that needed to be hemmed. Shelving that needed to be installed.

"Ah, *bella signorina,*" exclaimed Pietro with passionate dismay as he was leaving one evening. He came into the room that Sara was redecorating for Alyssa. One wall was painted a pale lemon yellow, and so was Alyssa's face, her hands, and her shoes. Sara climbed down from the stepladder, wiping her hands on her smock.

"You work so hard to make pretty the walls of the little one," he said sadly. "Look at your hands! Look at the tiredness in your eyes!" And suddenly his face cleared. "I will send you a painter of walls!" he decided. "Yes, that is it. My cousin Marco, he is an artiste par excellence and he will come and make walls for the little one. But not today. Today he is in Venezia, making love to his beautiful lady. Maybe next week, no? Or the week after. So you will put down the paintbrush now and come with me. The WC, she is *finito*!"

His last words wiped out everything he had said before. Sara scooped up Alyssa, yellow paint and all, and hurried after Pietro.

The toilet she had asked them to replace was in the main corridor, in between the room that she was occupying and the room that she hoped soon to have ready for Alyssa. It had been an awkward, cumbersome affair, with miles of black-and-white tile, a tiny lightbulb dangling from the ceiling, and a shower, sans doors, smack in the middle of the room. The dingy, nonfunctioning toilet was in a tiny closet with a hook-and-latch closure in the corner of the room.

Signor Contandino stood erect and solemn-faced before the tarp-draped entrance to the bathroom. As Sara approached, he ripped aside the tarp and gestured her, with a dramatic sweep of his arm, to enter.

The black-and-white tile had been polished to a blinding

sheen. The lavatory, once a pedestrian affair with rusted parts, had been upgraded to a sleek marble slab with a fountainhead faucet and cherub-ornamented handles. And, while one still had to walk through the shower in the middle of the room to reach it, the toilet was a dramatic fixture on an elevated platform on the other side, sleek and oval and accompanied by a matching bidet, in brilliant red. And even as Sara, wide-eyed, drew in a breath of appreciation, Pietro crossed the room, pushed a button, and demonstrated the truly magnificent flushing power of the new appliance.

"Bravo, bravo!" cried Sara, clapping her hands, and Alyssa echoed, bouncing up and down, "Bravo, potty!"

Pietro, with eyes sparkling, declared, "Come!" He caught her arm and propelled her down the corridor to the next bathroom, which also featured a sleek red oval fully flushing toilet, and the next, and finally into the apartment suite with its dust-covered furniture . . . but with bathrooms fully restored, polished, and functioning with red toilets that flushed perfectly and matching bidets that did precisely what bidets were supposed to do.

By this time Sara had set Alyssa on the floor, overcome with wonder "Pietro . . . Signor Contandino . . . it's more than I asked for, more than I expected . . . C'est magnifico! Grazie! Grazie!" She turned to Pietro, her eyes wide with wonder. "You got the water running in this part of the castle! Does the kitchen work, too?"

Pietro shrugged modestly. "Sì, it was nothing. Mi papa, it is he who makes the water stop when the rooms are closed. It is he who makes everything work fine."

Alyssa was scampering delightedly from one room to another, flushing toilets and declaring, *"Les WC sont rouges!"*

"What color?" Sara challenged absently, for her duties as English coach were never done.

"Red! The WCs is red!"

"Are," corrected Sara. "Are red." She turned to Signor Contandino. "You must have built the red kitchen," she realized suddenly. "And remodeled this entire part of the house?"

The signor remained stoic, but Pietro grinned. "It is so. When the big roof, she started to fall in, they say to my papa, Can you make us a place to live in the other part of the palazzo, and he says, *Sì. Et voilà!* You know Angelina Jolie, yes?"

Sara shook her head, catching Alyssa by the back of her T-shirt as she raced by and hoisting her once again to her hip. "Do you know what's on the other side of the castle? Behind those locked doors?"

Pietro translated the question for his papa, who gave a terse answer. Pietro returned to her with a shrug. "Boxes. And other things you don't want."

"What kind of things?"

He made an elaborate wiggling motion with his hand, which ended by tweaking Alyssa's nose and making her squeal with laughter. *"Serpenti e ratti."*

"Serpent . . . Snakes?" Sara pulled Alyssa close, her eyes widening involuntarily. "And—did you say rats?"

He grinned. "We go now. You want something fixed, you call Pietro, eh?"

"Yes," she exclaimed gratefully, still thinking about serpents and rats. "Thank you. Thank you so much."

However, as thrilling as it was to be able to flush any toilet in the house and to anticipate a shower with more than a trickle of water, Sara couldn't help but wish Pietro had not given her quite so vivid a picture as to what might be lurking behind those locked doors. And when, later that afternoon, she went to remove the drop cloths that covered the furniture she had piled in the middle of the room she was painting and a mouse the approximate size of a small lapdog scuttled across the room, her overreaction was predictable.

She slept with a sturdy length of two-by-four beside her bed that night, and in the morning she called Mrs. Harrison.

* * *

Ash arrived after dinner the next day. Sara, in shorts, lace-up boots, and elbow-length industrial gloves—just in case another rodent should make an appearance—had just finished dragging out a roll of the twenty-year-old Berber carpet she had removed from one of the bedrooms. She dumped it in the front drive, where it joined a pile of other castoffs that Pietro had promised to haul away in his truck the next morning. She sat on the front step, with the cool interior of the castle at her back, to catch her breath. That was when she heard the sound of an approaching car. She stood up.

Ash stopped his car—a red Porsche this time—in front of the trash pile and got out, looking immaculate in tan slacks and blue blazer with an open-collared blue shirt. Sara wiped a hand across her face, remembering the grimy gloves too late, and then quickly stripped off the gloves and lifted the corner of her T-shirt to scrub the dirt from her face—which probably afforded Ash more of a view than she had intended. She could see the amusement in his eyes as he removed his sunglasses and she faced him down.

"Housecleaning?" he inquired politely.

She approached the car. "Are you the exterminator?"

"Or maybe I'm the rat."

"Is that multiple choice?"

He grinned. "It's good to see you're keeping busy, Sara. But . . ." They were close enough now that he could reach out and remove the remainder of the smudge from her face with his fingertip, which he did, lightly. "Where is your cap? Your cheeks are the color of pimentos."

The color she felt stinging her face was not due to sun exposure but to something else entirely . . . Pleasure? Excitement? Simple relief to see him? Her heart had speeded the moment she heard the crunch of his tires on the marble drive and had increased in pace the closer he got until now it was practically skittering in her chest. She had missed him. She had simply missed him.

And she hated that.

She shrugged away his touch and replied, a little irritably, "I've been working all day. I'm overheated. And I think Mrs. Harrison is a tattletale."

His hand fell lightly to her shoulder, fingers touching the back of her neck. "*Spy*, I think, is a more accurate term." A brief caress against her hairline, so quick as to be almost imagined, and he dropped his hand. "Besides, I've brought along a little something to assist with your rodent problem. Where is Alyssa?"

But no sooner had he spoken than she came charging out of the open door, her arms open wide, crying, "*Petit-papa, petit-papa*, you came, you came, you came!" She flung herself into his arms and began covering his face with happy kisses, and he, laughing, reciprocated. He started to speak to her in French, but she caught his face between both of her plump little hands and reprimanded seriously, "We speak English at Rondelais."

Ash turned a meaningful look on Sara. "Do we indeed? Well, now, I think that is an excellent policy, providing, of course, that we know enough English words." He set her on her feet and reached in to the floorboard of the Porsche. "Do you, for example, happen to know the English word for this?"

He removed a covered basket from which a suspicious mewling sound emitted. He knelt on the ground close to Alyssa, and when he unlatched the top of the basket a tiny, fuzzy, gray-striped head poked out. Alyssa's eyes flew wide, her hands clasped her cheeks in amazement, and her gasp of delight could have won an Academy Award for its drama. Sara, barely able to suppress her own pleased laughter, was about to prompt Alyssa for the English word when she burst out, with her hands still clapped to her face, "Le cat!"

"Close enough." Sara sank down to the grass beside Ash and scooped the tiny ball of fluff from the basket. "Would you like to hold her?"

"Him," corrected Ash, and when Sara glanced at him he explained, "I felt the place could use a bit more of a male influence."

Sara lost her battle with a grin as she carefully transferred the kitten into Alyssa's wondering, expectant hands. The next half hour passed swiftly as they settled the kitten—and Alyssa, who would not be parted from it—in a corner of the kitchen with a saucer of milk, a box of shredded newspaper, and a ball of string. Ash helped himself to a glass of chilled white wine and poured another for Sara, gesturing her to the table on the other side of the room. They arranged their chairs so that they could watch Alyssa, and Sara sank into hers with a barely suppressed sigh of relief. It was the first time she had sat down all day.

"I'd say your gift is a hit," she said. "But if that's your solution to pest control, I'm telling you now, the rat I saw would not only laugh in that kitten's face, it would probably have him for dinner."

Watching those upward-curving lines appear at the corners of his eyes was like the first taste of chocolate after a diet. Her stomach actually did a little flip-flop, just from the pleasure of seeing them again.

"There's an excellent fellow who comes out spring and fall," Ash informed her, sipping his wine. "He'll be here in the morning."

She nodded, and shifted her gaze to Alyssa, who was twirling around and around while the kitten chased the string she held, and whose giggles were growing ever more shrill. Sara opened her mouth to call a caution, and Ash's hand touched hers lightly where it rested on the tabletop.

"Leave her be," he advised easily. "She's fine."

"She's going to fall."

"Then we'll find the first aid kit and tend her scraped knee, and the earth will continue to spin on its axis."

"She could step on the kitten."

"That," he admitted, "would be a slightly more complex problem. Relax, Sara. I'm watching her."

Sara had to take a quick sip of her wine because her eyes actually prickled, just for a moment, when he said that. The mere idea of turning over the enormous burden of responsibility that she had shouldered to someone else—if even for a moment—made her feel foolishly weepy with relief. But why did it have to be Ash? And why did it have to feel so good to have another English-speaking adult to talk to that it didn't even matter that he was the person who had, in an oblique and not-entirely-fair sort of way, caused all of her problems to begin with?

His hand, which still covered hers, turned over her fingers and she closed her fist self-consciously, withdrawing her hand, because her hands were paint-stained and her fingernails were broken and grimy. She was wearing no makeup and her hair was tied up in a bandanna and every inch of her felt gritty with dust. She belatedly recalled that she hadn't even bothered to put on a bra that morning, and remembering that caused her nipples to prickle with embarrassment, which she was certain he noticed. She twisted the neck of the T-shirt briefly between her fingers, abandoned the effort, and met his eyes boldly. This was what he got when he dropped in without notice and expected the world to stop because he was here. She dropped her hand to her lap.

"Why are you here?" she demanded.

He returned her gaze with effortless equanimity. "A couple of reasons. Primarily, of course, this would seem to be the only way I can accurately ascertain the well-being of my ward, since you persist on demonstrating how pissed you are at me by refusing to take my calls. And, oh by the way, might we call that game a draw? I'm growing exceedingly bored with it and besides, you are in violation of the law." And even as she drew a furious breath for protest he continued mildly, "Until proven otherwise, I am Alyssa's only legal guardian. She is with you by my good graces alone and you can damn well grow up and abide by our original agreement or I will take her back to London with me tonight. Additionally," he continued, raising his glass to her sputtering attempt to defend herself, "you have never called my office for help before. I think you wanted me to come."

Sara drew in several short, heaving breaths through her nostrils. "I wanted," she said tightly, "an exterminator."

"The list of support personnel is taped to the cupboard in the pantry," he reminded her.

Sara jerked her head away, her lips compressed tightly. She tried to focus on Alyssa, who was so happy with her new pet. She took a sip of wine, and could barely swallow it. She said, "I'm too old for this."

Ash said, watching her carefully, "If you're referring to your recent display of childish behavior, I quite agree. If you're talking about anything else, you're going to have to explain that to me because I frankly can't think what it can be."

Sara could feel the pressure build behind her eyes and she tried to forestall it by pressing her forefinger hard beneath her nose, which was beginning to drip. "I'm too old to play these games, I'm too old to be this angry. I can't do this anymore,

Ash, this is not the way I want to live my life. But if you think for one minute that I'm going to let you cheat Alyssa out of her inheritance . . ."

He said softly, "Shut up."

That made her look at him, even though her eyes were hot with tears, and big with surprise.

He repeated, "Shut up. Because you know as well as I do that my intention is to protect Alyssa, not to cheat her."

"I don't know that at all," she began, but her voice was mucousy and the tears were like acid in her eyes.

"And," continued Ash mildly, "if you continue in this vein, you're going to start crying and if you start crying, I shall have to kiss you and that will inevitably lead to activities not suitable for the eyes of a five-year-old. So just . . . shut up."

She stared at him, momentarily startled out of her self-pity. And then she felt a sudden, rather hysterical urge to laugh, and she had to press her lips together tightly to stop it. But the threat of tears was gone and in a moment she could take a sip of her wine. "That's not why," she said, not looking at him.

"I'm sorry?"

"The reason I didn't answer the phone . . . it's not because I was mad at you. Well," she admitted, "it was at first. But mostly it's because . . ." She took a breath and met his eyes. "Everything is different now. And I guess I didn't want to be reminded of that."

He nodded, saying nothing. But his gaze was steady and easy and, even though it was filled with understanding, she could not hold it for long. "So," she said purposefully, "you'll want to know how Alyssa's been doing."

He smiled and leaned back in his chair. "I can see for myself that she's been doing just fine. I'd rather know about you."

Nonetheless Sara told him about shopping trips and English lessons and feeding the swans and playdates with her new friend and learning to cook with Marie in the kitchen.

"A veritable paradise of a summer for a little girl," Ash said approvingly. "Which of course inspired you to begin dismantling the château, piece by piece."

She said defensively, "We need a home, not a display case. There isn't one cozy room in this entire castle. It's completely unlivable the way it is now."

"Which I might have pointed out on more than one occasion."

She frowned. "All it needs is some paint and carpets."

"It needs more than that. But I suppose that's a start. What have you done?"

She told him about her progress with paint and carpets and draperies, which of course segued into the tale of toilets, which made him laugh.

"Let me guess," he said. "They're all red."

She returned defiantly, "They all work."

He raised his glass. "Then I salute you."

His gaze wandered to Alyssa, who had temporarily collapsed on the floor with the kitten cuddled to her chest. He said, "You've done an excellent job with her English. You can be proud of yourself."

She shrugged it off, pleased and embarrassed, and admitted, "She's picking up English a lot faster than I'm picking up French, although"—and she smiled, slanting a glance at him—"I'm no longer paying five dollars for an orange."

He laughed. "I always had faith in you. I do wonder, however . . ." His gaze was steady and carefully neutral. "Whether you've given any more thought to my suggestion about a nanny."

Only about a thousand times, Sara thought, but her reply was a sharp frown. "For heaven's sake, Ash, what kind of person can't manage a five-year-old for a summer? My sister manages two of them every day!" And even as she spoke Alyssa had regained her feet, her giggles turning into shrieks as she raced back and forth across the stone floor, the gamboling kitten fast at her heels.

Sara drew in a breath to call to her, but Ash interjected, "Alyssa, *ma petite*! Come and give me a kiss!"

Alyssa immediately veered off and launched herself into his lap, smacking his face with a loud kiss. Ash settled her on his knee. "I think *petit* Puss is becoming tired, my dear, and may soon be ready for a bedtime story. So let me tell you the story of a very famous cat, and I will say it in English, so that you can tell the story to your Puss, *eh bien*? Now listen very carefully."

Alyssa leaned into the crook of his arm, her eyes rapt and intent on his face, as he related the story of Puss in Boots. Sara sank back into her chair and sipped her wine, a smile forming from the inside out, and began to relax for the first time in weeks. Perhaps months.

By the time he finished the story, which was imparted in two languages, the kitten was fast asleep on a folded towel near his empty milk dish, and Alyssa's eyelids were drooping. Ash carried her upstairs, Sara undressed her and put her to bed, and they stood for a moment beside the bed, watching her.

Sara said with a soft shake of her head, "I don't understand."

"Understand what?"

"How you can be so good with her and so hard-assed to everyone else."

He lifted an eyebrow. "Not to everyone," he pointed out. "Just to those who persist in engaging in pointless and wrong-headed behavior."

Sara stiffened and drew a sharp breath for rebuttal, but he forestalled her with a light touch on her arm. In the deep twilight of the sleeping child's room, his gaze was gentle, his eyes like lightly burnished gems. "Just because one occasionally does beastly things," he said softly, "doesn't necessarily make him a beast." Then, easily, "Is there anything to eat? I'm starved."

She replied, "We have dinner at five o'clock."

He stared at her in genuine horror. "Good God."

That made Sara smile. "There's some quiche and fruit in the fridge. Come downstairs."

· FOURTEEN ·

They returned to the kitchen in early twilight, and Sara rummaged around in the refrigerator while Ash poured more wine. The kitten had awakened and was weaving in between Sara's feet; Ash scooped it up and kept it contented in the crook of his arm by scratching its chin. He had not commented on the chaos he had discovered on the upper level: the toys in the corridor, the furniture piled against the walls, the smell of paint everywhere, and the fact that Alyssa, lacking any other place to sleep, had been tucked into Sara's bed—which Sara privately thought demonstrated a certain amount of class on his part.

She wondered if he was staying the night.

She said, "Alyssa has her own bed, you know. With rails, so she doesn't accidentally fall out. I just haven't put it together yet. And the rooms in this place are so big, and so far apart, and she's not really used to sleeping by herself, that I thought it was best to keep her with me for the time being."

"I absolutely concur." He was leaning against the counter, sipping his wine, stroking the kitten, absently glancing through the mail that had accumulated there. "Sara, is this today's post?"

She looked up from trying to adjust the temperature on the gas oven. "I guess so. Marie brings it up with her when she comes in the morning. It's probably just bills."

He said, in an odd tone, "I think you'd best look at it."

She came over to him. "Is there something from the States?"

He soberly handed her a peach-colored envelope with her address—Madame Sara Graves Orsay, Château Rondelais, Rondelais, France—beautifully calligraphied on the front, and on the back the return address: Mrs. Katherine A. Lindeman, 12 Surrey Lane, Northampton, England.

For a moment all she could do was stare at him. "Good God, Ash, how many ex-wives do you have?"

"It's not from my wife." He carefully returned the kitten to the floor, his expression pained. "It's from my mother."

She ripped open the envelope, extracted a single sheet of heavy peach-colored paper, and read the flowing script there with simple incredulity at first, slow, growing horror on the second reading, and finally, abject denial.

She was shaking her head before she could even find the words. "No," she said. "Impossible. This says she's coming to visit . . . no, it says a visit of *some duration* . . . what does that mean, anyway? And that she's arriving on the eighteenth of

July—that's two days from now! Are you kidding me? Did you put her up to this?" Sara demanded, her color high and eyes blazing. "Is this your idea of a joke? Because it's not happening, I'm telling you—"

He raised both hands in self-defense. "Before God, I had nothing to do with this." But there was a secret mirth, far in the depths of his blue eyes, that he tried to disguise. "She has become accustomed to visiting the château at her leisure in the past few years. Remember, I have managed it for some time now."

And still do, were the unspoken words. Sara found her breathing was escalating, a panic rising in her chest as she imagined one more thing she would have to deal with, and she said, "No. You're going to have to call her. Tell her not to come."

"I could do that," he agreed, nodding thoughtfully, taking up his wineglass. "Which would only ensure that she would arrive tomorrow, instead of the day after. My mother hates to be told what to do." And then he smiled. "There, you see? The two of you already have something in common."

"But . . ." Sara's voice, and her eyes, were wild. "Look at this place! Everything is torn apart. I've got a five-year-old I can't even keep up with and all the bedrooms are being painted and mice the size of Labradors are running down the halls and I can't have company! You can't do this to me, Ash, you can't!"

To her utter humiliation, her eyes began to flood again, and even though she tried to jerk her head away to hide it, Ash gently caught her face between his hands. "Hush," he said softly, and his breath whispered across her skin. "Hush. The only person my mother is allowed to make cry is me." His smile was gently coaxing, and his thumbs tenderly traced the corners of her eyes, gathering moisture there. "Stop this. Now." His hands tightened briefly, bracingly, on her face, and his eyes held hers firmly. "We have a good four hours of daylight. What do you need to be done?"

Sara wiped a hand across her face, furious with her weakness, and then dropped her gaze to Ash's perfectly manicured hands. "Can you put together a child's bed?"

He met her skepticism boldly. "Does it involve mathematics?"

"In a way."

"Then I can do it," he assured her briskly. He shrugged out of his blazer and began rolling up his sleeves. "Where are your tools? And don't forget to heat up the quiche, love. I really am starving."

In less than an hour the bed was assembled and Sara's opinion of Ash had risen considerably. They reconvened at the kitchen table with quiche—slightly overcooked—and fruit, and Sara said, grudgingly, "So you're one of those men who can do anything. Put a baby to sleep, build a castle from scratch, and negotiate world peace in our time. I'm impressed."

He inclined his head graciously. "All you had to do was ask." And he put down his fork. "Darling, no offense but this is terrible. Is there any bread?"

She glared at him for a moment, then took a fresh-baked loaf of bread from the bread box, along with a wedge of cheese from the refrigerator, and set them before him. He said, slicing the cheese, "You're going to like my mother."

"I hate you for doing this to me."

He smiled, very slightly, with just one corner of his mouth. "Actually," he said, "I wish I'd thought of it."

She tipped more wine into her glass but he held his hand over his. "I have to drive tonight," he said, and she stared at him.

"You're leaving?"

He glanced at his watch. "I have a one a.m. flight out of de Gaulle."

She sank back into her chair, setting the bottle of wine on the table, and thought for a time about the life he led, about one a.m. flights out of Paris to exotic locales, about the contacts that were required to rent a Porsche at the airport, about driving two hours to deliver a kitten to a child that wasn't even his. She had never felt so homesick in her life.

And the strangest thing was, she wasn't homesick for a place, but for a person.

He said, slicing cheese, "My mother doesn't require fussing over. She's accustomed to coming and going as she pleases. You'll likely never even see each other. I wouldn't get worked up over it if I were you."

"I'm not," Sara said. "Not anymore. I really don't have the energy to get worked up."

"Then why do you look so sad?"

She shrugged a little, and managed a smile. "I was just remembering the last time we sat together at this table. I couldn't have imagined the life I'm living now."

He did not reply to that.

She watched him eat bread and cheese and fruit and she drank one more glass of wine than she probably should have. When he said, "Come, walk me out," she sank too easily into the curve of his arm.

They went out onto the terrace, where a warm breeze was scented with lavender and a pale yellow crescent moon was just beginning to appear over the western turret of the castle. The simple, impossible beauty of it made Sara smile, and Ash, echoing her thoughts, murmured, "Now, there's a postcard."

"Sometimes," she admitted, "it still seems like a fantasy to me." She glanced up at him. "Most of the time it doesn't."

His arm slid from around her shoulders, his fingers lingering to caress her waist, briefly, and then he wasn't touching her at all. He said, "Sara, I have something to tell you."

She could tell by the look on his face, easy to read even in the bluish twilight, that this was why he had really come here. She felt her chest begin to tighten. And even though he still stood close to her, their arms brushing, she felt a little chill of loneliness when the breeze rustled again.

He spoke without looking at her. "I've finally located a judge in North Carolina who'll grant my request for an exhumation. I need to know . . . whether you'd like to be present for the disinterment."

Her throat convulsed involuntarily. It had been so easy, over these past strange and full and exciting and exhausting weeks, to forget what this was really all about, and the horror that lay at the root of it. *Disinterment*. The beautiful body of the man who once had loved her, the hands that had stroked her, the mouth that had kissed her . . . Disinterment. She felt dizzy for a moment, and she stretched out a hand to steady herself against the stone wall.

He persisted gently, though with obvious difficulty, "It's traditional for a family member to be present, in cases like these . . ."

She shook her head. Her voice was hoarse. "No. I can't."

"It might help you to find closure. And it seems only respectful, that someone should be there."

She was still shaking her head, though more adamantly now. The horror of it seemed to sink into her pores.

"Sara . . . are you having second thoughts? Because once the procedure is set in motion, there'll be no going back. If you want to stop this, this is your last chance."

She managed, in a moment, "Isn't there . . . another way?"

"For the kind of accuracy required by law, no. And since there is a considerable fortune at stake, the chances are that this will, eventually, be required as evidence in court."

Again, she shook her head. "No. No, it doesn't have to go to court. I own this place now. I signed the settlement papers. If I want to give it to Alyssa, I can do that; it doesn't matter who she is or who her father is and there doesn't have to be proof of anything." She turned on him, fists closed, "And if you try to fight me—"

"I have no reason to fight you," he said calmly, "but other people do. I've managed to control Michele for the time being, but I know her too well to imagine this is the end of it. In a year, or several—at a time when this entire business might be particularly hurtful to a young girl—she'll come back to challenge your claim unless the issue of paternity is settled now. Or unless," he added with barely a pause, "there's nothing for her to challenge."

She stared at him for a moment of outright disbelief.

Ash gave a slow, heavy shake of his head and drew in his breath through his teeth. "I never thought I'd hear myself say this, but I'm prepared to buy the bloody place from you. It will be the most foolhardy financial move I've ever made, but I'll do it. Let Michele come after me if she cares to try. Do what you like with the profits, put them in a trust for Alyssa if that's what you want, buy her a real house instead of this tumbling-down pile of stones—"

"No." Sara was shaking her head adamantly long before he finished speaking. "Forget it. I'm not selling, not to you or anyone else. This is Alyssa's home, her heritage—"

"It's rock and crumbling mortar!"

"It's who she is! It's her chance to one day look back and see where she came from and how she came to be, it's her connection with her past, her identity . . ."

"You're making assumptions that don't even exist! Her identity is precisely what's in dispute!" And then in a calmer tone, "Try to be reasonable Sara. This is the only sensible solution."

Sara ground her teeth together, her breath coming quick and hard in her chest. "Sell me your shares," she demanded. "If you want to do the best thing for everyone, if you really want to protect the château and Alyssa's heritage, sell me your shares on terms I can afford and let me take over the trust."

He made a short impatient sound. "I can't do that."

"You mean you won't."

"I mean I can't and it would be bloody irresponsible of me to even consider it. If the paternity test should prove negative, you would leave yourself vulnerable to having the entire estate stripped from you—including Alyssa's portion, which is currently safe and untouchable in a trust. Think it through, for the love of God. I know what I'm doing."

"And I don't?"

He looked at her steadily for a moment. "In this particular situation, no."

Sara pushed her hands into her hair and tightened her fingers. The sound that burst softly from her lips was filled with disappointment and contempt. "You *are* obsessed," she said. "With Daniel, with this place, with the Orsays and everything that was theirs. I expected better from you. But she was right, wasn't she? You're never going to let this place go."

He stared at her, frowning. "Who was right?" And then, with astonished recognition flaring in his eyes, he exclaimed, "Good Lord, Michele? Are you serious?"

He half turned from her, as though to physically distance himself from the absurdity of the accusation. For a moment Sara thought he might literally walk away. And then he turned back sharply. His voice was low and there was a glitter to his eyes in the moonlight. "Let me tell you something, Sara," he said. "Nothing would please me more than to be quit of this place, of the Orsays and all their bloody baggage. Do you imagine for one moment that there has ever been any advantage to me to continue to look after them all these years, to advise them and counsel them and try to keep them all from driving themselves to ruin any faster than was absolutely necessary? Do you think I didn't have more interesting, challenging, and profitable matters with which to occupy myself? I did it because it was left to me to do, and because I swear by all that's holy I sometimes think the only person who gave a bloody damn about what became of any of them was me. And even now that they're all gone, I'm still left to pick up the pieces of the shambles they made of their lives. Not because I want to, but because I have to."

Sara swallowed a sudden lump in her throat, hands closing at her sides. "I'm sorry to be such a burden to you," she said stiffly. "It wasn't my idea."

He blew out a short breath. "You know that's not what I meant."

He lifted a hand as though to reach for her, but she turned away, crossing her arms over her chest. He was silent for a long time.

Then he spoke, quietly, behind her. "Do you remember that day at the chapel ruins, when we had the picnic? You asked me what I was afraid of. I don't think I really knew the answer until the morning Mrs. Harrison walked into my office with a note from you, saying that Alyssa had been left behind." There was a pause, and Sara could feel his tension, the prickle of horror with the memory. "That's what I'm afraid of," he said then, with an effort she could feel. "That someone will be hurt because I made a mistake, that someone will suffer because I failed to do my job. Alyssa is my responsibility. Protecting your inheritance is my responsibility. I can't do any less than what I know is best."

Sara turned to face him, her throat tight and her eyes aching. How she wanted to rest her head on his shoulder, to feel his arms around her, to let herself be taken care of, even if for only a moment. How she wanted to rely on him. To be his responsibility. To just be held by him. To rest.

She said, holding his gaze, "I want to adopt Alyssa."

For a moment he did not react at all. And then she felt the breath of his sigh, and his eyes closed slowly. "Ah, Sara," he said, in a voice that was filled with weariness and compassion. And that was all.

She could feel small tremors starting inside her, deep within her muscles, and she clamped her hands down harder on her arms to control them. She tried to keep her voice steady. "Will you help me?"

He looked at her sadly. "You know there's only one way I can help you. And in the end, it might wind up only hurting you, and Alyssa."

His voice took on a note of gentle exasperation, and he took a step toward her. "Sara, look at yourself. You're exhausted, you're grieving, and you're not thinking clearly. Your life has been turned upside down in a matter of weeks, and now you're living in a strange country in a four-hundred-year-old building that's falling in around your ears and you're thinking of adopting a child of whose existence you weren't even aware three months ago. Give it some time, love. Think about this."

She said tightly, "If there's one thing Daniel taught me— taught both of us—I'd think it's that time is the one thing we can't afford to take for granted."

She saw his lips compress, briefly, perhaps against pain, and the corners of his eyes tightened. He said, "This is not China, or the far reaches of the Ukraine. The French do not relinquish their children to foreigners so easily, particularly a child who is already as well situated as Alyssa."

She drew a sharp, harsh breath to protest but he spoke over her, calmly. "There's no point in approaching the authorities at all until we have the results of the DNA test, and I think you knew that all along. You also cannot fail to realize that the matter of a ten-million-dollar estate complicates the situation considerably, which is even more reason for you to take my proposal seriously. The moment the judge signs the order of exhumation, this all becomes a matter of public record, and the evidence—whatever it may turn out to be—can be used against you as well as for you. But as things stand now, in this very small window of time, you are perfectly within your rights to sell the property, become a very rich American, and then proceed with the rest of your life. If that includes a petition to adopt Alyssa, you will have more than adequate resources to pursue the effort. So I ask you, what good will it do to go through with this paternity test? If you find out Alyssa is Daniel's child, you'll spend the rest of your life despising yourself for being married to a man you never knew. If you find out she isn't, you'll have nothing left of him at all. Don't do this to yourself, not when there's a simpler way—"

"Stop it!" she cried. "I'm not interested in any more of your schemes or your deals or your assurances! A little girl's entire future is at stake and that's the *only* thing that matters right now!"

"Which little girl?" Ash said softly. "The one who's sleeping upstairs right now, or the one who was abandoned forty years ago in a trailer park in North Carolina?"

The breath that caught in her throat sounded like a sob and for a moment all she could do was stand there, her arms falling limp at her sides, staring at him, while the tears she had been fighting all day finally spilled over into two hot tracks down her cheeks. Ash stepped into her and took her shoulders, and though she tried to pull away at first, he held her, and he bent his face close. His eyes were filled with empathy and tenderness, and something else . . . conviction. Or determination.

"I know you've been hurt," he said. "I know you've been betrayed, and I know how hard it is for you to trust me. But Sara, what if you're wrong? What if, this time, I'm really the good guy?"

And that was when she started sobbing, helplessly, brokenly, in a way she hadn't done since that day Michele had first arrived with Alyssa. He took her in his arms and held her there, stroking her hair, kissing her face, and she turned her mouth to his instinctively, losing herself in him because that was, at that moment, all she wanted in the world. She stretched her arms around his neck, pushed her fingers into his hair, and let his heat consume her, flooding through her skin and into her brain, burning out everything else. "I don't care," she whispered brokenly against his face. The texture of his skin, smooth yet coarse, so very male, against hers, the smell of him, the taste of him, the feel of him, strange and strong and dangerous and familiar, all of it enveloped her, and even as she spoke her eyes began to flood again, this time from need; simple, raw, and helpless need. "I just want the pain to stop. I just want it to stop . . ."

His mouth covered hers again, a deep and penetrating kiss that blotted out everything else, every thought, every memory, everything but wanting, everything but sensation. His hands were on her back, beneath her shirt against her bare skin, fingers strong and hot as they pressed her close, traced her spine and the curve of her shoulder blades and making her gasp as they cupped the crescent of her bare breasts where they were pressed so hard against his chest. He whispered, "I can do that for you, Sara." His lips were against her ear, his whisper a brush of fire. "I can make the pain go away. I think we can do that for each other, tonight . . ."

He took her face in his hands then, and tilted it upward so that her eyes were filled with the darkness of his, the awful, wondrous combination of tenderness and barely leashed passion, of dark demand and desperate restraint. "If that's what you want." His breath was hot and hard and unsteady on her face and it tasted of her and of him and of the tentative, wanton intercourse in which they had already engaged. "If that's all you want."

She dropped her gaze because she couldn't meet the fire of his any longer. Because she was ashamed and uncertain and because the only parts of her that really mattered still wanted him; wanted his hands on her, and his mouth, wanted him inside her, wanted the wild, hot ecstasy of release; wanted to be held by him, to be comforted by him, to lie in the shelter of his protection throughout the night. And she wanted not to be sorry in the morning.

She sank helplessly against his chest. "I don't know what I want."

Slowly, his arms came around her, gentle in their restraint, almost reluctant, but holding her. His heartbeat, so wild against her ear at first, gradually began to slow, his breathing to calm. He kissed her hair. "I know what I want," he said softly. "I want to make love to you when your heart isn't broken. When you're not weeping in my arms. And when Daniel isn't a ghost between us."

She lifted her face to look at him, and what she saw in his eyes was still and deep and completely unreadable. And in the end his hands traveled to her shoulders, and he stepped away from her. "Good night, love," he said softly.

"Don't leave," she said. There was pleading in her eyes, perhaps in her voice, and she thought for a moment she saw his resolve waver. "Please."

But in the end he simply kissed her forehead, and he left.

· FIFTEEN ·

Katherine Alexandra Lindeman arrived in the same sleek black limousine that had transported Sara to Rondelais, though with sixteen pieces of luggage and a great deal more confidence. She wore an elegant ivory pantsuit and oversized, white-rimmed Chanel sunglasses and she made a statement worthy of Katharine Hepburn as she stepped out of the limousine, tilted up the sunglasses, and surveyed her surroundings with a regal sweep of her chin.

The trash pile had been removed and the guest rooms that were not under renovation were immaculate, but there was little Sara could do—or cared to do—about the furniture and paint cans that were stored in the corridors, or about the disarray of her room and Alyssa's. At least the toilets worked.

She had managed to get Alyssa bathed and dressed in clean clothes—as well as herself—before the arrival, and came to the front steps when she heard the car. Alyssa, with uncharacteristic shyness, hid behind Sara's leg and chewed on her thumb.

Katherine pronounced, "Well, I see the old place is much the same as ever. Although it would appear someone has been keeping after those lazy gardeners. Well-done." She approached Sara with a bold, confident stride and extended her hand. "I'm Katherine Lindeman, my dear. It's good of you to have me."

Sara smiled without conviction. "I'm Sara Graves. This is Alyssa."

She tried to coax Alyssa forward but the little girl clung stubbornly to her leg. "Did you bring me a cat?" she inquired.

"Good heavens, no, child. Why on earth should I do that? And don't suck your thumb, my dear. It will ruin the shape of your mouth."

Alyssa glared at her defiantly and continued to suck her thumb, which Sara had never seen her do before. She stroked Alyssa's curls and started to say something—she wasn't sure exactly what—when Katherine unsnapped her purse and removed a small white paper bag. "I've often thought what a pity it is that one should be completely unable to suck one's thumb and enjoy a treat at the same time. I suppose I shall just have to keep these sweets for myself." She opened the bag and revealed the contents to Alyssa.

Alyssa's thumb left her mouth and she looked questioningly at Sara. Sara said, "Just one." She gave a brief grateful smile to the older woman. "And what do we say in English?"

"Thank you very much," replied Alyssa solemnly and

released her death grip on Sara's leg to extract a piece of candy from the bag. "I have a cat."

Sara saw the corner of a smile that was very familiar to her begin on Katherine's face. "Do you indeed? Well, isn't it fortunate that I didn't bring you another?"

"I do have some other things for the child," she added to Sara briskly as she straightened up. "Some frocks and stuffed toys and such as that. They're in one of these cases somewhere. You can decide what's appropriate, of course."

Sara was a little taken aback. "That's—very nice of you."

Katherine said, "Well, then. Let's not stand about in the sun, shall we? Jean-Phillipe, the cases, please."

Sara felt like part of an entourage as she followed the very elegant Mrs. Lindeman—and Jean-Phillipe, with two suitcases under each arm—up the grand staircase. She was determined not to apologize, so that was of course the first thing she did. "I've been painting. I'm afraid things are a little bit disorganized. But I thought you'd want to stay in the Queen's Chamber . . ."

"That overgrown Hollywood monstrosity? Nonsense, that will never do. Aside from which, I despise that bathtub. Almost broke my hip there once. No, my usual suite will do just fine."

She turned down the corridor and slowed to a stop, taking in the accumulated clutter of ladders, paint cans, drop cloths, carpets, and furniture—not to mention the doll carriage, the plastic playhouse, the building blocks, the giant stuffed panda, and the tricycle that Alyssa immediately ran and jumped on, pedaling it down the corridor at top speed. She turned slowly to look at Sara. "My dear," she advised gently. "I don't mean to interfere, but whatever you're paying your workers is far too much. I should sack the lot of them for leaving the place in such a disgrace."

Sara quickly tried to kick some of the drop cloths out of the way while at the same time shoving a bucket filled with paintbrushes beneath a table. "Actually," she said, raising her voice a little to be heard over the clatter of tricycle wheels and the ringing of a tricycle bell, "I'm doing this myself. I don't have any workers."

Katherine's eyebrows shot up. "But why are you doing it at all?"

"Tante Sara! Look at me!" Alyssa had found the kitten and stuffed him into the basket of her tricycle, and Sara interrupted her conversation to rescue the very annoyed-looking kitten before he bolted under the wheels of the vehicle.

"I didn't think it would be such a big project when I started," she explained when she returned, trying not to sound defensive. "A castle isn't a very comfortable place for a little girl, and I just wanted to make it a little more inviting."

"She doesn't appear to be suffering," observed Katherine as Alyssa raced by on the tricycle again, squealing happily. And she added, "But why didn't you simply move into the family apartment? It does seem to me that would be the most practical thing to do."

Sara said uncomfortably, "Well—those rooms are private. They belonged to the family and I really didn't feel right just moving in there . . ."

Katherine raised her eyebrows. "Did I misunderstand? Don't you own this property now?"

"Well, yes, but . . ."

"Well, then really, I can't see why there should be any discussion. The apartment is set up for family living. It has a kitchen and sitting rooms and even a nursery, if I recall, that's more than large enough for the little one to ride that dreadful contraption around to her heart's content. All in all, a far more serviceable arrangement than you have now. Jean-Phillipe," she commanded briskly, turning to the chauffeur who still waited patiently with two arms filled with luggage. "As soon as you've unpacked the car, dash down to the village and bring back four reliable laborers, won't you? Tell them I'm paying top wages for two days' work." Even as Sara drew a breath for protest Alyssa raced by again and Katherine stepped back quickly to avoid losing the polish on her sleek Ferragamo pumps. "And," she added, "put out the word that we'll be interviewing English-speaking nannies beginning at eight o'clock in the morning."

"Hold on," Sara interjected firmly as Katherine turned to proceed to her suite—wherever that might be. "I told Ash I didn't want a nanny. I can take care of Alyssa myself. That's what I'm here for."

Katherine regarded her for a moment, her expression unreadable, and then invited, "Come along, my dear. Help me get settled. And mind the little one near the stairs."

Sara got Alyssa off of the tricycle and interested in her playhouse, and followed Katherine and the chauffeur, a little suspiciously, into the room that she had chosen. It was, of course, the same room that Ash had used, which only made sense, as it was one of the nicest en suite accommodations in the castle, and was always kept ready for visitors. Katherine placed her sunglasses and her purse on the stately mahogany lowboy and instructed Jean-Phillipe to lift one of the matched burgundy leather suitcases to the luggage rack, and line up the others beneath the window. "Now, my dear," she said to Sara, "you may certainly do as you wish, but it seems to me a peculiar characteristic of American women is that they tend to undervalue themselves. Perhaps it has something to do with all those years of building log cabins in the woods, or some such nonsense. I really can't imagine."

Sara was about to object, but found herself smothering a laugh instead. As much as she wanted to resent her uninvited houseguest, she could definitely see where Ash had gotten his charm. "Maybe," she agreed. "I guess self-reliance isn't always a virtue."

"Precisely." Katherine removed her jacket, shook out the folds with one crisp snap, and hung it inside the tall, intricately carved wardrobe. "I raised four children with the assistance of a nanny, and they all turned out rather well, if I do say so. One of them I believe you know." She gave Sara a glance that was too subtle to read, and continued, "Another is a professor of mathematics at the University of Edinburgh, with three little ones of her own and another on the way. A third manages a hugely successful business in Sydney, and my youngest is presently serving with Doctors without Borders in Africa." She walked over to the suitcase and unsnapped the locks. "I think mothers serve best by building character and imparting values, not by wiping noses and bottoms. Further, I can assure you that my husband would never have achieved the measure of success he enjoyed had I not been there to support him every step of the way, which I surely could not have done had I been exhausted from chasing about after four children all day." She held up a small pink dress with an elaborately ruffled chiffon petticoat for Sara's examination. "What do you think of this, my dear? I'm sure it's quite impractical, but I was simply taken by it."

Sara couldn't help smiling. "It's incredibly impractical. Alyssa will love it."

Katherine regarded her kindly. "You are doing a noble thing," she said. "But there's no reason in this world why you have to do it by yourself."

Sara hesitated. "She is a handful," she admitted reluctantly. "Especially in a place as big as this. Maybe it wouldn't hurt to have someone for part of the day."

She gave a satisfied nod. "My thoughts precisely. Now, give me a moment to change, won't you, and let's have a look at what can be done with those rooms."

Katherine emerged from her room ten minutes later wearing jeans, a work shirt, sturdy gardening gloves, and a paisley silk turban over her beautiful platinum hair. She waded into the Orsay apartment without hesitation or trepidation and began flinging off dust covers, ripping down draperies, shaking out carpets, and giving orders to the day laborers like a general organizing a battle. Somehow she even managed to get Alyssa interested in the project, and had her self-importantly collecting all the knickknacks and placing them in a box to be hand-washed later. By five o'clock, a sitting room and a bedroom had been cleared out, windows had been washed, floors and walls had been scrubbed, carpets had been vacuumed, furniture had been brushed and polished and fireplaces cleaned.

"All in all," Katherine declared with her hands on her hips as she dismissed the workers, "not a bad day's work. But now it is time for little girls to retire to their suppers, and for big girls to find a good stiff drink. Upon such was the greatness of the British empire built." She caught Alyssa's willing hand and swung it lightly to her own easy gait as she led the way out of the rooms. "Sara, will you join us?"

Sara returned a grin as she stripped off her work gloves and hat. "I'm right behind you." And that was when she knew for certain that Ash was right.

She really liked his mother.

*   *   *

In three weeks, Sara's life had been transformed, as had the five-bedroom Orsay apartment in the center of the castle, as had Alyssa's and, she supposed in a way, Katherine's. A beautiful home had been carved out of the cold stone of the castle that included a warm and modern family room/sitting room hung with bright gold and black drapes and rich moss green carpets on the floor and cushiony, comfortable, child-and-kitten-friendly sofas and chairs. Pietro's cousin Marco had come to paint Alyssa's new nursery/playroom with an amazing fairy wonderland mural. Her bed was draped with a princess canopy and her cupboards were filled with treasured toys. She adored her new nanny, Martine, who came at noon and stayed to put Alyssa to bed three or sometimes four times a week, and who took her on outings with other children in the village.

Katherine took Sara on a shopping spree to Lyon, where they purchased comfortable modern pieces to intermix with the antiques the Orsays had collected, and chose fabrics to be made into bed coverings and curtains and upholstered pieces that turned the cold, echoing castle into a home. The bizarre red kitchen actually became pretty when outfitted with a bright yellow country table and chairs, and Marie seemed much more comfortable preparing their easy, casual meals there.

Katherine and Sara began restoring the gardens, hiring workers from the village to rebuild the walls and cut back the undergrowth, and in the evenings they often enjoyed cocktails on the terrace. When they went to the village, the two women and the bouncy-haired, rouge-cheeked child, the merchants knew them by name and smiled to see them coming. The baker saved treats for Alyssa and the fishmonger sent home delicacies for the kitten, who was now known, for rather obvious reasons, as Monsieur Le Chat.

Sara's boxes arrived from America: the contents of her dresser drawers, her shoes, her summer clothes—long after she had already bought replacements. Seeing her familiar belongings in these unfamiliar surroundings was strange at first, and then she decided she liked it. The place was slowly becoming her own.

And then, at the bottom of a box, she found the book of

Daniel's poetry that she had always kept on her bedside table. It was the volume he had inscribed to her in French on the night of his book signing at Books and Nooks, and he had always teased her that one day, when he knew her better, he would translate it for her. Then, of course, they had gotten to know each other very well, and translation no longer seemed necessary. Now, for the first time, she knew enough French to read it for herself.

Sara, he had scrawled in his big, elegant handwriting across the page, *tu fais chanter mon coeur—Daniel.*

You make my heart sing.

She touched the page, smiling softly, waiting for the essence of him to spring from the ink into her fingers, as it had done so many times before. Waiting for the memories, the pain, the tears, the longing. But the picture that came to her mind was not of Daniel, but of Ash on that day they had picnicked in the chapel ruins, holding up his mobile phone for her to read the e-mail he had saved. *She makes my heart sing.*

It was true, she had never had a chance to really know Daniel, and even now she wasn't sure who he had been, or who he might yet be proven to be. But for a brief shining moment in time, he had loved her. He had made her heart sing, too. And whatever had happened since, or might happen in the future, that was worth treasuring. Ash had understood that.

And for a single, fleeting moment she understood something, else, too: what it was like to love two men, separately and equally at the same time. One for who he had been, and another for who he was.

She did not put the book on her bedside table. Instead she took it downstairs to the vast, empty library that once had stored the great collection of Orsay treasures. She positioned it on a shelf in a place of honor, where it belonged. Where, perhaps, it would begin a new collection of treasures.

* * *

The weather in North Carolina was foul, which seemed somehow appropriate. There was some kind of tropical storm moving up the coast, which had grounded every flight after the one Ash had taken. Now the sky was blue black and rain came in alternate slashing spurts and steady downpours, bending trees to the ground one moment and deadly still the next. *Goddamn it, Daniel,* Ash had thought wearily as the car made its way to the cemetery, *it's still all about drama with you.*

A plastic canopy had been set up over the site, but rain still dripped down his collar and chilled his spine. The sound of it was like a soft, steady drumbeat on the plastic, but the counterpoint was the thrum of the diesel engine and the ghastly creak of the chain as the coffin, spilling black loam into the pit below, was raised out of the earth.

A representative from the coroner's office was there, as well as a technician from the lab he had hired. A priest stood by because he had insisted on it. Because Daniel might not care, but Ash did. And there was another man he did not know, a burly fellow with sandy hair who kept his hands thrust into the pockets of his Windbreaker, and who regarded Ash with a steady, unwavering gaze.

The coroner's assistant came over to him. "We can do the procedure here," she said. "It would save the time and expense of transporting the remains to the lab."

Ash nodded tersely and signed the papers she presented to him. He looked straight ahead when they opened the coffin, and he didn't blink until they had closed it again. *Dear God, Sara*, he thought, *I'm glad you're not here. I'm glad.*

The entire business took less time than he had imagined. It was all very matter-of-fact and efficient, which was the way he liked things done. But in this case it seemed grotesque. The coffin was closed. The officials went away into the rain with their samples. The priest came forward and made the sign of the cross, began to murmur the words. And when he was finished, the gravediggers returned to hook up the chains.

Ash forestalled them by stepping forward. He placed one hand on the coffin. It was cold and slick with dampness, and there was an odor—of dark, dank earth and formaldehyde and things left best undisturbed—that he would never forget. Not as long as he lived.

"Good-bye, Daniel," he said softly. And then, more heavily, "I'm sorry."

He let his hand fall away from the metal casket, and he nodded abruptly to the gravediggers, who were waiting impatiently in the rain. And when he turned the burly sandy-haired man was standing beside him.

"Are you that lawyer?" he inquired, frowning at him. "The English one?"

Ash said, "I'm Ash Lindeman."

The other man extended his hand. "I'm Jeff Delaney. Sara's—Daniel's, I guess—brother-in-law. It was good of you to call, and let us know . . ." He nodded uncomfortably toward the proceedings. "About all this."

Ash shook his hand, feeling tired. "There was no one else to call," he said simply. "Daniel had no other family."

Jeff said, "My wife, Dixie, thought somebody should be here. But we've got kids and—well, the fact is, I didn't want her to come."

"I understand."

"We didn't expect you to fly all the way over here."

Ash said, "He was my friend."

A respectful silence, Then Jeff said, "Is Sara okay?"

It was a moment before Ash answered. Then all he could offer was, "I think so. I hope so. I think she will be."

Jeff looked at him steadily for a time. Rain plopped on the plastic canopy. The diesel engines started to putter.

Jeff said, "You hungry? Dixie would never let me forget it if I didn't bring you home for a meal."

"Thank you." It required an effort, but Ash managed a smile. "I think I'd like that."

The chains began to creak, and the two men walked out into the rain and up the hill to the parking lot.

*   *   *

When Sara hung up the phone with Dixie, she was crying. Katherine muted the sound on the satellite transmission of *Britain's Got Talent*, her favorite television show, and looked at her with concern. "Is everything all right at home, my dear?"

She didn't know exactly how or when it had happened, but Sara awoke one morning and realized she was at home here. She never dreamed of the sound of gulls anymore. She could hardly remember the smell of the sea. And that was why the tears that clogged her throat and dampened her cheekbones were so inexplicable.

"No," she answered Katherine, and pressed furiously at her eyes with the heels of her hands. "I mean, yes. Yes, everything is fine. I don't know what's wrong with me. I seem to cry at the drop of a hat these days."

"Menopause," observed Katherine succinctly. "I suggest hormones without delay. They are the only things that will preserve your skin."

Sara gave a startled laugh and rubbed away the last of the tears. "I'm only forty-six!"

"Oh, it can go on for years," Katherine assured her airily. She un-muted the television but turned the volume low. "Which is why you must remember you can still get pregnant. How do you think Ash ended up with a sister thirteen years younger than he?"

Sara laughed again and dropped down on the sofa beside Katherine, leaning her head back against the cushions. She watched, without seeing, a rather disastrous tumbling act for a time. She said, "Ash is coming this weekend."

"How delightful of him." Katherine did not inquire how this information should come to Sara via her sister, some three thousand miles away.

In the time since their last meeting Ash had resumed his habit of texting, rather than calling—usually every day, sometimes only one word: *Okay? Well?* And she could imagine him checking that off his to-do list every day from whatever time zone he was in. At first she had resented the fact that he never called, and then she was glad. What would she have said to him? She was uncomfortable and a little embarrassed about their last encounter, and no doubt he was, too. After all, she was the one who had begged him to stay. He was the one who had walked away.

Sara drew a shaky breath. "There's this . . . thing . . . we have to do . . . to make sure—to find out who Alyssa's father was."

Katherine's hand, slim and strong and supple, squeezed hers. "I know."

Sara pressed her head back against the sofa cushions again, her gaze on the ceiling, and whispered, "I hope I'm doing the right thing."

"Well, of course you are, my dear." Katherine patted her hand briskly, as though, with that, the matter was settled. "You can't go the rest of your life wondering, now, can you?"

"No," Sara said, brushing another film of moisture from her eyes. "I can't."

"Then there you have it."

She turned up the volume on a boy vocalist, and they watched until the commercial.

Katherine muted the television. "Clearly, this is none of my affair," she said, "and you certainly don't have to answer if you don't want to. But have you given any thought to what you will do when this matter of paternity is settled?"

Sara said, "Do you mean with the château?"

"I mean," replied Katherine, "with your life."

Sara was, for a moment, taken aback. It wasn't as though the question had never crossed her mind—usually late at night when the stillness and the vastness of the place settled in on her and she could hear her own heart beating in the dark. *After this, what?* Or when she awoke, sick with terror, after a nightmare and had to go stand beside Alyssa's bed to make sure she was okay, and she thought, *What am I trying to do here?* Ash was right. There was no happy ending. Either she would find out that her husband had been a liar and a coward, or that the little girl with whom she had already fallen completely in love was nothing more than an illusion. Either way, what would be left for her?

She said, carefully feeling out the truth for the first time, "I'm not the same person I was when I came here."

"I don't see how you possibly could be."

"Ash thinks I should go back to work in the corporate world."

"Well, of course he does. Work is Ash's answer to everything."

Sara smiled a little, though wanly. "I don't know, maybe he's right. He certainly seems happy."

"My dear," replied Katherine with calm certainty, "my son is many things, but *happy* is not one of them."

Sara looked at her, startled.

"Oh, he pretends so well that sometimes it's difficult to see the truth. I wonder sometimes if even he knows how unhappy he is." A small furrow marred Katherine's perfect brow. "But he's tormented by things you and I can only imagine. It has to do with his father dying so young, I think, and so unexpectedly. It's as though there's an emptiness inside him that he's frantic to fill, and if he piles up enough victories—in business, mostly, but in other ways as well—the emptiness will go away. It doesn't, of course, and he can't understand why, so he starts all over again, chasing another victory. And then when Daniel died . . . Well, the two of them were the same age, you know. I frankly think it terrified him."

Sara said, slowly, "I think Ash tries to do the right thing, most of the time. And most of the time he probably is right. But I guess when you're that afraid of failing, you can't always see what the right thing is."

Katherine reached over and patted Sara's hand, briefly. "Do you know, Sara," she said matter-of-factly, "I've grown rather fond of you. I can't say why. I think you may remind me of myself, when I was a young widow. I thought the world had ended, of course—and I was right. Everything I believed I would have forever turned out to be only an illusion. Good heavens, Ash was barely out of university and thought he could fill his father's shoes. My Shelby was still in school and Margaret was a young mother with problems of her own. I cried for a year, and that's the truth of it. I thought my life was over." She paused a moment, her pale blue eyes lost in the pain of backward reflection—but only for a moment. "And then I woke up one morning," she continued, "and realized that I was right. My life, the one I had planned for and hoped for and worked for day and night for over forty years, was over. So I sold my house, moved to the country, and started a completely new life. And," she added, turning to survey Sara with a thorough, critical eye, "I got a new haircut."

Sara tugged self-consciously at the ends of her hair. "What's wrong with my hair?"

"Good heavens, girl, we're two hours from the most glamorous city in the world. A new style would do wonders for your morale. And while there's no truth whatsoever to the claim that a visit to Paris can cure all ills, I've always found it to be a marvelous diversion."

Sara let her head slide down slowly until it rested lightly against Katherine's shoulder. "I'm glad you came here," she said softly.

Katherine seemed surprised, and then, rather awkwardly she reached up a hand and patted Sara's cheek. "Well, then," she said. And she tried to hide her smile as she turned up the volume of the television again.

· SIXTEEN ·

Ash arrived at the end of the week with a very pleasant young female lab technician who made a game of swabbing Alyssa's cheek for DNA, and who kept it all so quick and light that Alyssa didn't even have a chance for a typical five-year-old's recalcitrance, much less fear. Sara had to sign an affidavit that she had witnessed the procedure, and so did Katherine. Afterward, they all went down to the village for peach glace, and the lab technician took her samples and got on a train for Paris.

Sara had been nervous about seeing Ash again, about what she would see in his eyes, about what she would say to him, and most of all about how she would feel. She didn't want to be awkward around him. She did not want any of those telling silences that would make his mother lift an eyebrow. She should have known better than to worry.

Ash was as smooth and as charming as ever. The first moments of his arrival were dominated by Alyssa, of course, and he scooped her up and laughed with her and listened to her stories as he always did until she squirmed away to go find Monsieur Le Chat. He kissed his mother's cheek and then, politely, Sara's. She noticed that his lips barely brushed her skin and that his eyes seemed oddly distant.

When they went for ice cream he gave most of his attention to Alyssa, and merely smiled without comment when she told him about her new nurse. He admired the work that had been done on the apartment, and pretended to be fascinated by every detail of Alyssa's new nursery. He suggested that they allow the nanny to put Alyssa to bed while they drove to a nearby town for dinner. He was, as ever, a delightful conversationalist and a charming host, and any other time Sara would have enjoyed herself immensely. But she could not help noticing that he did not address a single personal comment to her, and that the smile he gave her was the same one he gave his mother. And there was a vague and confused ache in the pit of her stomach she could not quite define.

A fine summer rain was falling when they returned to the château, which spoiled their plans for after-dinner drinks on the terrace. Sara worried, as she always did when it rained, about the roof. She had noticed a damp spot in one of the attics when she and Katherine directed the placement of some of the Orsays' old furniture during the renovation.

"I doubt a rainfall this light will do much damage," Ash remarked as they returned to the apartment. He served his mother a whiskey from the Orsays' glass and marble bar, and poured sherry for Sara. "It's probably just a loose tile. You should call Contandino."

"Yes, and I should have him check the stability of the west wing while he's about it, if I were you," Katherine said. "I can't think how long it's been since anyone was back there."

"I don't know how he will get in there," Ash said, "without taking the door off the hinges." He sat down in one of the deep gold club chairs that Sara had purchased, stretching out and crossing his legs at the ankles. "The keys seemed to have disappeared over the years."

"I should imagine Signor Contandino has a copy," his mother said, "since he installed the lock."

"Excellent idea." Ash sipped his whiskey. He glanced around the room admiringly. "You ladies have done a fine job with the place. Very nice indeed."

"So glad you approve," replied Katherine, sipping her drink. "We charged your account."

"I did not," Sara objected quickly, and she thought she saw Ash's lips twitch with amusement just before he lifted his own glass again. She added, "But thanks for refunding the tax money."

He saluted her with a small lift of his glass. "Glad to contribute." And then Ash looked at Sara as though seeing her for the first time. "You've done something different with your hair."

His mother gave an impatient sniff. "Isn't that just like a man? A two-hundred-euro haircut and it takes him half a day to notice."

Sara shrugged it off, absently fingering the stylish fringes

of hair that now swept forward to caress her neck and empha-
size her cheekbones and eyes. "I think it's too young for me.
Your mother and I went to Paris for the day."

"Did you, now? What did you do?"

And so they chatted for a while about Paris, and Ash
told them about his trip to Argentina. He said nothing about
North Carolina, and Sara kept waiting for him to look her in
the eye. And then Katherine said, "I think we should have
a party, Sara. We'll invite the locals, and the expats who are
living nearby . . . all the ones worth knowing, anyway. It will
be a lovely way for you to get to know your neighbors."

Ash suppressed a groan. "Please, mother, not one of your
parties. Whatever has Sara done to deserve such a thing?"

She returned an arch look and Sara, who was already feeling more than a little annoyed with him, said, "I think it's a
wonderful idea."

"We should do it at the end of the month," Katherine
pronounced, "when everyone has returned from holiday and
before that dreadful cutting of the vines—"

"Burning of the vines," Ash corrected.

"Yes, of course, before all that nonsense begins. It completely saturates the fall social season in this region and we
want to be ahead of the curve on that, don't we? Yes, I think
this is perfect. I shall start writing out the guest list immediately." She finished her drink and stood. "And now, my dears,
I'll be off and leave you two to do the things young people do.
And," she added over her shoulder as she exited the room,
"don't imagine I don't know what they are. I was young once,
too, you know."

Ash smothered a half laugh in his glass as closed the door. "Good God," he said. "I think I've just been given permission to have sex . . . by my mother."

Sara smiled to cover her embarrassment and took a quick sip of her sherry. "I'm still getting over being called 'young.'"

"The two of you seem to be getting along well. I suspected you would. But if you let her talk you into that party, please don't try to say you weren't warned."

Easy conversation, comfortable topics. Two polite strangers in a room. Except that her heart was pounding hard and there was a knot in her stomach the size of a fist and she couldn't stop sneaking quick glances at him . . . how long his fingers were, curved around the glass, the way his hair shadowed his forehead, the length of his legs, the texture of the skin on his neck. Remembering how he had felt, pressed against her. Remembering how he had tasted. Remembering how much she had missed him.

Sara said abruptly, "I hope you don't think your mother got the impression we were sleeping together from me."

Ash gazed into his glass, a slight tension appearing between his brows. "I rather suspect she got it from me," he said. "Your name does seem to come up quite a bit, come to think of it. At any rate, I apologize." He set down his drink, only half finished, and stood. "I'm rather tired. If you don't mind, my dear, I think I'll go to my room as well."

Sara got to her feet, feeling confused and trying not to show it. "Some of the guest rooms in the apartment aren't finished," she said, "but I thought you might like—"

"No, that's quite all right. I put my things in my customary room in the old part of the château. I have some work to catch up on and there's an Internet connection."

"So that's where it is!" Sara exclaimed. "I should have known."

He smiled. "There's a wireless router. I'll show you how to turn it on in the morning, and you can set up your computer anywhere in the château."

He touched her arm lightly in a casual gesture of good night, and then hesitated. He looked into her eyes then, and she thought she knew why he had avoided doing so all evening. Behind the tenderness was, just for a moment, the glimpse of a shadow, a dark ache that reminded her of the one she had glimpsed so briefly there before, in the chapel ruins. Almost before she could define it the shadow was gone, but the memory of it lingered, and made her afraid.

He said, "I like your haircut." He playfully brushed her fringe with the backs of knuckles, and turned to go.

She caught his arm. "What's wrong?"

He turned back to her, a furrow between his brows, and she thought he would return a sharp answer. But then his eyes moved over her face, slowly, her cheeks and her temples and her chin and her nose and her lips and her jaw and her throat, as though memorizing the contours, or caressing them. And finally, he met her eyes, and the pain she saw there was the ache of wanting, and regret. She knew that, because the ache was mirrored in her own chest.

"I thought I could do this," he said lowly. "I thought I could come here for the weekend, and be with you, and talk to you, and enjoy you, and that everything could be between

us as it was when we first met. But I can't. And it can't. So."
A breath. "I'll leave in the morning."

She placed her hand on his chest to stop him from moving
past her. Cotton as soft as silk. Muscles strong and hot. The
hard, heavy heartbeat beneath her fingers felt like her own,
and she stood there with breath suspended for a moment,
trying to tell him that with her eyes, and listening with her
fingertips. She made an effort to keep her voice even and
without implication.

"Dixie called," she said. "She told me . . . what you did."
She stopped, and swallowed to clear her throat. The effort
to hold his gaze was tremendous, and her fingers pressed into
his heartbeat. "What I didn't have the courage to do. I've
been thinking about what you said. And you might be right.
Maybe, this time, you are the good guy."

He dropped his eyes, almost as if to draw a curtain on the
pain that grew darker, and clearer, with every word she spoke.
He wrapped his fingers about hers where they lay on his chest.

"I've given this some thought," he said in a low tone, looking at their enmeshed fingers, and not at her eyes, "and I've
come to see that I've pursued you unfairly. You're very lovely,
very . . . enchanting, and I hope you won't blame me if I've
been quite swept away by you." His lips tried to smile, and his
tone tried to sound light, and neither quite succeeded. He
glanced at her briefly, and then, with a slight knitting of his
brows, at the hand he still held. "I know how difficult things
have been for you, and I may have taken advantage of that.
You're a recent widow. This isn't the time for you to have to
fend off another romantic entanglement. And so I've been a

bit of a cad. I apologize. Perhaps we can both move on from here."

She said, feeling stunned, "Ash, that's not . . ."

Now he met her eyes. His own were dark with firm resolve, and turmoil just beneath the surface. "Your family was very courteous to me," he said quietly. "I'm glad I got to meet them. But I went to North Carolina for myself, not for you." His fingers tightened then, squeezing hers almost to the point of pain, and then abruptly, he dropped her hand. "And there's no such thing as a good guy."

He looked at her then, his jaw knotted and his eyes as bleak as an empty sea. "You deserve better," he said.

And he left without another word.

*   *   *

Sara made her way down the corridor in the dark, guided only by the light that spilled beneath his door. She knocked, but did not wait for him to answer before pushing open the door.

He was propped up against the pillows atop the rumpled bed wearing dark-framed reading glasses and a blue silk robe that was open to the waist over his bare chest. Papers were scattered around him and he was working on a mini-laptop, which he closed slowly and put aside when he saw her.

She said, "Why don't you let me decide what I deserve?"

A cool, damp breeze came from the open casement window, and Sara, whose bare feet were already cold from the long walk down marble floors, started to shiver. She was wearing a knee-length sleeveless cotton nightgown that tied at the shoulders with ribbons and was trimmed with delicate rows of crocheted lace that she had bought in Paris because it was frivolous and it made her feel pretty. Now she wished she had thought to grab a robe before impulsively striding out of the relatively cozy apartment but, after tossing and turning in bed for twenty minutes, she had been afraid that if she hesitated for even another moment, she would lose her nerve.

"You know," she said forcefully, "I spent forty years working hard and playing it safe to make sure I got what I deserved, and when I finally decided to take a chance, yes, it broke my heart. Yes, it brought me pain. But . . ." She dug her fingers into her arms, trying to keep her voice from shaking. "It also brought me love, even if only for a little while. And it brought me here."

She blew out a breath, calming herself. "So maybe this is what I deserve. Maybe I deserve to take just one more chance. Maybe I deserve to figure it out for myself. I just wish . . . you wouldn't tell me what I deserve." It was only when the words were out that she realized she had not been shivering from cold at all. Her hands dropped to her sides and the gooseflesh on her arms disappeared. "That's all I wanted to say."

He removed his glasses. "Come here," he said softly.

A breeze rustled the leaves outside his window and sent a shower of raindrops splashing onto the deep sill. Sara grasped her arms again against another bout of nerves. "There's one more thing," she said tightly. "I think you should know . . . I finally figured out that hating Daniel was keeping him here as much as loving him. So . . . no more ghosts."

Ash extended his hand to her. "Come here."

She did, and he pulled her down into the circle of his arms and legs and he covered her mouth with his and the shivering stopped and the heat began, warm and smooth velvety, from the inside out. He turned her into the curve of his arm, his leg over her hip, holding her against his chest, and he stroked her cheek, and the curve of her eyebrow, with his fingertip. His eyes were the color of a deep ocean when storms lurk hundreds of feet below, and they filled her world.

"Don't think I don't want you," he said, hoarsely, against her mouth. "It's gone far beyond wanting you. I'm really quite obsessed with you, I'm afraid. I don't quite know how it happened."

Sara whispered, "Me either."

"I'm going to be very bad for you." His voice soft and rough, his fingers cupping her cheek, threading through her hair. "There are things about me, parts of me, you don't know. I don't want you to be hurt again. I don't want to be the one to do that."

She said, "Then don't."

"I can't help who I am."

Sara turned her face into the caress of his hand, a sign of gentle surrender. "Oh, Ash," she said, and let herself sink into him. "Do you know who you're talking to? Do you think I don't know that?"

"I don't want to be responsible for . . ."

She laid her fingers across his lips. "This isn't a contract negotiation."

He kissed her fingertips, his eyes dark with a gentle ferocity. "Please don't regret this."

Sara said, "Have you done something that you could go to prison for?"

That surprised him. "I don't think so."

"Is there another woman?"

"God, no." He whispered that against her throat, his breath like fire, and she shivered with pleasure.

"Any transmittable diseases?"

He laughed softly. "Not to my knowledge."

"Then what else matters?"

"Darling, I think you should raise your standards." But when he lifted his face to hers, he was smiling, and his gaze was filled with longing. "There is one thing you really should know, however." He pushed his fingers lightly through her hair, caressing it away from her face, exposing her eyes and all the vulnerability there. When he looked into her eyes, it was with a kind of thirst, as though he could drink her in with his wanting. He said softly, "I'm afraid I've fallen quite in love with you."

"Oh, I'm so glad," she whispered, draping her arms around his neck, lifting her face to his. "I was afraid I was the only one."

She kissed his lips, and the corner of his mouth, and the coarseness of his chin. She tasted salt and citrus, and the sharp, tangy essence that was simply him. "I didn't mean to," she whispered. "I didn't want to. I shouldn't have. But I love you. And it scares me."

He slipped his arms around her back, pressing her to him, holding her tightly, just holding her. His heart was like thunder against her breast. And he said, "I know."

"Do you believe in second chances?" she whispered, desperately, against his ear.

"Yes," he said, fiercely. And then relaxing against her, kissing her jaw, and her cheekbone, and the corner of her eye, he repeated gently, "Yes."

He smiled then, and took her fingers in his, tasting each tip with his tongue, traveling down the center of her palm to her wrist. She shivered, and the pleasure went straight down to her core. He said, softly, "I wanted to call you. Every day. But I couldn't bear to hear your voice. Or even worse, to not hear it."

Sara thought about all the times she had played back his messages on her voice mail, just to hear the sound of his voice. And she caught her breath as his lips traveled upward, delicately, to her shoulder, to her neck. "I would have answered the phone this time," she whispered.

His hands caressed the fine material of her nightgown, dipping ever so slightly toward the cleavage, tracing the lace that trimmed the underarms. His breath was against her shoulder. "Did you get this in Paris?"

She managed an incoherent "Hmmm."

"It's very pretty." His fingers tugged at the shoulder ribbon. "I'm going to take it off now."

She whispered, "Okay."

And then she caught his hand. He looked at her, puzzled, and she said, "Ash—did you . . . Are you . . . What I mean is, I've learned a lot of things since I've been here, but how to buy condoms in France isn't one of them."

He started to laugh, softly, against her neck. "This is why

I adore you." He swept away the papers beneath them and lowered her back against the pillows, poised above her with his hands on either side of her face, his eyes filled with tenderness and mirth. "You have nothing to hide. You make me wish . . ." And slowly the mirth faded as he lowered her face to his, and kissed her lips gently, and all too briefly. "That I didn't either."

He looked at her again, brushing her bangs with his fingertips, and he smiled. "The answer to your question," he said softly, "is yes. So now may I . . . ?"

Fingertips toyed again with the ribbon of her nightgown and she answered his question by slipping her hands between their bodies and deftly untying the sash of his robe. "Yes," she whispered, when her fingers met his skin. "Oh, yes . . ."

They came together greedily at first, with heat that built too quickly between them, hungry for the sensation of him inside her, of her wrapped around him, mouths drinking, hands grasping, letting that final aching, cascading burst of pain and pleasure seize and transport them, separately and together and then, on a dizzying tide of gasping breaths and shattering heartbeats, release them again to touch, to warmth, to holding.

And then, inevitably, they flowed into each other once again, fingers tracing familiar contours, tongues gathering the perspiration from each other's skin, tasting what was him and what was her, and what was theirs together. They discovered each other with movements that were long and slow and quick and hot, sometimes with wanton abandon and sometimes with breaths suspended, drawing each sensation to its most exquisite, most attenuated expression of pleasure. There was greedy impatience and then there were long sweet moments of slow and sensual delight. There should have been awkwardness, moments of uncertainty, even small disappointments. But it was as though they had been doing this together for all of their lives.

They slept, and they made love, and they awoke in each other's arms and made love again. As a soft pink light began to creep across the sill of the casement, Ash kissed her hair and murmured, "Why do people always think sex will end an obsession? The more I have of you, the more I want."

Sara, curled into the curve of his arm with her fingers spread flat across his abdomen, said sleepily, "I didn't know people thought that."

"Men do. All the time." He bent now and kissed her lips. She could taste herself on him, a deeply erotic mixture of tangy perfume and salty sweat and sex, and she responded in kind.

"That explains it, then." She let her fingers slide upward, exploring again the slick contours of his chest, the tendons of his throat. "I think we're shameless."

"You make me feel sixteen."

"You make me feel like Superwoman."

He laughed softly, kissing her neck.

"I should go." And yet she turned her head, exposing more of her throat to his kisses, and she couldn't stop her hands from caressing his shoulders, and his back, and that sensitive area she had discovered just beneath his arm, not far from his heart. "It's almost morning."

"Where will you go, love?" he murmured, hands gently cupping her breasts, kissing them each, tenderly, one by one. "You live here."

"You know what I mean." And she made no move to rise.

"Sara." He lifted his face to hers, his hands cradling her head, his eyes suddenly and surprisingly intense. "Come with me to London."

At first she thought he was joking. "I can't do that."

"Why not?" And that was when she began to suspect he might be serious.

"What about Alyssa?"

"You don't trust my mother?"

"I can't ask her to—"

"I can." His fingers tightened in her hair. "Or we'll send for her. Or we'll take her with us. We'll take her to the zoo and the museum and the park on Sunday. My place is huge, mammoth, really. There's plenty of room. We'll even bring my mother if you insist, but I'd rather not."

She started to laugh, but he stopped her with a kiss, deep and long and hungry. That was when she knew he wasn't kidding. "Come with me to London," he said, lowly, a little breathlessly. "I want you to see my flat. It's all black and white; you'll hate it. I want to take you to dinner and dress up for the theater and hail a taxi for two. I want to take you to my office and show you how important I am. I'll even introduce you to the ridiculously handsome Mr. Winkle."

She started to giggle, her fingers playing over his collarbone. "Is he handsome?"

"Unfairly so." His thumbs traced the shape of her eyebrows

while his lips kissed her cheeks, and her nose, and the corner of her mouth. "I want to make love to you for twenty-four hours without stopping for breath," he whispered. "I want the scent of you on my pillows. I want . . ." and he moved above her, his eyes deep and solemn and rich with need. "I want you out of Daniel's house," he said softly. "I want to know if you're real."

She wrapped her arms around his neck and lifted herself into him and she whispered her answer into his ear.

Because she wanted to know, too.

· SEVENTEEN ·

In all of the best fairy tales, the downfall of the hero begins with greed. The beautiful princess is not enough; he must also have the bag of gold. Escaping the wrath of a giant means nothing; he has to go back for the golden goose. Ash should have been satisfied with simply loving Sara, even if it meant she was locked away in a castle. Even if he had to share her with Daniel. But he wanted her all to himself.

The first few days were glorious. She made fun of his stark, cold, hospital-clean flat, and then they made love in every room of it. He took her out to brunch at the Dorchester, because there was never any food in his house, and later they went shopping and he pretended to hate the red cushions she bought for his white leather sofa. But on the way home, he scooped up two armfuls of red roses from a flower stall to complement the cushions and later, as they lay tangled in a cashmere throw on the floor with red cushions scattered all around, he knew he would always adore those cushions because they smelled of her.

"Do you think we'll ever get tired of this?" she murmured, lying soft against his shoulder.

"God, I hope so." He stroked her hair. "Because I really am exhausted."

She laughed and he looked at her with the most amazing sense of wonder. "You belong here," he said. And his brows drew together because even as he said it he could hardly believe it was true. "I didn't think you would. I thought it would feel strange—exciting, of course, but strange—having you here. It simply feels natural."

She wound her fingers between his. "Do you know how you meet someone on vacation or on a business trip and have a fling?"

"I've never done such a thing," he assured her soberly, rubbing their entwined fingers against the faint stubble of his chin.

"And then you get home and you try to keep in touch, try to pick up where you left off . . . and it's, like, who *is* this person?"

"I swear, I've never—"

She picked up one of the red cushions and bounced it off his shoulder, and he smothered his laughter in her hair.

She said, seriously now, "Do you think it will be like that with us when the passion fades?"

He took her face in his hands and looked into her eyes and said simply, "No. I've made those kinds of silly mistakes, Sara, and so have you. We can take a few days to act like teenagers but in the end I think we both know what we want. And whatever surprises are waiting for us along the way we'll just learn to manage."

She smiled. "Spoken like a man who always gets what he wants."

"It's what I do," he assured her, and he drew her again onto his shoulder, utterly convinced of his invincibility.

*   *   *

An easy routine began to transform Ash's London life. He discovered his refrigerator could actually hold food. His kitchen smelled of coffee. He went late to the office because he did not want to miss the sight of Sara sitting at his table wearing one of his robes, reading the morning papers and munching on her toast. He stayed at the office only a few hours because there was always something he would rather be doing: taking Sara to lunch, or strolling in the park, or helping her to rearrange the guest room for the anticipated arrival of Alyssa on the coming weekend.

"I do believe the time off you've taken agrees with you, sir," commented Mrs. Harrison. "You're looking quite fit."

Ash declared expansively, "I'm in love, Mrs. Harrison. Best thing in the world for the constitution."

"Congratulations, sir. And just as a point of reference, you might note that during your absence the business has not suffered appreciably. In fact, one might even say it has thrived."

He gave her a suspicious look. "Are you implying my presence here is a hindrance to productivity?"

"Certainly not, sir. Merely that should you wish to continue half days, I doubt anyone would object."

He muttered, "I'm certain there was an insult there somewhere."

"On the other hand," she continued easily, "did you happen to see the Dejonge proposal that I left on your desk? Their attorneys have gone over it and returned it with comments."

Ash frowned in annoyance. "I still say we could work this all out in two hours if they'd agree to a meeting. Any progress on that?"

"I'm afraid not, sir. They believe it's still too early in the process."

"Very well. I'll take the proposal home with me tonight. Sara's stopping by to meet me for lunch. Let me know when she arrives, will you?"

"Actually, sir, she arrived about half an hour ago. She's with Mr. Winkle now."

Ash frowned at that. "She didn't mention."

And Mrs. Harrison simply lifted her eyebrows. "Should she have?"

Ash went into his office, closed the door, and picked up the telephone to buzz Winkle's line. But in the end, he replaced the receiver, impatient with himself, and turned to his own work. Nothing would make Sara's temper flare faster than to think he was interfering in her private business discussions, and she was more than capable of managing her own affairs.

Besides, it wasn't as though they had any secrets.

* * *

Alyssa arrived the next week in a swirl of happy chatter and a mound of stuffed toys, in the hands of his mother, who happily turned her over. Katherine planned to stay in town for a few days to shop, then she would retire to the country to attend to her own affairs before returning to Rondelais in another few weeks to help Sara prepare for the party.

She took her son's newfound domestic tranquility in stride— a town house that had never been more than a hotel room now transformed with fresh flowers and dishes on the drainboard and a guest room outfitted with a Little Mermaid comforter, and his arm, lightly draped around Sara's shoulders— as though it were only natural, as though it had always been so, and that gave Ash an unaccountable pleasure. She stayed for tea and gave an easy, chatty report on matters at Rondelais, and he thought how odd it was, and yet how right, that the two parts of his life should be linked in this way.

"I was right, by the way," she informed Ash, "about the keys to the west wing. That dour Italian did have them after all. He came out and opened up the rooms, and checked around for damage. Do you know the Orsays left everything just as it was when they moved out? Rotting furniture, pictures on the walls . . ."

"No hidden van Goghs, I trust," suggested Ash, sipping his tea.

"I'm afraid not. Just family photographs and bric-a-brac, nothing of import. Nonetheless, they might have sentimental value to . . ." She glanced at Alyssa, who was importantly serving tea and cake to her stuffed bear at the small designer cocktail table on the opposite side of the room—scattering crumbs all over the highly polished floors and table surface in the process. "Someone at some point, so I boxed them all up for you."

"Mother, you didn't go wandering around in there." Ash's voice was alarmed.

"Actually, the damage is not as severe as one might imagine. Mr. Contandino thinks the roof can be repaired. Of course it would cost a bloody fortune."

Sara sighed. "What else is new?"

"Never mind, my love," Ash said, smiling at her. "It would just be another twenty rooms for you to keep clean. Let the roof fall in, I say."

Sara looked worried, and Katherine said, "It wouldn't hurt to talk to someone about some kind of emergency measures to control the water damage when you return. I'm sure that would be a manageable expense."

She moved on to talk about her plans for the party, and to arrange to go shopping with Sara the next day for the necessities, and Ash fell into a reverie whose most remarkable component was simple contentment.

They made frozen waffles for breakfast, and Sara decorated them with funny faces made out of fruit, the way she had seen Dixie do for the twins. They fed the ducks in the park. They had dinner at five. And there was that inevitable moment when Alyssa burst into Ash's bedroom early one morning while they were still asleep and declared scoldingly, "*Petit-papa*, Tante Sara, where are your clothes?" Sara was mortified, but Ash laughed about it the rest of the day.

On Sunday they took Alyssa to the zoo and ate cherry popsicles, most of which ended up on Ash's shirt as he was lifting Alyssa to his shoulder to view the elephants. Sara, laughing, was trying to brush the stain away with a paper napkin when she noticed a woman across the path from them, wearing big sunglasses, chic, formfitting cropped jeans, and high-heeled sandals, watching them. As soon as she noticed Sara's gaze, she turned and walked the other way.

"Tante Sara, Tante Sara, tigers!" Alyssa tugged excitedly at her hand, and Sara quickly hid the faint shadow of puzzlement that had crept into her eyes as she turned her smile back to Alyssa.

"By all means," declared Ash, swinging Alyssa up into his arms, "we mustn't keep the tigers waiting. Which way, Magellan?"

And so they were off, with Ash and Alyssa trying to outdo each other with their tiger growls, and with Sara laughing so hard that her heart barely speeded at all when she spotted the woman again as they were leaving the tiger exhibit.

Alyssa, skipping along between them, a hand held in each of theirs, suddenly stopped and gasped, her eyes big as they followed a red balloon floating free against the sky. "*Petit-papa*, look!"

He dropped to one knee beside her to better share her view. "It's a balloon," he told her. "Shall we go and see if we can find another? Perhaps one just for you?"

Those beautiful big eyes widened even further in delight. "*Rouge?*"

"Red," corrected Sara. This time the woman did not try to avoid her eyes. She waited patiently in the shade of a sycamore a few dozen feet away, absently twirling her sunglasses between two fingers, her expression cool and unashamed.

"I think I know just the place to look," Ash said, catching Alyssa's hand in his as he stood. "Shall we, my love?" His eyes, crinkled in the sun, looked happy and relaxed as he turned to Sara. "I saw a vendor just around the corner, there."

"You go ahead," Sara said, smiling quickly. "I need to find a ladies' room. Alyssa, do you need to go to the toilet?"

Alyssa shook her head, tugging at Ash's hand. "A red one!"

Ash laughed and let himself be pulled away, and Sara called after him, "I'll meet you there!"

She waited until the two of them had disappeared into the crowd before she turned and walked over to Michele. There was a wooden bench underneath the tree, and Michele had made herself comfortable there, her shapely jeaned legs crossed, a cigarette in her hand. She gestured for Sara to join her. Sara remained standing.

"Are you following us?" she demanded without preamble.

Michele looked amused as she pushed the sunglasses into her sleek red hair. "And so it is true. You have domesticated him. This I could not believe until I saw it for myself. Congratulations." She drew on the cigarette and blew out the smoke in an elaborate sigh. "And what a very great pity."

"What do you want?" Sara said.

Michele glanced up at her. She seemed completely unintimidated by the fact that Sara was standing over her. If anything, in fact, it was Sara who felt ill at ease in her cotton capris and sneakers, her hair pulled back in a ponytail, her nose pink with the sun. But women like Michele had always been able to do that to her. She started to cross her arms over her chest, realized that looked defensive, and stopped herself. Michele smiled, unruffled.

"You are correct," she said easily. "I have followed you since I heard Ashton tell the doorman where you were going. I always like to give my regards whenever I am in the city, but your happy little family was already leaving as I arrived. Perhaps I should have made my presence known." She shrugged. "But one learns so many more interesting things when one watches unseen, *n'est-ce pas?*"

Sara closed her fingers, and opened them again. "What did you learn?"

Michele smoked in silence for a while, her eyes wandering in a leisurely, disinterested fashion over the families and couples that passed by. "You will be surprised perhaps to learn I came to see you. I wanted to tell you about Ashton's last visit to me in Paris." She slid a glance upward toward Sara, and her smile was slow and sly. "Ah, I see our darling boy did not bother to mention this to you, eh? And it was only a few weeks ago. One wonders what other secrets he has kept."

Sara knew she should turn on her heel and walk away. She did not.

Michele shrugged and drew again on the cigarette. "I was going to tell you of how he took me in his arms and made such love to me that I wept, how we lay naked and exhausted on the floor of my little apartment when the sun came up, how I took his hand and led him to the bath . . ."

Sara felt a chill go down her spine—not because of the words, but because of the desperation that must have prompted them. Until now she had thought of Michele as a shallow, bitter, and selfish woman whose only pleasure came from hurting others. But Sara realized she was just a sad woman, hurting inside herself.

Sara said simply, and as kindly as she could, "I don't believe you."

Michele smiled, curling her tongue upward as she blew out smoke. "Then you are clever. Because it is untrue. Ashton is disgustingly loyal. It is all very boring, really. A woman, she likes a little adventure in her life now and again, don't you agree?"

Sara said nothing, and Michele took another draw on the cigarette.

"Ash did come to see me in Paris," she said with a shrug. "The encounter, it was not so pleasant as I would have liked. He—how is this said?—used his threats against me, to protect you, and the child. My Ashton, he has been very angry with me in the past, but never has he been so forceful. And so I determined to discover for myself what manner of woman you are, to inspire such passion in him."

Michele tossed away the cigarette and stood. This time when she tried to smile, the expression did not quite reach the corners of her lips. "He is a fool for the child," she said. "This I knew." She shrugged. "But when I watch him, and he does not know I'm there, and he smiles at you . . ." She glanced briefly away, and an expression crossed her face that Sara could not entirely read. It might have been a flash of pain. "Never has he looked at me in that manner. Never. And that is what I wanted to know. So you have won. Congratulations."

And then she smiled, a stiff, brittle expression that did not come close to her eyes. "But," she said, "still he has the secrets, no?"

Sara said softly, "You still love him."

She laughed. "*Chérie*, don't be absurd! Of course I love him. I have loved him when I hated him. I have loved him through three other husbands. I even loved him when I was married to him." She shrugged again, her lips forming a brief, elaborate pout. "Alas, he loves another. This I know now. *C'est la vie*."

Sara felt compelled to say, "I'm sorry."

The flash of surprise in Michele's eyes was covered quickly by another light laugh. "*Chérie*, do not waste your tears. I know very well the cure for a broken heart. I am off to Spain, and my new lover—who is very rich, and very old. And I will advise you"—she tilted her head speculatively, her smile cool—"to enjoy your good fortune while you may. These things rarely endure."

Sara watched Michele walk away, and then moved quickly through the crowd, almost running at the end, until she spotted a blond man in a cherry-stained shirt at the balloon stand. She surprised him by flinging herself on him and kissing him hard on the face, and she whispered in his ear, "I have something to tell you when we get home." He gave her a puzzled smile, and bought her a yellow balloon to complement

Alyssa's red one. They walked home swinging Alyssa's hands between them, and she told him about the encounter with Michele while they chopped apples and carrots for a salad, because she did not want there to be any secrets between them.

· EIGHTEEN ·

Overnight, it seemed, Ash's bachelor life was turned upside down. His flat was reduced to chaos in very short order. The housekeeper who usually came once a week was engaged daily and could barely keep the disorder under control. There were jam smears on his chrome cabinets and orange juice circles on his countertops and fingerprints on his glass tables. And he barely noticed because in the evenings Alyssa would crawl into his lap and he would read her some ridiculous story about talking puppies or flying cats or moons, and he could feel Sara watching him and smiling and he could almost convince himself, just for a moment, that the life he was living was his own.

And then there were other times.

Sara had gotten into the habit of lying down with Alyssa, just until she fell asleep, and sometimes Ash would use that quiet time to go over paperwork or return phone calls or send e-mails. But other times, when the house rang with a silence now unfamiliar to him, he would feel compelled to go upstairs, and step quietly into the child's room, and stand over them, cuddled together as they were, and his chest would fill with a longing so intense it actually hurt. Because he knew by whose graces these two had entered his life. And sometimes, late at night when he awoke only to make sure Sara still slept beside him, or sometimes at moments like these, when he watched the two of them together, he became desperately convinced that if he were not very, very careful, Daniel would take them back.

It was their last night in London. Alyssa was grow-ing cranky; she missed her nanny and her cat and her fairy princess nursery, and five days of overstimulation in the city had exhausted all of them. They decided to travel back to Rondelais on the afternoon train the next day. Ash would stay the weekend; beyond that they had made no plans.

He came out of the shower to find Sara sitting cross-legged on his bed wearing the nightie he liked so much, the one with the ribbons, and his reading glasses. Papers were spread out around her, and she was scowling over some of them. He said, "Darling, you're taking on some dreadful habits from me." But he loved seeing her there. He loved the fact that she could read with his glasses. He finished drying his hair with the towel and tossed it aside. "What are you doing?"

She said unhappily, "I'm running out of money."

"Do you need cash, love?" He turned to the mirror and began combing back his hair. "There's some in the drawer there."

She shook her head impatiently. "I don't mean cash. I mean *money*. The Contandinos charged a fortune to repair the plumbing—not that it wasn't worth every penny—and I spent a lot more on restoring the apartment than I meant to. And your mother's right—something has got to be done with the roof, even if I can't afford to have it completely repaired. The electricity and the oil and the occupancy tax—whoever heard of charging a tax to live in your own house, anyway?— it's all more than I thought it would be."

"Is this an accounting?" He came and sat beside her, reaching for the paper in her hand. "How much do you need?"

She snatched the paper back from him. "I don't need your money, Ash."

"Don't be absurd. I told you from the beginning, Alyssa's trust is set up to provide for her, so whatever you've spent on her—"

"You're already paying for the nanny and the house-keeper—"

"Aside from which, any repairs you make to the property are an improvement on my investment so—"

Her jaw was set and her eyes took on that stubborn glaze that he had almost forgotten. "I don't need your money," she told him again, very distinctly. "I need a plan."

He smiled and plucked the glasses from her face. "Oh my. Are we about to have one of those dreary domestic squabbles over finances I hear so much about? I understand the make-up sex is simply spectacular."

He leaned forward to kiss her neck, but she snatched the glasses back from him and returned them to her face. "I need a long-term sustainable plan for the château to pay for itself. I asked Mr. Winkle to run some figures for me. I haven't gone over all the paperwork yet, but from what I'm seeing here so far I think I can put together a viable business plan—at least enough for the initial financing."

He frowned, taking up one of the papers. "For what?"

"For restoring the château and turning it into a B&B," she said simply. "If your hotel company thought they could make money doing that, why shouldn't I?"

He simply stared at her. "For one thing, why should you?"

"Because it's Alyssa's heritage," she replied simply, "and it needs to be there for her when she grows up. By that time," she added, retrieving the paper from his hand, "the winery should be a growing concern as well. I can start out by leasing the land for vines," she explained, "and gradually buy back the business with the proceeds from the château. It's been done before. I have several business models to back that up."

Ash took a breath, bit back the words, and stood, pinching the bridge of his nose. He took several steps across the room before he said, "Sara, I don't doubt your ability to do this, if you're set on it. But you do understand that you have absolutely no experience in the hotel business."

"I know how to hire people who do. And I *do* know how to sell things. Actually," she said, and when he turned he could see the cautious excitement in her eyes, "the idea came to me from Pietro, who's always asking whether I know these rich and famous people, and then it started to make sense when your mother insisted I move into the old apartment. I started to think about that bride who fixed up the Queen's Chamber

and how much the super-rich would pay for a fantasy vacation or the super-famous would pay for a luxury retreat, and
I'm telling you, Ash, it could work."

He had to smile at the enthusiasm that was so at odds
with her usual reserve. He said, "I think it probably could.
However, it's an extremely long-term project and—"

"Actually," she said, "if I can make these numbers work,
I can get most of the work done this winter, and open to my
first guests by spring."

He stared at her. "You can't mean to stay there through
the winter."

"Well, I'll have to be there, to supervise the labor."

"Impossible," he said flatly. "I won't allow it."

She removed the reading glasses slowly. "Excuse me?"

"You can't mean to live there, Sara," he said impatiently,
"all by yourself. And I certainly can't have you in charge of a
gaggle of foreign laborers—"

She started laughing. "What century are you from?"

"Besides, what about Alyssa?"

"She'll be in school."

"In London."

A silence as sharp as a guillotine fell over the room.

"I was going to tell you about it," he said, with only the
slightest edge in his voice. "I've enrolled her in an excellent
girls' school for the fall. They have a superlative arts program
and even horsemanship, should she care to take that up when
she's older. She will be home on weekends and holidays. I
thought we could take her to visit there the next time you
come to town."

She said evenly, "What's wrong with the school in Rondelais?"

And he replied, "It's in France."

"She's French!"

"And I'm British. This is where I live. This is where . . ." He stopped on an indrawn breath, his brows drawing together sharply, because he realized he had never said it out loud to her before. "This is where I want you to live, and Alyssa. Here, with me."

She simply stared at him. "But . . . what about Rondelais?"

He had no ready answer, and she must have seen that. "We can go there on holiday, now and again," he said, perhaps half a beat too late. "If . . ."

"If what?" Her tone was cool.

He met her gaze evenly. "If we decide to keep it."

"It's my home," she said. "And Alyssa's. It's where I live."

He was growing impatient. "And I live in London. This is where my business is. Even if there were any practical reason at all for you to keep the château, you surely wouldn't expect me to just pull up stakes and move across the Channel—"

"Which is so much harder than moving across an ocean," she retorted. "And do you mind explaining to me just exactly what stakes you're talking about, anyway? From what I can tell, the longest you've ever lived in this apartment is the past two weeks that I've been here."

And then he drove his fingers fiercely through his damp hair, forcefully pushing back anger. "Now we *are* going to fight," he muttered.

"No," said Sara. Quietly, she began to gather up the

papers. "It's just the same fight we've been having from the beginning. It's about who has control—of the château, of Alyssa. And I think you may have been right all along. It will have to be settled in court." She replaced the papers in the leather binder from which they had come, the one stamped Lindeman and Lindeman in gold. Her smile was weak and unconvincing. "The trouble with sleeping with the enemy is that you sometimes forget he *is* the enemy."

"Or she," he replied, before he could stop himself.

And she said, "Touché."

He said, "Should I sleep elsewhere tonight, Sara?"

"It's your bed."

He looked at her for a moment, and then he came and sat beside her on the bed. She started to slide over, so their legs would not be brushing, but he placed a hand lightly on her knee. He said, "Can we agree, at least, that we want to be together? Wherever we live?"

Her nostrils flared with an indrawn breath, and she shifted her gaze briefly to the ceiling. "The master negotiator," she said. And when she looked at him, there was no gentleness in her eyes. "I don't think there's compromise on this, Ash."

He said, holding her gaze, "It's Daniel's house."

And she replied, "No. It's mine. And Alyssa's."

He had to say it. "You don't know that. Until the DNA test comes back, nothing has changed. I'm still Alyssa's guardian, and she's going to school in London. I'm sorry."

Sara looked at him for another moment, her expression unchanged. And then she said, "So am I."

She turned back the covers on her side of the bed, and lay

down with her back to him, switching off the lamp. After a moment he got into bed beside her and lay there stiffly in the dark, because he simply did not want to leave her. And after a time he said quietly, "I'm not your enemy, Sara. I'm just trying to do what's right."

It was a long time before she spoke. He thought she might be too angry to respond at all. And then she moved and laid her head on his shoulder. "I know," she whispered. "But why can't we do it together? Why do we have to be on opposite sides when we both want the same thing?"

"Alyssa is my responsibility," he said, his voice low and tight in the dark.

"And you're always in charge. And always right."

A moment passed. "I'm sorry. I wish it could be different." She sighed again. "I know."

She spread her fingers over his heartbeat, and he wrapped his fingers around her shoulder, and kissed her hair, and they lay together, holding each other, and said nothing else. But it was a long time before either of them slept.

* * *

There are some things that are simply inevitable. That was why Sara did not spend a lot of time anymore thinking about the shadow life she had left behind . . . the life where gulls swooped and called on summer days, where lovers walked on sun-bright beaches and little yellow houses baked on salty streets. She didn't think anymore about the time when there had been no stately, ancient château in her life, or about the time before she had known a dark-eyed French child with bouncy curls and nonstop enthusiasm. She didn't think about the time before she had gone to Ash's room and told him what she deserved, because it had simply been inevitable. As had the way her life had changed, had been turned around and inside out, in the short time that they had been together. Because she had changed completely inside, it was inevitable.

She knew of course that nothing between them was really settled. She knew that, in a lot of ways, they had only been playing house these past few weeks and that it could not go on forever. But she also knew that, because of him, everything was different. She knew who she was now, and she knew what she wanted. As outrageous as it sometimes seemed when she thought about it, she knew she was never going back to North Carolina. She was going to stay in France, and she was going to restore and manage a four-hundred-year-old château, and she was going to raise a child who wasn't her own.

She didn't want to do this alone. But she could, if she had to, because she had met and loved Ash. The irony was that the only thing that stood in her way was, in fact, Ash.

She had spoken to Mr. Winkle—who was every bit as handsome as Ash had indicated, and thoroughly intimidated by his boss—about her options for adopting Alyssa. Although he admitted family law was not his strong point, his opinion was that, under the current circumstances, the chances were not good. She was a single woman, and an American who had not, as of yet, established legal residence in France, and had no claim of relationship to the French child at all. He indicated, but was polite enough not to say, that should new information about her parentage arise, the situation certainly would be worth revisiting.

Which was, of course, exactly what Ash had told her.

He also went on to say that while she was indeed free to deed the château to anyone she wished, when a minor child was involved the simplest and safest thing to do would be to simply transfer her title to the property into the existing trust—which, of course, Ash administered. She couldn't seem to make him understand that was not an acceptable solution to her. And that was why he had sent her away with a copy of the entire Rondelais file, including the record of the transfer of shares from Daniel to Ash, and of the documentation of the trust that had been set up for Alyssa. To reassure her. Because, as owner of Rondelais, she had a right to see all of the details of every transaction that had ever taken place concerning the property. Something Ash had never bothered to mention to her before.

She had arisen early, because the tension between them still had not dissipated by morning, and although she knew Ash was awake, he said nothing when she left the bed. She went into the kitchen and spent the hour before Alyssa woke studying the file on Rondelais, noting the documents she would need to copy for inclusion with her business plan. And then she noticed something she had never expected to see.

Ash came into the kitchen a few minutes later, showered and dressed, and texting something as he spoke. "Sara, I'm afraid I'm not going to be able to go with you to France this afternoon, after all. I've just had a message from Dejonge offering to meet with me in the morning. I've been trying to set up this meeting for months, and I won't get another chance. If I drop you and Alyssa at the station at eleven o'clock, I can just catch my flight to Johannesburg. I'll try to make it to Rondelais early next week. I've just arranged for Jean-Phillipe to meet your train in Paris." Finally he looked up, perhaps noticing her silence. He saw the expression on her face. He saw the open folder on the table.

She held up a paper. "Ash, what is this?"

He closed the phone, and put it in his pocket. His face went very still.

"It would appear to be a transfer of ownership certificate," he said, his voice completely expressionless, "for a certain number of investment shares in Château Rondelais."

"You told me Daniel put the money you gave him into a trust for Alyssa. But this says you transferred your holdings to her name, too. And it looks to me like you did it all on the same day." She stared at him, trying to make sense of it all. "You never owned shares in the château."

He said briefly, "No."

"But all this time . . ." It made no sense. She couldn't comprehend it. "You let me believe you owned a legitimate part of the property. You used that to convince me to . . . You lied to me."

"As administrator of Alyssa's trust, I was negotiating on her behalf."

Sara pushed herself up from the table, simply because she had to move away from him. She was still in her robe and slippers, and she felt oddly vulnerable. Completely confused. "But . . . I don't understand. It makes no sense. Why would you do such a thing? Why would you sign everything over to Alyssa? And why didn't you just tell me what you'd done?"

"Because," he murmured, almost absently, almost as though to himself, and without looking at her at all, "then I'd have to tell you the truth, wouldn't I?"

Her heart was tight in her chest, and as hard as she tried, as closely as she looked, she could see nothing on his face but . . . inevitability. Her fingers went to her throat, which was suddenly dry. "What truth?"

He walked over to the table, absently turning some of the papers around so that he could see them. "Winkle," he observed. "I suppose I always knew it was only a matter of time."

She said, with her thoughts still twisting and turning, trying to understand, "That's why you couldn't sell me your shares. Because they weren't yours."

"Partially," he agreed. "In the beginning, I could have arranged the paperwork easily enough, without violating the terms of the trust. But once you found out about Alyssa, once you became so determined to be involved in every bloody little detail . . . I didn't want to have to explain it all to you. Easier to let you be angry with me over a simple property dispute, than to despise me for the truth. Particularly since it was something I've spent all these years trying to deny, myself."

"Please, Ash. I don't understand."

He said abruptly, "It wasn't Daniel's idea to set up the trust. It was mine. He didn't ask me for money. I insisted upon his taking it. And I couldn't keep the shares he gave me in exchange because . . ." She could see his jaw knot, and flex. "Because it was blood money."

He looked at her then, and it was as though the act of looking at her was a punishment. His eyes were cold and still, but behind that practiced, determined, detached gaze there was a slow, churning torment. He said, "When Daniel told me about the woman, Alyssa's mother, I advised him to settle the matter of paternity, that much is true. He refused, and I didn't care why. I was annoyed with him and his constant scrapes, his constant coming to me to bail him out, and this was just one more muddle I had to pull him out of. But as I told you before, taking care of the Orsays is what we do." With each word he spoke, his voice became flatter, more detached. "So I went to the woman—a girl, really, I can't imagine she was more than nineteen—in that squalid little room where she and Alyssa lived in my hand-tailored suit and custom-made shoes and a tie that cost more than she'd probably ever seen in a lifetime because that's what I do. I fix things. And in my most intimidating, lawyerly fashion I told her that she was to desist immediately from annoying Monsieur Orsay and leave the region by the end of the week, and if she did not, I would have the authorities come to her room and break down her door and take her child away from her. The entire time she just sat there, terrified, holding her baby and crying. I gave her a hundred-Franc note and walked away. And that evening, the police think it was, she took a straight razor to her wrists."

Sara's fingers covered her lips, catching the whisper of breath that was almost like a cry. "Oh, Ash."

But he jerked his head away, refusing her emotion, refusing to meet her eyes. "I hated Daniel," he said tightly. "I blamed him for what he'd made me do—what I thought he made me do—and I wanted to punish him. I didn't tell him I had been there. I let him think he was responsible for the girl's death. I made him give up the only thing he had of value—a portion of Rondelais—to pay for it. I thought if I could make him suffer, my own suffering would ease, but of course it didn't. And the worst thing was, I never had a chance to tell him the truth. No." And now he did look at her, with a bleakness in his eyes so deep it seemed to go all the way to his soul. "The worst thing was, I let you hate him, too."

He drew a breath, released it slowly. "So there you have it. Now you know me. Now you know what I'm capable of. And now, every time I look at you, I'll see it in your eyes."

"Ash." It was hard to draw a breath, hard to form a thought. Her chest was aching, her throat on fire. "I don't know what to say."

"That's all right." A faint softening of his features almost formed a smile, but not quite. And none of it reached his eyes. "I think we both knew all along that it all was only make-believe."

He looked at his watch. "Please pack your things and get dressed. I'll wake Alyssa."

She said hoarsely, "We have to talk about this."

He shook his head briefly. "There's nothing more to say. There are some ghosts that simply can't be laid to rest. Besides, I have a plane to catch." And he looked back at her with a cold, humorless smile as he turned to leave the room. "You didn't really think you could change me at this late date, did you, my dear?"

*   *   *

Ash purchased their tickets and saw them to check-in. The busy St. Pancras Station allowed no time for conversation and he attempted none. Alyssa, who loved trains and was excited about seeing her cat again, bounced up and down with a ceaseless stream of chatter between them. At the gate, he transferred Sara's carry-on from his shoulder to hers, and said, "This is where I leave you. Your train is in twenty minutes."

There was a stricken look in her eyes when he said that. He wondered if it had been there all along, and he simply hadn't noticed. He said, with care, "I think we may come to see that there's a difference between being in love, and loving. I'm not sure I'm capable of the latter. But I've enjoyed being in love with you. And I hope one day you'll forgive me. But I don't expect it."

Alyssa raised both arms to him. "I love you, *petit-papa!*" He knelt down and hugged her hard, and kissed her hair, and told her to be a good girl on the train.

Sara said, when he stood, "It's not going to be this simple, Ash. I'm not going to let you make it this simple."

But he couldn't look at her anymore. "I'll call," he said, and he walked quickly away. He didn't even tell her good-bye. Later, he would remember that.

He hadn't even told her good-bye.

· NINETEEN ·

He had the car wait while he stopped by his office to pick up his mail and the paperwork he needed for the trip. He spoke tersely to Mrs. Harrison and told her he didn't know when he would be back. He made it to the airport with half an hour to spare. He sat in the departure lounge and opened his briefcase to take out his laptop and then he noticed the return label on one of the envelopes he had scooped up on his way out of the office. He opened it, and read the contents.

"Damn it," he said softly. His fingers tightened on the paper in his hand, wrinkling it. He looked at the clock on the opposite wall. "Damn it," he repeated, with more ferocity. He snapped his briefcase closed, stuffed the letter inside his coat, and left the airport.

In the taxi, he tried to reach Sara on her mobile but, to his frustration, got an out-of-service message. She was always forgetting to charge the battery, despite his admonitions and reminders. But then he glanced at his watch and realized she would be on the train by now, perhaps even in the Chunnel and out of range. He tried her again when he got out of the taxi, but got the same message.

There seemed to be slightly more activity than usual in his building when he arrived. Televisions were playing on every floor, with groups of people clustered around them here and there, which usually signaled some kind of bloody financial crisis or another somewhere around the world in which he was not remotely interested at the moment. He strode into his suite without looking left or right and said, "Mrs. Harrison, see you if can arrange a video conference with the Dejonges tomorrow morning instead. Meanwhile, get my team into the conference room for a briefing. And make it within the next fifteen minutes." He glanced at his watch. "I have to catch the next train to France."

She was already dialing the telephone. "Very good, sir, but you'll have to make it a plane instead."

He scowled at her. "What?"

She nodded meaningfully at the flat-screen that was muted on the opposite wall. It showed a reporter interviewing a firefighter against a background of chaos, but he did not give it more than a glance. "There's been a dreadful accident in the Chunnel," she said. "I'm sure no more trains are running today. They've been trying to reach the victims for over an hour but there seems to be . . ."

He did not hear anything else she said. He stared fixedly at the images on the television screen. The high glass arches of St. Pancras Station, the chaos inside, a reporter pushing a microphone into some woman's face. She was weeping hysterically.

He felt the blood leave his face. His fingertips went cold. He said hoarsely, "Which train?" And when she did not answer immediately he shouted, "Which train, goddamn it!"

She hung up the phone. She lifted the remote control and pushed the Mute button. In a moment a grave voice intoned, "Again, if you're just joining us, Eurostar 1902, the 11:32 nonstop from London to Paris, has met with disaster in the Channel Tunnel . . ."

He stared at the screen. The images, the words, buzzed by him. From very far away he heard Mrs. Harrison say, "Sir?" Out of the corner of his eye, he saw her rise.

He turned to look at her. He said woodenly, "Sara and Alyssa were on that train."

He remembered pushing his way out of the office and someone grabbing his arm and Mrs. Harrison saying something to him about a crisis center hotline and trying to push a piece of paper into his hand with a telephone number on it but he shook her off and he knew what it was to be blind with terror because he didn't see anything, not the people he shoved out of his way, not the button on the elevator, not the stairwell he plunged down, until he was in the street and traffic was screeching around him and horns were blaring and he grabbed the door handle of a taxicab before it even stopped. And he was saying, fiercely, under his breath as he flung himself inside, "No. *You can't have them.*"

"Beg pardon, guv?"

"St. Pancras. *Now.*"

He punched the number again for her mobile, and this time he got nothing, not even the out-of-service message, just a high-pitched warbling that sounded like sirens rushing to a disaster, that sounded like the end of the world.

He threw a handful of bills at the driver, he did not know how much. He was running now, running through the big doors, down the vast concourse with its throngs of people, pushing his way to the front of a ticket window, blurting something, demanding something, and before he could hear the answer he saw a man in uniform and he grabbed his arm and he started running again and at some point a woman with a Red Cross emblem on her shirt took his hand gently and said, "Did you have family on board, sir?"

And he answered hoarsely, "Yes."

She took him to a room packed with folding chairs and people who were eerily quiet, except for the occasional broken sob, the sounds of shock, the sounds of horror. Someone led him to a chair and gave him a clipboard with a form to fill out but he couldn't make his hand work. He heard whispers: *Two hundred forty-six dead. No survivors. No, two hundred forty-six on board. Twelve survivors. No, twelve dead. So far. No, the first car had been untouched. No, the first car had exploded on impact.* There was a board at the front of the room with papers pinned to it. People kept gathering around it, stiff-muscled, holding one another. He said to the man next to him, "What's that?" And he said, "The passenger list. The names with the check marks next to them are the bodies they've recovered."

Ash stood up and he walked to the front and stood there,

unable to make himself approach the board. He saw pain and terror and sympathy on the faces of the others, strangers to him, but just like him. They stepped back to let him near the board but he stood still, staring at those small typed lines from a distance, some with check marks, some without. How life could change in an instant. How only a breath ago he was worried about diamonds in South Africa and calling for his team. How only a heartbeat ago he stood in the dark and watched Sara and Alyssa sleep and ached with loving them. How he hadn't even told Sara good-bye. Someone touched his arm. He stepped forward.

Gabon, Gentry, Giddons . . .

And he couldn't do it. He couldn't read further. He couldn't stand here in this sea of pain reading a list of names and waiting to see the one with the check mark beside it, this was not what was supposed to happen, this was not what he had planned, and there was nothing he could do about it, not this time.

He remembered a spring day, the chapel ruins, a picnic spread on the stones. Sara's eyes. Always, Sara's eyes. *What are you afraid of, Ash?*

This. This moment. This future that even then had been rushing toward him, that he could have avoided had he only taken more care, had he been more vigilant. This moment. This was what he had been running from all his life.

He turned and fled the room, suddenly drenched in sweat, suddenly desperate for air, and he felt other pained, sympathetic eyes following him, but not for too long, because they were all the same, they and him, his agony was theirs and there was nothing any of them could do to stop it. On the concourse again he grasped a pillar simply to stop his forward motion and he turned, leaning his head back against it, and closed his eyes, shaking inside, breathing into his cupped hand because he was afraid if he didn't, he would shout out loud, he would scream like a madman, *You can't have them.*

Yet he was the one who had failed to keep them. He was the one who had let them go.

Almost as if an answer to prayer, his mobile rang. He fumbled it out of his pocket, breath stopping, trying to focus, thinking for a moment the letters on the screen spelled *Sara*, thinking they did but they didn't; they spelled *I'tnl Caller* and how absurd it was that life should go on, that somewhere in the world someone in an office was picking up a telephone and dialing his number, not just absurd but fantastic, really, completely obscene. He took the phone and he threw it as hard as he could across the floor where it collided with a kiosk and broke into several dozen pieces. That was when he heard a voice.

"Ash?"

He stood very still, not daring to turn.

"*Petit-papa!* There you are!"

They were there, just across the way, surrounded by a moving throng of people. Alyssa with her ribboned ponytails and her little backpack in the shape of a floppy rabbit, clutching Sara's hand and bouncing up and down, waving to him, and Sara, in the yellow dress she had worn that morning, looking frail and worried. He moved toward them, not taking his eyes off them, terrified that if he did, they would disappear, knowing that if he reached for them, he might grasp only air, bumping shoulders with strangers, trodding on toes, and then he stood before her, with her big gray eyes looking so strained and anxious, and she said, "We missed our train. I tried to get another, but there was an accident in the Chunnel and—"

A sound exploded from his throat, one he didn't recognize, and he caught her to him and she didn't melt away at all. She held him back, hard, as hard as he was holding her, and when his knees started to give way she sank to the floor with him and he blindly reached out an arm to gather Alyssa into his embrace. Sara said breathlessly against his ear, "I was so mad at you for sending us away, for thinking I wouldn't forgive you, for not giving me a chance . . . And then I was mad at myself, for letting you send us away, for not fighting for you. I tried to call you, I wanted to tell you I'd stay here if you wanted, and Alyssa could go to school in London, and we'd work it out together what to do with the château, God it's so simple, Ash, if we could just work it out together . . . but I couldn't get a signal on my phone so I left the gate and then I realized the battery was dead, but they wouldn't let me back through security, and by the time I made it back the train was already gone . . ."

He said hoarsely, "It was your train. I thought you were on that train."

It took her a moment to comprehend, and then the color drained from her face. "Oh, Ash." Her arms came around his neck, she buried her face in his shoulder, and he held her, held them both, until his arms began to tremble from holding them. Alyssa wriggled away, took his face in both of her small, plump ones, and demanded with a scowl, "Why do you cry, *petit-papa*?"

He laughed and wiped his hand across his eyes, and his wet face, not because he was embarrassed, but so that he could see. "Because I'm happy to see you," he told her. He scooped her up and stood, his other arm around Sara's waist. "That's all. Just happy. Let's go home."

* * *

That night he stood beside Alyssa's bed while Sara cuddled her to sleep, thinking how life could change in an instant, thinking about second chances, and no power on earth could have moved him from their sides. He lay down beside them, careful not to wake Alyssa, and put his arm over them both. Sara twined her fingers with his.

Fifteen were confirmed dead; forty-two injured. Life could change in an instant.

"Sara," he said softly, "when I was in that room, looking at those people's faces . . . knowing what they felt, seeing myself in their eyes . . . I'll never forget it. I don't think I can ever be the same person again."

She turned gently to face him, forming herself to the curve of his body. She said, "I know." And he knew that she did.

She whispered, "I don't want you to hate Daniel anymore. I don't want you to hate yourself."

He shook his head, kissing her hair. "How can I hate Daniel?" His voice was low and rich with emotion. "He brought me this. This moment. This incredible treasure. And this time I'll protect what is mine with all my heart. As for the man I once was . . ." He stretched out his arm, across Sara, and gently tucked away a curl that was caught in the moisture near Alyssa's parted lips. "I think I can forgive him as well." He looked at Sara. "If you can."

"There was never anything to forgive." Very softly, very sweetly, she kissed his lips. She said, "Remember the man I fell in love with. Please don't take him from me. Not entirely."

He was silent for a long time, holding them. Just holding them. "I don't think I can go back to my old life." And when her eyes lifted, questioningly, to his in the dark, he smiled. "For one thing, I seem to have lost my mobile. For another . . ." He released a long soft breath, lightly tangling his fingers in her hair. "It simply doesn't seem important anymore. I'm not sure how I ever thought it was."

"What will you do?"

"I'm not entirely ready to become a missionary to the Sudan," he admitted, "and I won't abandon the company, or my employees. But I've always known I was a good deal more involved there than I needed to be. And lately I've been thinking about a midlife change of career. Perhaps I'll try my hand at wine making. Or the hospitality industry."

Sara tucked her head beneath his chin, smiling. "You seem very employable to me," she said. "I'm sure you won't have any trouble at all finding a job."

And then he said softly, because it had seemed so unimportant before, because it hadn't even mattered until now, "The results of the paternity test came in today. That's why I canceled the trip to Johannesburg. I knew there would be a copy waiting for you at Rondelais, and I didn't want you to be alone when you opened it. I was on my way to tell you when I . . . when I heard."

She looked up at him. Her eyes were as soft and as luminous as moonlight in the dark. She whispered, "Do I need to know? Does it matter?"

"No," he returned, kissing her cheek. And he added simply, "She's ours, isn't she?"

Sara smiled, and closed her eyes again, and said, "Yes."

Sara relaxed, content in the circle of his embrace, and he reached across her again, and found Alyssa's hand, and felt her fingers close around his in her sleep. He smiled, and watched over them until his eyes grew heavy, and he fell asleep.

The dream came, and he awoke with a start, as he always did, as he leapt to catch the white hat. And then he started laughing, silently to himself in the dark, turning over carefully so as not to disturb his girls. But Sara was already awake, and she eased herself up onto one elbow, looking at him. "What?" she whispered. "What's so funny?"

"Nothing." He stroked her hair, but he couldn't stop smiling. "I just suddenly realized where I've seen you before."

She waited for him to say more, but when he did not, she merely kissed his cheek softly and said, "Did I tell you I've figured out how we can solve all of our differences?"

"No," he answered, twining his fingers through hers, still smiling, "but it doesn't matter. Because so have I."

Happily Ever After

The ceremony was private, with only family and, of course, Mrs. Harrison in attendance. They gathered on the knoll amidst the ruins of the old chapel: Dixie and Jeff, who had flown in from the States the day before, and Ash's sister Margaret from Scotland with her husband, and his mother in cascades of lavender ruffles. Alyssa wore her pink dress with its ruffled petticoat and solemnly held a bouquet of wilting daisies that she and her soon-to-be *grandmère* had picked that morning. Mrs. Harrison wore a pale blue suit, which for Ash was cause enough for celebration. A holy man said words, and gold rings were exchanged, and a single, gentle kiss. It was a simple ceremony that in and of itself changed nothing. But with it, a family was formed where none had been before. And afterward, nothing would ever be the same.

Five hundred guests were expected at Rondelais for the

reception, and most of them had already begun to arrive. A dozen white tents were set up across the emerald lawn and throughout the gardens, sheltering food, musicians, a champagne fountain with thousands of sparkling glasses, and a wedding cake that was decorated like Cinderella's castle. The place looked liked a feast day gathering from medieval times, with bowers of flowers everywhere and a Maypole, even though it was September. A steady breeze cooled the bright blue day, and the flapping of the tent canvases sounded like wings.

"And you said I couldn't give a party." Katherine stood beside Ash with champagne in hand, surveying the whole with enormous satisfaction. "And on such short notice, too."

"You have outdone yourself," he assured her, and leaned down to kiss her cheek. "I only regret that we didn't alert the tabloids. Your fame would have spread far and near."

She gave him an annoyed look. "I had hoped marriage to Sara would improve you. But I can see now you'll never change."

That made him laugh, and he replied, gazing into his champagne, "No, I suppose not."

There had been one near-disastrous moment, when Conde de Castrilli of Spain arrived with his new paramour— the former Mrs. Lindeman. Katherine's eyes had gone wide with disbelief and Ash's jaw had tightened, but Michele had merely kissed them both, politely, on the cheek, without ever unwinding her arm from that of the count. She introduced him as her "fiancé, the fourteenth count of Castrilli" and murmured graciously, "What a lovely party. I do hope you'll do us the honor of joining us in the spring for our wedding celebration. Castillo Castrilli is quite a bit larger than this," she assured them, "so of course we'll expect you to stay the week. And bring the lovely American, won't you?"

They watched her stroll away on the arm of her adoring— and much older—fiancé, and that was when Katherine and Ash had each snatched a glass of champagne from a passing waiter and consumed half without comment.

"Where is your lovely bride, anyway?" Katherine said now. "The guests are starting to grow curious."

"I think she took Jeff inside to meet the Contandinos. He said something about wanting to look at the west wing."

"Well, I suppose it wouldn't hurt to have a genuine builder give an opinion. And the Contandinos should be the guests of honor for this entire affair, if you ask me. Imagine, the key to preserving this entire estate was hidden away in the west wing all this time, and the Orsays never even knew it."

"Our request to be listed hasn't been granted yet," he reminded her.

"But the letter was authenticated."

"For which," he said, slipping his arm around her waist and kissing her again, soundly, "we have you to thank."

Katherine replied, "Really, my dear, these public displays of affection are growing quite tiresome." And he laughed again.

The letter to which she referred was, of course, the original written to Louis XIV from his mistress Adelaide Duvant, detailing the joys they had shared during his latest visit and thanking him for the lovely style in which he kept her at

Château Rondelais. It had been found behind a 1920s wedding photo of an Orsay couple and several layers of newsprint when Sara, unpacking the photographs to rehang them in the library downstairs, had accidentally broken the frame.

"Of course," his mother pointed out practically now, "you realize it's rather a weak claim to fame, and if you were actually to receive a restoration grant, it would be all just a bit too fairy-tale, don't you agree?"

"Absolutely," concurred Ash, his eyes twinkling. "On the other hand, having given the matter some thought of late—and having read aloud a great many of them over the past few months, too, mind you—I've discovered that fairy tales have a good deal more to recommend them than we might first have thought. Besides"—he sipped his champagne—"I've a feeling I'm going to need the funds to pay for this wedding."

"Lindeman, old man!" A stranger clapped him on the back—a stranger in the sense that, at least, Ash could not currently recall his name. That once had been his strong suit: remembering names, faces, hobbies, the names and ages of children. It was his stock and trade. It was his charm.

"Congratulations," said the stranger. "Well-done!"

Ash extended his hand. "Good of you to come. May I present my mother, Mrs. Jonathon Lindeman?"

Proper acknowledgments were made, Katherine excused herself, and the man turned back to him. "I wondered what became of you. I heard you were ill, or had retired."

Ash smiled. "Neither one, in fact. I'm taking a few months off, and next year I may open a small branch office in Lyon, with rather more of an eye toward philanthropy. My wife seems determined to go into the hotel business, and I'd like to be nearby."

The stranger surveyed the château behind them with an appreciative eye. "Aye, clever woman, your wife. I might not be averse to putting money in a venture like that."

"Then you should meet with her," said Ash. "I'll be happy to arrange it. But not today. It's my wedding day."

The stranger eyed him with interest. "Philanthropy, do you say? An interesting notion, that. A mind like yours for business, you might actually get a thing or two done. I should put you in touch with some chaps I know."

"I'd be most grateful. But as I said . . ."

"Your wedding day, yes, right."

"Papa! Papa!" A small torrent of pink chiffon with a red and angry face flung herself at him and began to spill forth in rapid French the story of how cruel her new cousins were to her. Ash hoisted her onto his hip and told her she was his princess and then he said to the stranger, smiling proudly, "Have you met my daughter?"

* * *

Jeff said, "I don't know, Sara. It doesn't look that much of a big deal to me—modernizing the rooms, that is. I could probably draw up some plans for you while we're here."

Sara beamed at him. "Thanks, Jeff. That's just what I was hoping."

Jeff and Dixie were staying at Rondelais with Alyssa while Ash and Sara took a two-week honeymoon to Italy. When they returned, Sara intended to launch into full-scale renovations with the château—with or without the restoration grant. She had already made a few tentative inquiries and had returned a positive interest in spring/summer bookings. There was no time to waste.

"Making the repairs, now," Jeff reminded her, "that's going to take some money."

"You need the stuff fixed," Pietro interjected, beaming, "you call the Contandinos, sì?"

Pietro and his father had dressed for the occasion: Pietro in an ice blue tux with a green bow tie, and Signor, looking somber and dignified in a bright yellow blazer with red slacks and a dashing blue ascot. Sara grinned at them. "What would I do without you?"

She pulled closed the heavy arched doors to the west wing, careful not to smudge her dress. She had chosen a long, slim blush pink satin suit with a white brocade trim around the cuffs and the deep décolletage, because she had wanted her dress to match Alyssa's, and because Ash had loved it. She said, "The party is waiting for you. Let's go down."

"Sara!" Dixie rounded the corner, looking a little harried. "There you are! This place is as big as a—well, a hotel, isn't it? How do you keep from getting lost? Everyone's asking for you." She slipped her arm through Jeff's, and added to him, "It's your fault. Like Sara doesn't have more important things to do on her wedding day than talk about construction plans? Ash has been very patient," she told Sara, and smiled. "He's nice. And I like his mother."

"So do I," Sara said.

"But neither one of them is going to be nice very much

longer if we don't get down there," Dixie added with a stern look at Jeff. "And I want you to have a talk with your sons. They don't have the faintest idea how to play with little girls."

Sara turned to follow them downstairs, but was stopped by a solemn, gravelly voice. *"Signora."*

She turned, rather astonished, and Signor Contandino said in perfectly accented English, "Your keys."

He presented her the heavy bronze skeleton keys that opened the doors to the west wing and it felt, to Sara, like a monumental gift. She felt the weight of them in her hands and she was momentarily overcome with awe—for what she had taken on, for what the future held, and, most of all, for what she had been given. She said, smiling at him, her eyes misting, "Thank you."

He bowed to her, deeply, from the waist.

"Sara," called Dixie impatiently, from several dozen feet down the hall.

"I'm coming." Sara hurried to catch up.

"Signora!"

She looked back and Pietro said, "Do you know Sting?"

"Yes!" exclaimed Sara, delighted, laughing out loud. "Yes, I do!"

Pietro grinned and gave her two thumbs up, and Sara hurried after her sister, still laughing. She caught up her hat as she left the château and moved, as quickly as her delicate satin pumps would allow, across the lawn to find her husband.

She loved the way his eyes crinkled when he saw her. "I finally convince you to wear a hat," he said, "and you have to choose one as big as a boat." He bent deep beneath its brim to kiss her, and Sara lifted her hand to its crown so that the hat didn't fall off as she bent back to return his kiss.

"It's very stylish," she insisted. "And it goes with the suit."

"So it does."

"I see the boys are trying to make peace with Alyssa."

"She's a little spoiled, you know."

"We're not going to have that argument now."

"Oh my, no," he agreed pleasantly. "Not when there are so many more interesting arguments waiting for us to have."

She slanted him a look that was filled at once with both reprimand and adoration. "You make me look forward to the next fifty years."

"You make me glad to be alive," he responded, and their eyes met and, really, there was nothing more that needed to be said.

They stood for a moment beneath the brilliant cobalt sky while the chamber orchestra played in the background and the guests laughed and moved all around them, and the sunlight sparkled and glinted off the moat, watching the twins toss a red ball back and forth while Alyssa scampered between them, trying to catch it. Sara said, not wanting to move at all, "Your mother wants to start the reception line. We should go greet our guests."

Ash said, "Watch your hat."

The moment after he spoke a gust of wind snatched the big white hat from Sara's head and sent it charging into the air like a sail. She laughed out loud and they both leapt at once to catch it, and Ash had never been happier in his life.